ACROSS THE DISTANCE

ACROSS THE DISTANCE

MARIE MEYER

FOREVER
YOURS

New York   Boston

Copyright © 2015 by Marie Meyer
Cover design by Elizabeth Turner
Cover copyright © 2015 by Hachette Book Group, Inc.

Forever Yours
Hachette Book Group
1290 Avenue of the Americas
New York, NY 10104
hachettebookgroup.com
twitter.com/foreverromance

First ebook and print on demand edition: May 2015

Forever Yours is an imprint of Grand Central Publishing.
The Forever Yours name and logo are trademarks of Hachette Book Group, Inc.

The publisher is not responsible for websites (or their content) that are not owned by the publisher.

The Hachette Speakers Bureau provides a wide range of authors for speaking events. To find out more, go to www.hachettespeakersbureau.com or call (866) 376-6591.

ISBN 978-1-4555-9017-9 (ebook edition)
ISBN 978-1-4555-9096-4 (print on demand edition)

This book is dedicated to all the families who suffered losses as a result of the tragic events of September 11, 2001, especially the children who lost their parent(s).

Acknowledgments

All thanks and praise to my Lord and Savior, Jesus Christ, through whom all things are possible.

This last year and a half has been a whirlwind of non-stop excitement! From writing *Across the Distance*, then tossing into Pitch Wars on a whim, to finding representation…every step has been a dream come true. But, without the love and support of so many amazing people, Jillian and Griffin would still be on my computer and not in your hands.

My phenomenal agent, Louise Fury, who favorited my Pitch Wars entry and changed my life. Thank you for believing in my work and loving Jillian and Griffin as much as I do. You're always there for me, answering my questions at all hours of the day. You've patiently guided me through the publishing process, and I'm eternally grateful. I'm so blessed to have you in my corner.

To my editor extraordinaire, Megha Parekh, at Grand Central

Publishing, thank you for taking a chance on me and my story. You gave Jillian her wings to fly. I've loved working with you. You're a gem!

My publication team at Forever Yours, thank you for making *AtD* the best it can be. From the gorgeous cover, detailed edits, and publicity, you've packaged Jillian up nicely, so I could share her with the world.

Team Fury, especially Lady Lioness, for not only choosing my Pitch Wars entry, but fighting like a momma lion for *AtD*, and making me part of The Pride. Thank you for believing in me, your kick-butt edits, and all your brilliant ideas. You've taught me so much. Because of you, I am a better storyteller.

Jen McLaughlin, my agency sister, thank you for taking the time to read *AtD* and supplying a blurb. I'm humbled by your kind words and praise.

To my husband and two Darlings, who are currently buried under a mountain of laundry, if you can hear me, "Thank you for your unwavering love and support! I'll dig you out soon! I love you forever!"

My parents, Jim and Judy, thank you for fostering my love of the arts. Without your support, love, and encouragement, I wouldn't be where I am today. I love you.

My Arizona family: Dot, Kris, George, Brendin, and Pat, I can hear you cheering all the way from the desert! Thank you for believing in me. I love you.

The Pride, Sarah Blair and Annie Rains, hear us roar! It was a pleasure working with both of you during Pitch Wars. Thank you for your cheers and constructive criticism. You helped make *AtD* what it is today.

My SS Sisters: Heather Brewer, Sarah Bromely, Cole Gibsen, Emily Hall, Jamie Krakover, Shawntelle Madison, L.S. Murphy, and Heather Reid, thank you for your friendship. What happens on the farm, stays on the farm! Love you, ladies.

Brenda Drake and the Pitch Wars crew, thank you for your time and dedication to helping aspiring authors become real authors. Pitch Wars will forever hold a special place in my heart.

My lovely CPs: Molly Dean Stevens and Meredith Tate, my writing is better because of the two of you. Thank you for the time and consideration you put into helping me perfect my craft.

The NA Collaborative: Ara Grigorian, Amanda Heger, Sophia Henry, Kate L. Mary, Laura Salters, Annika Sharma, Jessica Ruddick, and Meredith Tate, you're all amazing! I'm so fortunate to be a part of such a talented group of authors. The future of New Adult is very bright. Much love and thanks to you, my friends!

To Brandy, my first reader, your enthusiasm for my story was all the encouragement I needed to send Jillian and Griffin out in the world. Thank you! Love and cosmos, my dear friend!

ACROSS THE DISTANCE

Chapter One

The tape screeched when I pulled it over the top of another box. I was down to the last one; all I had left to pack were the contents of my dresser, but that was going to have to wait. Outside, I heard my best friend, Griffin, pull into the driveway. Before he shut off the ignition, he revved the throttle of his Triumph a few times for my sister's sake. Jennifer hated his noisy motorcycle.

Griffin's effort to piss Jennifer off made me smile. I stood up and walked to the door. Heading downstairs, I slammed the bedroom door a little too hard and the glass figurine cabinet at the end of the hall shook. I froze and watched as an angel statuette teetered back and forth on its pedestal. *Shit. Please, don't break.*

"Jillian? What are you doing?" Jennifer yelled from the kitchen. "You better not break anything!"

As soon as the angel righted itself, I sighed in relief. But a small part of me wished it had broken. It would have felt good to break something that was special to her. Lord knew she'd done her best to break me. I shook off that depressing thought and raced down the steps to see Griffin.

When I opened the front door, he was walking up the sidewalk with two little boys attached to each of his legs: my twin nephews and Griffin's preschool fan club presidents, Michael and Mitchell.

Every time I saw Griffin interact with the boys, I couldn't help but smile. The boys adored him.

I watched as they continued their slow migration to the porch. Michael and Mitchell's messy, white-blond curls bounced wildly with each step, as did Griffin's coal black waves, falling across his forehead. He stood in stark contrast to the little boys dangling at his feet. Their tiny bodies seemed to shrink next to Griffin's six-foot-four muscled frame.

"I see that your adoring fans have found you." I laughed, watching Griffin walk like a giant, stomping as hard as he could, the twins giggling hysterically and hanging on for dear life.

"Hey, Jillibean, you lose your helpers?" he asked, unfazed by the ambush.

"Yeah, right," I said, walking out front to join him. I wrapped my arms around his neck and squeezed. I took a deep breath, filling my lungs with the familiar scents of leather and wind. A combination that would always be uniquely *him*. "I'm so glad you're here," I sighed, relaxing into his embrace. I felt safe, like nothing could hurt me when I was in his arms.

Griffin's arms circled my waist. "That bad, huh?"

I slackened my grip and stepped back, giving him and the squirming boys at his feet more room. "My sister's been especially vile today."

"When isn't she?" Griffin replied.

"Giddy up, Giff-in," Mitchell wailed, bouncing up and down.

"You about ready?" Griffin asked me, trying to remain upright while the boys pulled and tugged his legs in opposite directions.

"Not really. I've got one more box to pack and a bunch to load into my car. They're up in my room."

"Hear that, boys? Aunt Jillian needs help loading her boxes. Are you men ready to help?" he asked.

"Yeah!" they shouted in unison.

"Hang on tight!" Griffin yelled and started running the rest of the way up the sidewalk and onto the porch. "All right guys, this is where the ride ends. Time to get to work." Griffin shook Michael off of his left leg before he started shaking Mitchell off of his right. The boys rolled around on the porch and Griffin playfully stepped on their bellies with his ginormous boots. The boys were laughing so hard I wouldn't have been surprised to see their faces turning blue from oxygen deprivation.

Following them to the porch, I shook my head and smiled. Griffin held his hand out and I laced my fingers through his, thankful he was here.

"I'll get the trailer hitched up to your car and the stuff you have ready, I'll put in the backseat. You finish up that last box; we've got a long trip ahead of us." Griffin leaned in close and whispered the last part in my ear. "Plus, it'll be nice to say 'adios' to the Queen Bitch," he said, referring to my sister.

"Sounds like a plan." I winked. "Come on boys," I held the door open and waved them inside. "If you're outside without a grown-up, your mom will kill me." They both shot up from the porch and ran inside.

"Giff-in," Michael said, coming to a stop in the doorway. "Can we still help?"

Griffin tousled his hair. "You bet, little man. Let's go find those boxes." Griffin winked back at me and the three of them ran up the stairs.

I trailed behind the boys, knowing that I couldn't put off packing that "last box" any longer. When I got to my room, Griffin held a box in his hands, but it was low enough so that the boys thought they were helping to bear some of its weight. "Hey, slacker," I said to Griffin, bumping his shoulder with my fist. "You letting a couple of three-year-olds show you up?"

"These are not normal three-year-olds," Griffin said in a deep commercial-announcer voice. "These boys are the Amazing Barrett Brothers, able to lift boxes equal to their own body weight with the help of the Amazing Griffin."

I rolled my eyes at his ridiculousness, and smiled. "You better watch it there, 'Amazing Griffin', or I'll have to butter the doorway to get your ego to fit through."

Still speaking in a cheesy commercial voice, Griffin continued, "As swift as lightning, we will transport this box to the vehicle waiting downstairs. Do not fear, kind lady, the Amazing Barrett Brothers and the Amazing Griffin are here to help."

"Oh, Lord. I'm in trouble," I mumbled. And as swift as lightning (but really not), Griffin shuffled the boys out of the room and down the stairs.

I grabbed my last empty box and walked across the room to my dresser. I pulled open a drawer and removed a folded stack of yoga pants, tees, and dozens of clothing projects I'd made over the years. Shuffling on my knees from one drawer to the next, I emptied each of them until I came to the drawer I'd been dreading. The one on the top right-hand side.

The contents of this drawer had remained buried in darkness for almost five years. I was scared to open it, to shed light on the objects that reminded me of my past. I stared at the unassuming rectangular compartment, knowing what I had to do. I said a silent prayer for courage and pulled open the drawer.

Inside, the 5x7 picture frame still lay upside down on top of several other snapshots. I reached for the stack. The second my fingers touched the dusty frame I winced, as if expecting it to burst into flames and reduce me to a heap of ashes. Biting my lip, I grabbed the frame and forced myself to look.

There we were. Mom, Dad, and a miniature version of me. Tears burned my eyes. My lungs clenched in my chest and I forced myself to breathe as I threw the frame into the box with my yoga pants. I pulled out the rest of the photos and tossed them in before they had a chance to stab me through the heart as well.

Downstairs, I could hear the boys coming back inside and then footsteps on the stairs. Quickly, I folded the flaps of the box and pulled the packing tape off the dresser. With another screech, I sealed away all the bad memories of my childhood.

"Well, my help dumped me," Griffin said, coming back into my room alone. "Apparently, I'm not as cool as a toy car."

Before he could see my tears, I wiped my wet eyes with the back of my hand, sniffled, and plastered on a brave smile, then turned around. "There. Done," I proclaimed, standing up and kicking the box over to where the others sat.

"You okay?" Griffin asked, knowing me all too well.

"Yeah." I dusted my hands off on my jeans shorts. "Let's get this show on the road." I bent down to pick up a box, standing back up with a huge smile on my face. "I'm ready to get to college."

* * *

Griffin took the last box from my hand and shoved it into the backseat of my car. "I'll get my bike on the trailer, and then we'll be ready to hit the road." He wiped his upper arm across his sweaty forehead.

I looked into his dark eyes and smiled. "Thanks," I sighed.

"For what?" With a toss of his head, he pushed a few errant curls out of his eyes.

"For putting up with me." He could have easily gotten a plane ticket home, but he knew how much I hated airplanes. The thought of him getting on a plane made me physically ill.

He swung his arm around my neck, squeezing me with his strong arm. "Put up with you? I'd like to see you try and get rid of me."

With my head trapped in his viselike grip and my face pressed to his chest, I couldn't escape his intoxicating scent. Even though it was too hot for his beloved leather riding jacket, the faint smell still clung to him. That, coupled with the heady musk clinging to his sweat-dampened t-shirt, made my head swim with thoughts that were well beyond the realm of friendship.

I needed to refocus my thoughts, and I couldn't do that pressed up against him. I shivered and pulled away. Taking a step back, I cleared my throat. "I'm going to tell Jennifer we're leaving." I thumbed toward the house.

He scrutinized my face for a minute, then smirked. "Enjoy that. You've earned it."

I turned on my heel and let out a deep breath, trying desperately to rein in my inappropriate fantasies.

Months ago, our easygoing friendship had morphed into an awkward dance of fleeting glances, lingering touches, and an unspeakable amount of tension. I thought he'd felt it, too. The night of my high school graduation party, I went out on a limb and kissed him. When our lips met, every nerve ending in my body fired at once. Embers of lust burned deep inside me. I'd never felt anything like that before. The thought of being intimate with someone made me want to run to the nearest convent. But not with Griffin. When our bodies connected, I felt whole and alive in a way I'd never felt before.

Then he'd done what I'd least expected…he'd pushed me away. I'd searched his face for an explanation. He, more than anyone, knew what it had taken for me to put myself out there, and he'd pushed me away. Touting some bullshit about our timing being all wrong, that a long distance relationship wouldn't work, he insisted that I was nothing more than his friend. His rejection hurt worse than any of the cuts I'd inflicted upon myself in past years. But, he was my best friend; I needed him far too much to have our relationship end badly and lose him forever. Regardless of his excuses, in retrospect, I was glad I wouldn't fall victim to his usual love-'em-and-leave-'em pattern. Griffin was never with one girl for more than a couple of months; then he was on to the next. That would have killed me. So I picked up what was left of my pride, buried my feelings, and vowed not to blur the lines of our friendship again.

Climbing the steps to the porch, I looked back at him before going into the house. Griffin had gone to work wheeling his bike onto the trailer. His biceps strained beneath the plain white tee he wore. I bit my bottom lip and cursed. "Damn it, Jillian. Stop torturing yourself." Groaning, I reached for the doorknob.

"Hey, Jennifer, we're leaving," I said, grabbing my car keys from the island in the middle of the kitchen. She sat at the kitchen table poring over cookbooks that helped her sneak vegetables into the twins' meals. Poor boys, they didn't stand a chance. Jennifer fought dirty…she always had.

"It's about time." She turned the page of her cookbook, not even bothering to lift her eyes from the page.

"What? No good-bye? This is it, the day you've been waiting for since I moved in. I thought you'd be at the door cheering."

Usually I was more reserved with my comments, but today I felt brave. Maybe moving to Rhode Island and going to design school gave me the extra backbone I'd lacked for the last twelve years. Or maybe it was just the fact that I didn't have to face her any longer. By the look on Jennifer's face, my mouthy comments surprised her as well. She stood up from the table, tucked a piece of her shoulder-length blond hair behind her ear, and took a small step in my direction. Her mannerisms and the way she carried herself sparked a memory of my mother. As Jennifer got older, that happened more often, and a pang of sadness clenched my heart. Where I'd gotten Dad's lighter hair and pale complexion, Jennifer had Mom's coloring: dark blond hair, olive skin. But neither of us had got Mom's gorgeous blue eyes. The twins ended up with those.

Beyond the couple of features Jennifer shared with Mom, though, their similarities ended. When mom smiled, it was kind and inviting. Jennifer never smiled. She was rigid, harsh, and distant. Nothing like mom

Jennifer curled her spray-tanned arms around my back. I braced for the impact. Jennifer wasn't affectionate, especially with me, so I knew something hurtful was in store. I held perfectly still as she drew me close to her chest. The sweet, fruity scent of sweet pea blossoms—Jennifer's favorite perfume—invaded my senses. For such a light, cheery fragrance, it always managed to weigh heavy, giving me a headache.

Jennifer pressed her lips to my ear and whispered, "Such a shame Mom and Dad aren't here to see you off. I'm sure *they* would have told you good-bye." She slid her hands to my shoulders and placed a small kiss on my cheek.

And there it was. The dagger through my heart. Mom and Dad. She knew they were my kryptonite. For the second time in less than an hour, I felt acidic drops of guilt leaking from my heart and circulating through my body. But what burned more than the guilt was the fact that she was right. It *was* a shame they weren't here. And I had no one to blame but myself.

I held my breath while my eyes welled up with tears. *Not today, Jillian. You will not cry.* I refused to give her the satisfaction. I stood up taller, giving myself a good two inches on her, and swallowed the lump forming in my throat. She was not going to ruin this day. The day I'd worked so hard to achieve.

"Ready to go?" Griffin said, coming around the corner. "The boys are waiting by the door to say good-bye."

Jennifer stepped away from me and gave Griffin a disgusted once-over. "And yet another reason why I'm glad Jillian decided to go away to school," she said. "At least I get a respite from the white trash walking through my front door." Piercing me with an icy stare, she continued, "With the endless parade of women he flaunts in front of you, the tattoos, the music," she scowled, "I've never understood the hold he has on you, Jillian." She stifled a laugh. "Pathetic, if you ask me."

Griffin took a step in her direction. "Excuse me?" he growled, his expression darkening. I knew he wouldn't hurt her, but he was damn good at intimidating her. He wasn't the little boy who lived next door anymore. He'd grown up. With his deep voice and considerable size, he towered over her, the muscles in his arms flexing.

She shuffled backward. "Just go." With a dismissive flick of her wrist, she sat back down at the table.

"Yeah, that's what I thought, all bark and no bite." Griffin pulled on my arm. "Come on, Bean. You don't have to put up with her shit anymore."

I glanced back at Jennifer; she'd already gone back to her broccoli-laced brownie recipe. Griffin was right; I wouldn't have to put up with her shit while I was away. But he was wrong about her bite. When he wasn't around to back her down, she relished the chance to sink her teeth into me. It hurt like hell when she latched on and wouldn't let go.

We walked down the hallway. Michael and Mitchell were waiting by the door. "I need big hugs, boys," I said, bending down and opening my arms wide. "This hug has to last me until December, so make it a good one." Both of them stepped into my embrace and I held onto them tightly. "You two be good for your mommy and daddy," I said.

"We will," they replied.

I let go and they smiled. "I love you both."

"Love you, Aunt Jillian," they said.

"Now, go find your mom. She's in the kitchen." Knowing the boys' penchant for sneaking out of the house, I wanted to be sure their mother had them corralled before Griffin and I left.

I stood back up and looked into Griffin's dark eyes. "I'm ready." I tossed him the keys.

"I'm the chauffeur, huh?" Griffin smirked, pulling his eyebrow up. He opened the door for me and I stepped out onto the porch.

"You get the first nine hours; I'll take the back side." This time he gave me a full smile. *What would I do without him?* On the porch, I froze. It finally hit me. What *would* I do without him? Sure, I wanted out of Jennifer's house, but at what expense? Couldn't I just go to the junior college like Griff and get my own apartment? Why had I made the decision to go to school eleven hundred miles away? How could I leave him—my best friend?

The lump in my throat had come back but I forced the words out anyway. "Griff…" I sounded like a damn croaking frog.

Griffin wrapped his arms around me. "Yeah?"

"Why am I doing this?"

"What do you mean? This is all you've talked about since you got the scholarship."

"I know." I sniffled. "But, I don't know if I can do this. We'll be so far apart."

"Uh-uh. Stop that right now. I am not about to let you throw away the opportunity of a lifetime just because we won't see each other as often. You're too talented for Glen Carbon, Illinois and you know it. Now go, get your ass in the car." With his hand, he popped me on the backside, just to get his point across.

I jumped, not expecting his hand on my ass. My heart skipped and my cheeks flushed. "Hey!" I swatted his hand away.

"Get in the car, Jillian."

Damn, I already miss him.

Chapter Two

Jillian. Jillian, wake up."

Griffin shook my shoulder while I blinked away a dream. "I'm sorry," I replied groggily. "I didn't mean to fall asleep on you. What time is it?"

"It's just after eleven."

I pulled my legs from the dashboard and sat up, my back popping and snapping in protest. "Ugh, I hope there's a good yoga class on campus." I stretched my back and legs the best I could and took in my surroundings. "Where are we?" Griffin pulled off the turnpike and headed into the business district of some small town.

"We're in Pennsylvania. Do you want to keep driving or call it a night?"

"Shit, I'm sorry. I should have taken over the wheel a hundred miles ago."

"It's all right. You looked too peaceful to wake up."

"I'm such a slacker." Yawning, I rubbed my eyes, hoping to lubricate my dried-out contacts. "I don't think I can make it any farther tonight. Let's get a room."

"That's what I hoped you'd say. My ass hurts and I really need to piss."

Griffin found a cheap hotel right off the turnpike. At the check-in desk, Griffin showed his ID and paid for the room.

As soon as the desk attendant handed over our key cards, Griffin picked up his duffle bag and slung my backpack over his shoulder. We headed down the dimly lit corridor toward our room and a small chuckle escaped from my lips.

"What's so funny?" Griffin asked.

"The wallpaper. It's the same stuff Jennifer has on the walls in the guest room...my room."

"Leave it to Jennifer to troll cheap hotels for interior design inspiration," Griffin replied with a smirk.

We turned down another hallway and were immediately assaulted by the overpowering scent of chlorine. "I wonder if this hotel has a pool?" I inquired sarcastically.

Griffin shook his head and smiled. "You're such a smart-ass."

"I know. I learned from the best."

"Damn straight."

Griffin stopped in front of our door and slid the key card into the lock. The little red light flashed each time he pushed the card into the door. "Did I ever tell you how much I hate these things?" he said, turning around.

"Scoot over, let me try." I checked him with my hip and he playfully stumbled to the side. I shook my head and snatched the card from his hand. These kinds of locks required a certain rhythm—in, out...green light...and we were in. I turned to him and stuck my tongue out. "It's okay. You can't help it." I patted his shoulder. "It's not your fault you lack rhythm."

An indignant smile spread across his face. "Yep. Definitely a smart-ass." He nudged me aside with his shoulder and stepped into the room.

I followed and flipped on the light. There was one queen-sized bed in the center of the room and a large plasma screen TV sitting on the dresser. Griffin tossed the bags on the bed and headed straight for the bathroom. I flopped down next to our bags and contemplated never moving from that spot. It baffled my mind: I had done nothing but sit on my ass for almost ten hours, minus the occasional bathroom breaks and food stops, and yet I was completely exhausted. I heard Griffin turn on the shower. I closed my eyes and waited for my turn.

My body relaxed into the fluffy down comforter and my mind drifted to the dream Griffin had awakened me from. My mom's sweet voice still echoed through my head. She and my dad had been gone almost twelve years. Years of therapy had gotten me to the point where I could think about them and not cry…or run a blade across my skin. But no amount of therapy would ever diminish the guilt I harbored for them not coming home. It was my fault; I knew it and so did Jennifer.

A few minutes later the shower shut off. Griffin stepped out of the bathroom with a towel wrapped around his waist. His wet, coal-black hair stuck to his face and neck as he padded over to the bed where his duffle bag lay. *Oh, sweet Jesus.* The temperature of the room spiked and my pulse raced. Why did he have this effect on me? *He's just your friend, Jillian. Get it together.* But as I watched him cross the room, his olive, tattooed skin still damp and glistening, that was no easy feat.

I licked my lips, my mouth suddenly dry. With his body on full display, I couldn't keep my eyes from roaming even if I'd wanted to. I didn't know where to look first; every part of him demanded attention. His broad shoulders…his sculpted arms…the hard plains of his chest…and his chiseled abs, that gave way to the beautiful v-shaped outline right where the towel hugged his waist. My eyes lingered at his waist. *Curses…that wretched towel.* Every part of him was perfect.

Avoiding my gaze, he rummaged through his bag, ignoring me completely.

I had to pull myself together. Yes, he was gorgeous, but he was also MY BEST FRIEND. He'd made it quite clear that was all he wanted. Besides, if I put myself out there again, not only would I feel the sting of rejection bone-deep, I'd risk losing him altogether. I needed him in my life way too much. I refused to jeopardize our lifelong friendship because I couldn't keep my hormones in check. I needed to lighten up the awkward tension in the room.

"Whoa, where did those come from?" I pointed to his arms, much more defined than they had been a few months ago. I'm sure his new workout regime had something to do with the fact that his garage band, Mine Shaft, had recently moved out of the garage and onto the frat circuit.

"What?" he answered, still avoiding my eyes.

By the deepening blush of his cheeks, I could tell I'd embarrassed him. "You're looking good, Daniels. Real hottie material now."

"Shut up," he said, rolling his eyes.

"I'm serious, Griff. Your tat looks amazing now that your arms are bigger."

"Enough, Jillian. I don't want to talk about my arms. The shower's all yours." He thwacked me with the shirt he held in his hands. "Move over." I slid off the bed, giving him more room. Plopping down in the space I'd just vacated, he reached in his bag and pulled out a pair of boxers.

"Touchy, touchy. Remind me not to give you any more compliments." I stood up and leaned over him, grabbing my backpack off the bed. That's when I noticed the ink on his back. "You didn't tell me you got a new one," I said, trying to get a better look at the beautiful griffin spread across his back. "Turn around. I want to see it." My fingers traced over the muscular curves of his back, following the lines of the wings that spanned from one shoulder blade to the other. "Griff, this is amazing. When did you get it?"

"Um, it was finished up about a month ago."

"And you didn't tell me?" I swung my backpack at him. He threw his hands up, prepared for more attacks.

"Sorry, the band's been busy."

"Well, you certainly look the part now: Mr. Hardcore Rocker all tatted up and sexy." I added a little hip-shimmy for effect.

"I do have an image to uphold." He grinned and pulled the t-shirt over his head, hiding the griffin underneath.

I nodded in agreement and slung my backpack over my shoulder. "I'll be out in a bit."

The shower was a godsend. The heavy ache that my earlier dream had glued to my heart lost some of its stickiness and circled the drain with the orange hair chalk I rinsed from my hair.

Toweling off, I slipped on my comfy flannel pajama bottoms

and an old tie-dyed t-shirt I'd made in high school. I brushed the tangles from my hair and pulled it back into a ponytail before I went to lie down.

Griffin was already in bed, his breathing deep and even. Quietly, I tiptoed from the bathroom. I set my bag down and pulled an extra blanket from the bed and grabbed a pillow. The chair in the corner looked comfortable enough for me to curl up in for a few hours. "What are you doing?" Griffin asked.

"Uh…getting ready for bed?"

"Get over here." He sighed and patted the bed.

"Griff, I don't feel right about this. What about Erin?"

The last thing I wanted to do was get him in trouble with Erin. Even though they hadn't been together for more than a month, I didn't want to ruin anything. From the few times I'd met her, she seemed like a nice girl.

"Jillibean, I'm tired and I want to go to sleep. Erin's fine. Now, get over here, I'm not letting you sleep in a fucking chair."

I tossed the blanket and pillow back onto the bed and climbed in beside him. "You're already in trouble, aren't you?" I asked, burrowing under the blankets.

"Nothing I can't handle." He turned and faced the other wall, pulling the blankets up to his chin. "Good night, Bean."

"Goodnight."

Staring into the dark, I remembered the sleepovers Griffin and I had as children. We'd stay up all night watching movies and eating junk food until one of us felt like we would puke. But the second puberty knocked on the door, my grandparents had put the kibosh on our late night visits. Still, we saw each other every day—living next door to each other helped out a lot. Since I'd moved in with my grandparents at the age of six, Griffin had always been by my side—my protector, my cohort, and my best friend.

I snuggled into the covers, my back pressed to his. Heat pooled beneath the blanket we shared. I wondered if he felt it too…probably not. Sharing a bed with him now was very different than when we were children. We weren't kids anymore and my body reacted to him in a very different way.

I took a deep breath and let it out slowly, an attempt to slow my racing heart. Burying my want, I let myself be content with feeling safe with him beside me. My eyelids drooped and I fell into a dreamless sleep.

Chapter Three

My eyelids fluttered open when I heard a key sliding in and out of the lock, followed by a few choice words. Sleepily I walked over to the door and peered through the peephole. Griffin cursed on the other side.

"Fucking piece of…"

"Shit?" I said, opening the door with a smirk.

"Yes," he nodded in agreement. He smiled, chucked the key card across the room, and handed me a Starbucks coffee cup.

"You're up early," I said, pulling the stopper from the lid and sipping my skinny soy mocha. He walked past me into the room, pressing his lips to the side of his lidless coffee cup. "Why don't you ever get a lid on your coffee?" I asked.

"I like the smell as much as the taste." He winked and took another sip.

"You're so weird." Before I curled up into the small chair beside the desk I peeked into his cup and wrinkled my nose. "Black coffee? You should be a little more adventurous."

"I'll save the adventure for my love life."

"Ew." I rolled my eyes, shooing away adventurous images of him and his newest girlfriend. "But since you brought it up, have you heard from Erin?" They hadn't been dating long. I bet this trip hadn't gone over well…not that she had anything to worry about.

"Yeah, she called before you got up. I didn't want to wake you, so I took a walk down the street while I talked to her. And as luck would have it, I ran into these two beauties." He pointed to our coffees and smiled.

"So, how is Miss Erin?" I asked, curling into the small chair beside the desk.

"Eh, good, I guess." He shrugged.

"You guess? That doesn't sound good."

"I don't know. Things are just so damn awkward with her right now."

I chewed on the end of the stopper from my cup. "You're doing it again." I pulled the stopper from my mouth and pointed it at him.

"What?" he asked, staring at me with his dark eyes.

"You're looking for some reason to break up with her."

"I am not."

"Whatever you say. But when you talk about her, you sound more like the Grim Reaper than Cupid." My heart still clenched at the thought of him with someone else. What did they offer him that I couldn't? But, putting my jealousy aside, I wanted him to be happy. "Give her a chance," I encouraged.

"Yeah. We'll see," he said with a noncommittal shrug. "You ready?" he asked, draining the last of his coffee. His convenient change of topic wasn't lost on me, but I didn't press for more information; he'd talk when he was ready.

"As I'll ever be," I grumbled, unfolding myself from the chair. Setting my coffee cup on the table, I raised my arms above my head and stretched. "I guess I should get changed, huh?" I dropped my arms, smacking them against my legs like they were made of lead.

Griffin took a quick sip of coffee and cocked his head, swallowing. "Hmm, I don't know?" He tilted his head the other direction and pointed at me. "I like those shorts," he said with a wink.

I glanced down at my comfy sheep-adorned sleep shorts...my very short sleep shorts. *Why did he have to say stuff like that?* I knew it was nothing more than him messing with me—friendly, playful banter—but shit, my heart had to go and morph it into something more. *Damn him. And damn my traitorous, fluttering heart.* I narrowed my eyes. "Don't make fun of the sheep."

He took another gulp of coffee and held up his hands. "Hey, you asked. Just offering some sound fashion advice. You wear sheep well, Jillibean."

"Mm-hm. And you said I was the smart-ass." I shook my head and padded across the room, kneeling beside my bag. Rooting around, I pulled out a pair of denim shorts and a tank top. "I'll be right back." I turned and made my way to the bathroom, trying to keep my heart in check. *Friend, Jillian. He's just a friend.*

* * *

"Remind me again why you chose to go to school in Rhode Island?" Griffin asked wearily. Eight hours trapped in the car had taken its toll on the both of us.

"Because it's where budding fashionistas, like myself, must learn the trade," I replied with affected enthusiasm. At this point in the journey, I too had begun to wonder why I'd decided to leave southern Illinois and go to school 1,100 miles away. But then images of planes crashing into New York City buildings popped into my head and I remembered why FIT hadn't even been an option.

"Gotcha." Griffin tried to stretch out his long legs and failed miserably. My little Honda Civic didn't provide very much leg room for a person who stood six foot four.

"Thanks for coming with me."

"Jillibean, I wouldn't trade this for anything. Plus, you won't be back for a while, so I have to get all the time with you that I can."

"I'm going to miss you."

The corners of his mouth pulled down. "I already miss you." His voice was somber…why? He'd been my biggest supporter when I'd made the decision to go away to school. I figured he'd be glad to get rid of me, so he could focus his time on Erin and the band. Melancholy Griffin wasn't what I expected.

By the time we got into town, the sun hung low on the western horizon. I pulled into the student union parking lot so I could check in and get my dorm key. Griffin and I unfolded ourselves from the car and stretched. Before we walked up the steps to the union, Griffin gave his bike a once over. Since I planned on keeping my car at school, Griffin needed a means of transportation back to Illinois; hauling his bike had been the easiest and cheapest solution we had come up with.

"So, how does it feel? You made it. You're officially a design student," he said, opening the door to the Resident Life Office.

"A dream come true." I stood, looking around, taking it all in.

As a little girl, I'd always dreamed of going to design school. At the ripe old age of five, I realized I wanted to design my own clothes. I remembered my mom taking Jennifer and me to church on Sundays. I had sat on the floor of the church and used the pew as a desk. By the end of the service I had usually sketched twenty or thirty different designs. Mom had saved most of my drawings, but when my parents died and Jennifer and I were forced to move in with Grandma and Grandpa, I wasn't allowed to bring them. My grandparents didn't have much space and they only allowed us the barest essentials. My earliest creations most likely ended up as compost in the local landfill.

Now, thirteen years later, despite all the heartache and pain of my childhood, I was standing in the Resident Life Office of a prestigious Rhode Island design school, that much closer to realizing my dreams.

The RLO was a flurry of activity. With the onslaught of new arrivals, it was a good thing office hours had been extended. Looking up at Griffin, I sighed. "I'm going to get in line. It might be a while."

"No problem. I'm going to find something to eat. You want anything?" Griffin asked.

I shook my head. I was too excited and nervous to eat.

After thirty minutes of paperwork, I had my dorm access card and my room key, and Griffin had a full stomach and adequate time to smooth things out with Erin.

"Things okay with Erin?" I asked. As we walked to the car, I stowed my paperwork and dorm key, while I dug my car keys out from the bottom of my purse.

"She's all right. Thinks it's a little weird that I came with you, but that's okay." He shrugged.

Shit. I had gotten him in trouble. It felt like a brick had dropped into my stomach. I didn't want to screw things up for him. I looked up from my purse. "I'm sorry. I shouldn't have asked you to come."

Griffin halted his footsteps and put his hand on my shoulder, making sure I stopped, too. With the hand on my shoulder, he turned me to face him. "Jillibean, when haven't I been through a life-changing event with you? Did you honestly think that I wouldn't be here for this?"

I shook my head. Tears stung my eyes. He pulled on my shoulders, drawing me into his strong embrace. It took all of my strength not to cry. I refused to spend our last six days together in tears.

"Don't worry about Erin. She's fine."

"I just don't want to be the one to screw things up between you two."

He pulled away enough to see my face. "You aren't. Okay?"

I nodded.

He smiled. "Let's go see how big your new closet…um, place is."

"Very funny."

"I thought so," he said, shrugging.

My car crested a hill and Victor Hall, my dorm, came into view. Victor stood like a proud sentry on the north end of campus. The rear parking lot was deserted. Most freshmen would be arriving within the next few days, but classes didn't actually start until September 11th (just my luck). The second I'd found out that residence halls opened on August 30th, I was ready to pack up my shit and skip town faster than a toddler hopped up on energy drinks.

* * *

The low-flying airplane roaring overhead startled me from a nightmare. The walls rumbled and my breathing hitched; I could feel my heart pounding in my ears. Griffin lay beside me, still fast asleep. The green, digital readout on my alarm clock said it was September 6th, 8:30 a.m. Griffin was leaving today.

I knew he needed to get back home. With the fall semester starting at the State University, Mine Shaft was booking shows at frat parties every weekend. Griffin couldn't afford to be gone, and I didn't think his bandmates appreciated his absence any more than Erin did. He'd gotten a bazillion text messages from them while we'd been out last night. Selfishly, though, I talked him into staying at least until today, the day my roommate was moving in. I didn't want to spend even one night alone.

I slipped out of bed quietly, careful not to wake Griffin. My head hurt, but for the most part, I wasn't in bad shape considering how much I had drank last night. Griffin and I had decided to celebrate his last night in Providence by putting our fake IDs to good use. I popped four ibuprofens and my antidepressant, grabbed the things I needed for a shower, and closed the door behind me.

* * *

When I returned to my room, Griffin was packing his duffle bag. "I've been dreading this part since we left Illinois last Friday," I said, tossing my toiletries and wet towel into the closet.

"Me too." He pulled me to his side and hugged me tightly. He ran his fingers over the wet strands of my hair before he let go. "I am going to miss you so damn much," he said.

This time I didn't hold back the tears.

"Come on, Jillibean. This is too fucking hard when you're sad. We'll talk every day. Especially this coming week."

"Promise?" I choked.

"Have I ever deserted you on that day?"

"No."

Griffin and I walked down to the parking lot. "I miss you already," I whispered. Tears slid down my cheeks. I threw my arms around him.

He smiled and kissed my forehead. "I miss you too." Letting go, he stepped closer to his bike, straddled it, and ripped the engine.

He stretched his hand to me. "We'll get through this together."

"Promise?"

"Forever."

I stepped closer and hugged him again. With my face pressed to the crook of his neck, I asked, "Where's your helmet?"

"You know I don't like those things," he replied.

I shoved away from him. "Damn it, Griffin. You better start wearing a goddamn helmet."

"I'll buy one just for you when I get home." He pinched my chin between his forefinger and thumb, giving me his most innocent smile.

I batted his hand away and glared at him. "Damn right you will," I said.

"I gotta go, Jillibean. I'll check in all day. Keep your phone close."

Tears streaked down my face. "Okay."

"Have fun this year. You're going to rock those design classes."

He hugged me one last time before he gunned the throttle and pulled away. "Bye, Jillibean!" he yelled over his shoulder.

"Get a helmet, Griffin!" I yelled back as he disappeared around the corner. Why did it feel like my heart had just been ripped from my chest?

Chapter Four

September 11th. My first day of classes. Of all days, why did this one have to be the first?

I walked through the quad on my way back to Victor Hall and saw the flag at half-mast. I couldn't escape this day...ever.

My phone chimed with an incoming text message from Griffin.

I'm with you, Bean, he wrote.

Promise?

Forever. I'll call you later.

After reading his text, I felt slightly better. I typed my response and hit send. *Certain to be the highlight of my day.*

I unlocked the door to my room, dropped my backpack by the closet, and did my best impersonation of an extra on *The Walking Dead*, shambling over to my bed. Not five minutes later, my roommate, Sarah Theissen, came bursting through the door.

"Oh, hey," she said, caught off guard. "Sorry, I didn't know you were back."

"It's okay." I didn't make any effort to remove my head from the pillow.

Sarah shut the door, flung her bag onto her bed, and started rummaging through her closet. While swiping hangers from one side to the other, she asked, "Are you okay?"

"Fan-fucking-tastic."

That got her attention. Her aggressive clothes-mining expedition ceased. She turned around and stared at me.

"Uh…okay? That didn't sound encouraging. What's wrong?"

"Nothing." I sat up, trying to hide the sadness weighing on my heart. "I'm sorry. Just a rough day." If I pretended everything was fine, maybe she wouldn't push for more of an explanation.

During our correspondence over the summer, I'd only briefly mentioned that my parents were no longer living. I never gave her any details, so I couldn't blame her for not knowing how difficult today was. I wished Griffin were here. He knew.

Sarah grabbed a pencil off her dresser. Twisting her black and blonde ombre hair into a bun, she shoved the pencil into the knot at the back of her head. "Okay then. I have the perfect cure for a shitty day. The Phi Psis are having a party tonight and we're going."

"On a Wednesday?" I asked.

"Yeah, a welcome back party."

"Uh…I don't think so. I'm not really in the mood for a party."

"Nonsense. A party is exactly what you need. My boyfriend is meeting us there. Who knows, maybe you'll find a hottie for yourself."

I rolled my eyes. "Uh…no," I protested. The last thing I wanted was to be fixed up. There was only one man who appealed to me, and he wasn't interested, so I was destined to be single forever.

She cocked her head and frowned. "Jillian, all you've done is mope since I got here last Friday. When we talked this summer, you couldn't wait to get here and live it up. What's wrong? What happened to that girl?"

That girl had had to start college on September 11th.

"Fine. I'll go." If only to stop her from asking more questions I didn't feel like answering.

"Awesome. I'll text Brandon." Sarah went to her bed and started rummaging through her purse. Pulling her phone free, she tapped out a quick text.

"Okay, my fashion-forward friend, we need to get ready." She patted the mattress and stood up, holding her hands out to me. Walking toward my bed, she grabbed my hands and pulled me off the bed. "That's my girl. Help me find something to wear?" She smiled sweetly. She was a pretty cool roommate. I counted myself lucky; I could have ended up with way worse.

An hour later, Sarah was rocking a black mini-dress. I'd ruched the bodice on the side that didn't have a sleeve. The simple alteration helped accentuate her tiny waist. The dress's snug fit and short length also made Sarah's tanned, flawless legs look stunning. With her long hair loosely curled, the black color at the crown of her head faded to a pale yellow, very striking against her dark ensemble. Standing next to her, I felt short and severely underdressed in a simple royal blue tie-back halter and black skinny jeans. Oh well, I wasn't really in the mood to party anyway. If nothing else, at least the bright blue streaks of chalk I'd put in my hair made me look like a rock goddess.

Sarah dug her candy red stilettos from the closet, slipped them on, and admired my handiwork in the full-length mirror attached to our door. "Jillian, you are brilliant."

"Whatever. All I did was add a few stiches on the side with a needle and thread, not too difficult."

"Come here." Sarah waved me over to her side of the room. "We need a picture before we leave." Sarah was a photography student. She'd been snapping pictures since she'd gotten here last Friday night. It seemed that she saw the world through a constant viewfinder.

Once Sarah was satisfied with the shots she'd gotten, we grabbed our purses and left the room with discarded piles of clothes and shoes to clean up later.

* * *

The Phi Kappa Psi house didn't disappoint. The booze flowed freely and music pounded at ear-splitting decibels. In actuality, it was the perfect way to forget today's date.

"Sarah!" a voice called over the noise.

Sarah and I turned around, looking for the person who'd shouted her name. Seeing him in the distance, Sarah waved her hands above her head and yelled back, "Brandon, over here!"

Brandon pushed his way through the crowd toward us. Coming up beside Sarah, he bent down and kissed her. "Hey, babe. How long have you been here?"

"Maybe five minutes? Right, Jillian?" She looked at me and smiled.

"It hasn't been much longer than that," I agreed.

Extending his hand toward me in a friendly gesture, I placed mine in his and gave it a firm shake. "So, you're the roommate Sarah's been talking about all summer?"

"That would be me. I'm Jillian, nice to meet you," I replied.

"You're the fashion designer?" he asked.

"Yep. What's your major?"

"Architectural Engineering," he said, putting his arm around Sarah's waist. He smiled broadly and pushed his thick-framed glasses up on his nose.

"Wow." I looked at Sarah and smiled. Not only was Brandon gorgeous, with his pale blue eyes and neatly trimmed hair, he was smart, too.

"I can see Sarah spends her days talking about me." Brandon pinched her side and she giggled.

Sarah squirmed under his arm, batting him away playfully. "Oh, Brandon," she mocked in a fake southern drawl, "what would I do with myself if I couldn't talk about my beau all day long?" She pantomimed waving a fan in front of her face.

I laughed. Their comfortable interaction reminded me of how Griffin and I were. "Don't worry, Brandon. I vaguely remember her mentioning something about a boyfriend when we talked this summer."

"I'm sure she did." He rolled his eyes, but I could tell he was just playing with her. His affectionate smile negated the feigned annoyance I heard in his voice.

"You two dated in high school, right?" I asked.

"Yes. I'm one of those girls," Sarah said. "I followed my high school sweetheart to college." She looked up at Brandon and batted her eyelashes.

"And there's nothing wrong with that," I added.

"I like her." Brandon said to Sarah, smiling at me. "You would not believe how much shit Sarah's parents gave her about 'following' me here."

"Tell me about it," Sarah said.

Brandon took Sarah's hand. "Come on. You girls need a drink." He led us through the crowd. Sarah looked over her shoulder and smiled, making sure I was close behind.

Brandon pushed the back door open and led us out onto the deck, where the kegs were. A large crowd was gathered around the alcohol, making it difficult for all three of us to work our way through. "Wait here, I'll get your drinks," Brandon said, before he disappeared into the mass of people.

"Sarah, he's great," I said once he was out of earshot.

"He is." She beamed.

"How long have you been together?"

"We started dating during my sophomore year of high school. He was a junior."

I nodded my head in approval. "That's really awesome."

"Do you have a boyfriend?" she asked. Griffin immediately popped into my head, but I was pretty sure he wasn't the kind of boyfriend she was referring too.

"Yes," I hesitated. "But not in the romantic sense. Do you remember me mentioning my best friend, Griffin?"

"Kind of." She furrowed her brow, trying to recall our conversations from the summer.

"Griffin Daniels. He lived next door to my grandparents. When I moved in with them, he and I were pretty much inseparable."

"Oh, yeah. He's the one in the band, right?"

"Yeah, Mine Shaft. He's the lead singer and he plays the bass guitar." I smiled. I loved bragging about him.

"Do you have a picture? I want to see this rock god best friend."

I pulled my phone from my back pocket and touched the button to illuminate the screen. The picture of Griffin and I at my high school graduation shone on the screen. Griffin's older sister, Ren, had used my phone to snap the picture. Griffin looked straight ahead and I was on his back. When Ren instructed us to say "I is educated," Griffin smiled and repeated her phrase while I ignored her and planted a kiss on his cheek instead. This picture was my favorite and instantly became my wallpaper setting. It made me smile every time I saw it.

I passed the phone over to her. "This is Griffin?" she asked, grinning at me strangely.

"Yeah. Why are you looking at me like that?"

"Holy hell, Jillian, he's freaking hot."

She handed my phone back and I looked at the screen. Griffin always did have great hair. Black waves fell across his forehead in an artful mess that only a guy could get away with. I tilted my head, examining the picture. With his black leather jacket, messy bedhead, and stubbled jaw, he had looked rather sexy that night.

The screen went black and I slid it back into my pocket.

"Hey, who does my girlfriend think is hot?" Brandon said, walking up behind me.

"No offense, Bran, but Jillian's friend is smokin'." Sarah said, patting Brandon on the back.

Brandon handed me a cup. "Thanks," I said, taking it from his hand.

He handed Sarah hers. "Sarah's eyeing up your guy, huh?" he asked, taking a sip of his drink.

I took a sip of my beer and shook my head. "Oh, he's not my boyfriend," I said.

"I don't know why," Sarah interjected.

"He's only my friend." It was better that way, I reminded myself. Why complicate things? "He has a girlfriend."

"Good, I'd hate to lose my girl to some dude that lives..." Brandon looked at me. "Where are you from?"

"Glen Carbon, Illinois," I answered. "About fifteen minutes east of St. Louis."

"Maguire." A voice shouted from behind us.

Sarah and I started at the deep voice and turned in its direction. Brandon sat his beer down on the deck's railing and walked around us. "Hill, good to see you, man." The two guys gave each other the customary guy-hug—a few slaps to the back.

"You too, man." Backing away from Brandon, he smiled at Sarah. "Sarah, nice to see you're a permanent fixture this year."

"Yep. Now Brandon can't get away with anything," Sarah said, knocking her hip into Brandon's side.

"Who's this?" Mr. Deep Voice turned to me and smiled.

"This is my roommate, Jillian," Sarah said.

"Nice to meet you, Roommate Jillian." He smirked and offered his hand in greeting.

"Nice to meet you, Brandon's Friend," I retorted, placing my hand in his. He gave it a firm and confident shake, never averting his gaze.

"The name's Ryan." He reminded me of a California surfer boy. His blond hair stood out against his tanned skin, and his body suggested he spent an ample amount of time riding the waves. His cerulean gaze burned like the hottest part of a flame. It was almost a certainty that anyone who got involved with this guy was sure to get burned.

"When did you get back?" Brandon asked him.

Ryan flashed me a smile and turned his attention back to Brandon. "Yesterday."

"Cool. You get moved into your apartment?"

"Yeah, my parents sent most of my things to the apartment while I was in Chicago."

"Oh, that's right; you had that internship this summer. How was that?" Brandon asked.

"It was pretty fucking cool. Kept me busy, though."

"An internship doing what?" Sarah asked.

"My dad hooked me up with an architectural firm in Chicago. He called in some favors." Ryan shrugged.

"Impressive," Sarah said. "That will look great on a résumé."

"I hope so. You want another beer?" He asked me, completely disregarding Sarah.

I looked down at my full glass. "No thanks, I'm good."

He placed his hand on my elbow and leaned in closer. "You want to go find someplace quieter?"

My throat tightened and my heartbeat quickened. I looked at Sarah, hoping she'd save me.

"Come on, Brandon. These shoes are killing me. I need to sit down." She took Brandon's hand and led him toward the house. I knew I was on my own when she giggled and nodded her head, indicating I should go. *Thanks a lot, Sarah. Very subtle.* She and I were going to have a long talk later on.

"Um…" Before I could come up with a convincing reason not to go with him, my phone buzzed. I pulled it back out. A sweaty picture of Griffin doused in stage lights illuminated the screen. "I'm sorry. I really need to take this." I gave Ryan an apologetic smile and took off in search of that quieter place without him.

As I walked toward the back of the house, I answered the call. "You buy a helmet yet?" I shouted over the pounding bass, making my way toward the quieter backyard.

"Hello to you, too. Where the hell are you?" he shouted back.

Once I was clear of the house I could hear him better. "Hi, Griffin. Thanks for saving me. Even eleven hundred miles away, your timing is impeccable."

"Where are you? Saving you from what?" he asked again. He sounded worried.

I found a secluded corner in the back of the yard and plopped onto the grass. "My roommate, Sarah, talked me into going to the Phi Psi party tonight. I'm here now."

"Be careful, Jillibean, fucking frat boys can't be trusted."

After meeting Ryan Hill, I thought Griffin's animosity toward frat guys was warranted. "Don't worry, I will."

"How are you?" he asked.

"I'm okay, but I'm not going to lie, it completely sucked ass having to start classes today."

"I'm sorry, Bean. I wish I could be there with you, but I know how strong you are. You're going to do great."

"I appreciate the vote of confidence." I sighed, running my fingers over the thick grass.

"Damn right I have confidence in you. You're the strongest person I know."

I smiled, picturing him giving me a stern look; his forehead creased, eyes pinched. He always was my biggest cheerleader. "Thanks, Griff."

"I don't need thanks for telling the truth. Are you alone?" he asked. "Where's Sarah?"

"She's off somewhere with her boyfriend. Did you start classes today?" A warm breeze whipped some of my blue strands of hair into my face. I brushed them away, careful not to get blue chalk on my face and fingers.

"Yeah, I had one. The guys and I spent the rest of the day rehearsing." He sounded tired. He was the most driven person I knew. I hoped he wasn't pushing himself too hard.

"Do you have a show tonight?"

"Yeah, but I wanted to call you before we went on."

"I miss you, Griff." I suddenly felt very alone.

"I miss you too." The timbre of his voice dropped. "I may not be physically there, but I'm still with you, Bean."

"Promise?" I waited for his usual reply.

"I'm sorry, Bean, I've got to go." he said hurriedly. "The guys are waiting. I'll call you later."

He didn't say "forever," like he always did.

"That's okay. Knock 'em dead." I tried to sound excited, but the lump in my throat served as a cork, keeping the excitement bottled up inside.

"Be careful, Jillibean. I mean it."

To keep from crying, I busied myself tearing at clumps of grass. "I will. I promise. Bye, Griff."

"Bye, Bean."

Before the line went dead, I could hear the repetitive beat of drums in the background. For the second time tonight, I watched Griffin's picture fade to black before I slipped it back into my pocket.

The sun had set while I was on the phone. Dozens of darkened silhouettes filled the backyard, oddly lit by the light spilling through the windows of the house. Hearing Griffin's voice reminded me of how much I missed him. I didn't have the energy to join the masses anymore. In retrospect, this party wasn't such a good idea.

I poured the warm beer in cup onto my tiny mound of grass clippings before I stood up. I was ready to go back to the dorm. I hoped Sarah wouldn't be too upset.

Pushing through the crowd, I pulled open the back door and went inside. Only a few people stood in the kitchen, but when I entered the main room, it was filled with tons of horny co-eds looking to score, and countless drunks. It seemed when people got wind of a party the news spread like kindling over dry brush.

"Sarah?" I yelled over the booming music. I stretched up on my tiptoes and craned my neck, hoping to get a better view of the room. Sadly, my five-and-a-half-foot frame didn't offer me any advantages. Great, that's all I needed—to lose my roommate at my first college party.

In the distance, I thought I saw a girl wearing bright red heels and a black dress, sitting on someone's lap. I squinted, trying to see through the dark. Sure enough, my eyes hadn't deceived me: it was Sarah sitting on Brandon's lap, their heads connected at the lips.

When I was a few feet away, I called her name. "Sarah." By her lack of response, I could tell her thoughts were elsewhere. "Sarah,"

I tried again. I really didn't want to tap her shoulder, but she wasn't paying attention.

"Hey, it's Roommate Jillian."

Behind me, I could hear Ryan Hill's deep voice approaching. *Shit. Why wouldn't he leave me alone?* I turned around and there he was, standing right in front of me. "It's just Jillian," I corrected.

"Where'd you run off to earlier?"

"Nowhere. If you'll excuse me, I need to talk to my roommate." I turned around, hoping he'd realize I wasn't interested.

"Sure thing, babe. I can take a hint," he replied sarcastically. "You didn't look like you'd be a whole lot of fun anyways."

"Dick," I mumbled under my breath. As much as I wanted to turn around and flick him off, my desire to leave won out. I tapped Sarah on the shoulder and prayed he walked away. "I'm sorry to ask, but would it be okay if we left?"

"Uh, sure." She hesitated. "Is everything okay?"

I shook my head no. I wasn't okay, and if I didn't leave now, I risked having a meltdown in the middle of all these fucking strangers.

"Okay. Um…" I could tell she didn't know what to do. She hadn't ever seen me on the verge of a panic attack. She gave Brandon a concerned look and then stood up from his lap. "I'll call you in the morning," she said, bending down to kiss him one more time.

When she straightened up, she appraised me. "Jillian, what's wrong? You don't look so good."

"I just need to go." I needed to get out of the crowd, but who I needed most was back in Illinois.

"Do you want me to drive you two back to the dorm?" Brandon asked Sarah.

"No, I drove. We haven't been here that long. Plus, you kept me pretty occupied. I never even got to finish my drink." Sarah winked at Brandon.

"I'll walk you guys out," Brandon said, standing up.

The three of us shoved our way through the throng of people, to the front door. Once we were outside, I felt better. The breezy night air cooled my flushed skin and worked magic on my shot nerves.

"Jillian, will you please tell me what's wrong?" Sarah begged. I could tell by the sound of her voice that she was really worried about me.

"I'll be okay. I promise. I just needed to get out of there." I took a deep breath. Sarah gave Brandon another uneasy look, but didn't ask me any more questions. I was thankful for the silence as we walked to her car.

Brandon and Sarah held hands and I walked a couple of steps behind them, enjoying the night air. After feeling like the walls were closing in at the frat house, outside felt like heaven.

When we got to the car, I climbed into the passenger seat, giving Sarah and Brandon a minute to say good-bye and most likely talk about my erratic behavior. I was sure they both thought I was Looney Tunes by now. I rested my face on the cool glass of the window and waited when my phone buzzed in my pocket. Pulling it out, I saw I had a text from Griffin. It read: *Forever.*

He knew he'd forgotten.

Chapter Five

Sarah pulled the driver's side door open and started the car. In the side mirror, I saw Brandon walking back to the frat house.

"Jillian, you really need to tell me what's going on, because I am seriously worried." She turned and looked at me, unwilling to move the car until I gave her some sort of explanation.

I felt sick. All I really wanted right now was for Griffin to hold me. He'd gotten me through this day for the past eleven years. The only people I've ever discussed my parents' deaths with were my therapist and him. I lifted my head from the window and looked at Sarah. Now that I was on my own, I didn't know how to handle my emotions.

The streetlights bathed the car in a soft glow, providing just enough light that I could make out Sarah's features. Her eyes were wide with worry, the blackness of her pupils hiding the striking violet color of her irises. The corners of her lips were turned down. She waited for me to say something.

"I'm sorry I asked you to leave. I just couldn't stay in there."

Not after talking to Griffin. And definitely not after meeting Ryan-Jackass-Hill.

"I'm not upset that you asked me to leave, I'm worried about you," she said, taking my hand in hers. "Did something happen? Did someone hurt you?"

I shook my head. "No, nothing like that." I lifted my hand from hers and shifted in the seat, angling my body so I could see her better. "Can we go back to the dorm, please?" I asked, not wanting to open my old wounds in the car.

With a defeated sigh, Sarah replied, "Sure."

I watched her pull the car onto the street. Her shoulders sagged as she leaned toward the steering wheel. I should give her a chance. Wasn't that why I came here? To start over? Get away from my past? I needed to talk to her. "Sarah," I whispered.

She kept her eyes on the road. "Hmm?"

"Are you tired?" I asked. If I was going to spill my guts, I wanted to get it all out at once.

"Not really."

"Can we talk when we get back to the room?"

She turned her head toward me. "Only if you want to."

I was pretty sure I needed to talk to someone. The one person I wanted to talk to wasn't here, so maybe it was time I learned to trust someone else.

* * *

I was thankful for the quiet, five-minute drive back to the dorm. Somehow, Sarah must have known I needed that time to gather my courage.

Sarah parked the car and we got out. When I rounded the front of the car, she threw her arms around my shoulders, squeezing me in a tight hug. "Jillian, we may not have known each other long, but I'm always here to listen," she said.

"Thanks," I whispered.

Once we got to our room, we both ditched the party clothes for sweats and t-shirts. My well-loved, oversized, Mine Shaft t-shirt was too comfortable to pass up, and because it used to be Griffin's, it sort of felt like he was here with me.

I plopped down on my bed and pulled my comforter around my shoulders, waiting for Sarah to get back from the bathroom. *What made me think that my past wouldn't follow me here?* No matter where I lived, no matter where I went, my parents would still be dead. College wasn't the escape from reality that I'd prayed for. If anything, college was real life—real reality. For the first time ever, I had to survive on my own.

The door creaked open and Sarah poked her head around, "It's just me," she said, tossing a towel into her hamper.

I smiled half-heartedly.

She climbed onto her bed. "If you're too tired, we can talk some other time. I don't want to force you…" She trailed off.

I shook my head. "I need to do this." Sitting cross-legged on my bed, I pulled the blanket tighter and took a deep breath.

"You already know that my parents died when I was little and that my sister and I had to move in with our grandparents. I told you that this summer."

"I remember." She nodded.

That was the easy part. The rest of the words felt like barbs stuck to my vocal cords. I cleared my throat hoping to dislodge them.

"When I was little, I collected snow globes. Every vacation, every trip, wherever we went, I had to get a snow globe. By the time I was six, I had ninety-nine different globes from all over the U.S., and even a few from other countries. My dad had a business trip in New York City and my mom went with him." My voice wobbled. I didn't want to cry, but as my therapist always said, tears were a *healthy* way to let go of the hurt inside of me.

Tears rolled down my cheeks.

I didn't feel better. Even after all these years, it still hurt so damn much.

Sarah got up from her bed, grabbed a box of tissues from her dresser, and moved onto my bed. She pulled a tissue from the box and held it out. I released the death grip on my blanket and took the tissue.

"Thanks." I sniffled, wiping my nose.

"No problem." She scooted closer and wrapped me in a fierce hug.

Once Sarah let go, I blew my nose and continued with my story. "Before my parents left for New York, my mom promised she'd get me a snow globe from the city. As it turned out, my stupid collection would cost my parents their lives."

"That's not true," she said quietly.

I pulled another tissue from the box and pressed it to my eyes. I couldn't stop crying. "Sorry." I sobbed into the tissue.

Sarah rubbed my back, trying to comfort me. "You really don't have to do this if you don't want to."

I lifted my head from the tissue and looked at her through swollen eyes. "I know. But I do want to." And I really did. "It just takes me a while to get through it. It's not something I talk about often. Years of counseling have gotten me this far, but I'm not sure I'll ever be able to forgive myself."

"Oh, Jillian." She sighed and hugged me again, pulling a tissue from the box and drying her eyes, too.

"If I hadn't asked them to get me that stupid snow globe, they wouldn't have decided to meet their friend that worked at the World Trade Center."

Sarah didn't answer right away. She bit her bottom lip and inhaled deeply, trying not to cry herself. "God, Jillian," she whispered.

"My mom called the night before and told me their plan for the day. They were picking up my snow globe and then their friend was giving them a tour of the buildings before the work day started. The fact that they had to buy my souvenir first made them schedule their tour at the exact wrong time." I tore up the tissue in my hand and tossed the shreds on the bed. I hated the emptiness in my hands, so I pulled a fresh one from the box and repeated the cycle.

"You want to know the worst part?"

Sarah nodded, pulling out a wad of tissues for herself, giving in to the tears she'd tried to fight off.

"My parents knew they weren't going to make it out."

"Dear God," she mumbled.

"Jennifer and I were at school when it happened. My grandparents had just dropped us off and were on their way back home."

I had to pause for a minute. This was so hard. I rubbed my eyes and tried to swallow the lump in my throat. "I need to get some water." I choked.

Without another thought, Sarah flew off the bed and went to the mini-fridge. She pulled out two bottles of water and came back to sit with me on my bed. "Here." She held out one of the bottles.

I grasped it with my tissue-less hand and held it to my cheek. The cold of the bottle broke through the numbness I felt at revealing my past. I enjoyed the cold for a second before pulling off the cap and taking several large gulps.

"Thanks," I said, replacing the cap. "I'm sure this is exactly what you had planned for tonight," I scoffed.

Sarah took a drink of her water and put the cap back on. "I'm not just your roommate, Jillian, I'm also your friend. I'm glad you trust me enough to tell me all this. I know it's hard. Like I said before, you can tell me anything."

I smiled a little. She wasn't Griffin, and no one could replace him, but right now, I was glad she was here.

I took another sip of water and continued. "I was in first grade that year. Jennifer was in fifth. I don't remember much about school that day, other than the teachers kept us in from recess. It wasn't until we got home that afternoon that things changed."

"My school closed early," Sarah added. "Being from Yorkville, I wasn't too far from lower Manhattan. Even though I was only in first grade, I remember everything like it was yesterday. It was so scary. At the time, my mom was teaching at my school, so I was able to be with her through all the chaos. My dad, being a doctor, was called in to help with the injured, but he was eventually sent home because—" she paused and blew her nose— "there weren't any."

In the back of my mind, I remembered Sarah saying she was from New York, but not truly understanding the geography of the state, I didn't realize she was so close to everything. "I'm sorry; this is probably hard for you, too. You were there. You lived it."

"I did and it was horrible. But at the end of the day, I didn't lose anyone. In my six-year-old world, I still felt a sense of security because I had my parents. I can't even imagine what you went through."

I buried my head in a tissue again and held my breath, holding back a fresh wave of tears. Sarah's hand moved in counterclockwise circles on my back while she listened to me sob. I concentrated on her hand, counting each circle she drew. *One…two…three… four…five…*

Fifteen… Feeling like I could get through the rest, I straightened up and drew in a large breath. "I'm sorry," I said. Sarah's hand fell away and I grabbed at the tissue box, pulling out five at once. I wiped tears and snot from my face.

"It's okay," she soothed, patting the blanket wrapped around my knee.

"Okay, where was I?"

"Things changed when you got home from school," she prompted.

"Oh, yeah. When Jennifer and I got home from school, my grandparents told us about the planes crashing into the buildings. We already knew that much from what our teachers told us at school. Then, Grandpa told us that Mom and Dad were in one of the buildings." I choked on my tears, coughing as the words fell out. "He also told us they left a message for us on the answering machine."

Sarah gasped, covering her mouth. "No."

I nodded. "At the time I was too little to really understand. It wasn't until years later that I worked up the courage to listen to the message. They told Jennifer and me good-bye."

"Oh, Jillian. I'm so sorry." She wrapped her arms around me, letting me cry quietly on her shoulder for a long time.

Sarah shh'd and soothed. She even drew her counterclockwise circles on my back again. I liked that. It gave me something to focus on when I felt like I was spinning out of control. Sarah's lazy circles would work in the absence of Griffin's strong arms. They both had their own special way of holding me together.

"I'm sorry I dragged you to that party tonight. I know now why you didn't want to go."

"It wasn't your fault. You didn't know," I mumbled against her shoulder.

"So, what's this Griffin guy like?" she asked. I could tell she was trying to shift my thoughts to a more pleasurable topic.

I lifted my head from her shoulder. From all the crying I felt my heartbeat pulsing behind my eyes. "What about him?" I croaked.

"He's your best friend?" I heard the skepticism in her voice—the unasked question: *Why?*

"Yeah." I nodded, rubbing my forehead.

"What's wrong with him?" she asked.

I laughed, confused by her question. "What?"

"Well, from what I've gathered." She held up her finger and began ticking off what she knew about Griffin. "He's talented, being in a band and all; he's kind and caring, because you've said as much; and he's got the smoldering bad boy look working for him. So, I'm wondering why he's *just* your friend. What's wrong with him?"

"Nothing," I replied defensively.

Sarah cocked her head. "Bullshit, nobody's perfect. There's got to be a reason why you two are 'just friends.'"

Last spring popped into my head. The night I'd kissed him. I shrugged off his rejection and smiled at Sarah. That was a story for another night. "He's a terrible slob. I'm talking month-old pizza boxes under the bed, dirty dishes everywhere, and he never puts the seat down."

"That's awful." She gasped in mock horror. Her giggling sold her out. "He's totally not relationship material. Wait a minute, what the hell am I doing with Brandon?" she asked. "He never puts the seat down either."

I laughed too. "I don't know how you survive." After tearing away the wall I'd built around my emotions, it felt nice to laugh about something completely ridiculous.

"What time is it?" I asked.

Sarah reached for the iPad sitting on my dresser and pressed the button at the bottom. "It's one."

"I'm so tired and my eyes hurt. Do you have classes on Thursday?" I asked.

"Yeah, but I may be ditching tomorrow," she said, standing up and stretching.

"It's the first week of classes. You can't skip yet."

"Watch me." Her devious grin morphed into a big yawn.

"You bad girl, you." I looked at my bed and noticed a mountain of tissues, but I was too tired to dispose of them properly. I shoved them onto the floor and flopped on my side, pulling the comforter up over my ears.

"Hey, missy," Sarah said. "You just told me that Griffin was the messy one." She pointed to the tissues on the floor.

I shrugged. "I never said I was a neat freak."

"Right." She smirked and pulled the blankets back on her bed. "Thank you for telling me your story."

Even though I had only touched upon one part of my dark past, the fact she knew that much made me feel better. "Thanks for listening."

"Anytime."

When Sarah flipped off the lights, images of the past flashed across my mind, but the only thing I could think about was what it felt like when Griffin's lips touched mine.

Chapter Six

My iPad blipped on my desk. Still half asleep, I sat up and reached for it, feeling around until my hand touched the corner. I pulled it onto my lap. Through my swollen eyes, I tried to focus on the screen. A FaceTime call from Griffin.

I glanced at Sarah who was still asleep and crept toward the door, not wanting to wake her. I was also thankful for some time alone with him and I would take it any way I could get it.

Shutting the door behind me, I slid my finger across the bottom, and Griffin's smiling face filled the screen. "Jillibean," he said.

At seeing his face, relief washed over me. I felt like I hadn't breathed since he'd left a week ago. "Hey, Griff."

I headed for the stairwell, hoping to find an empty music practice room so we could talk in private. The hallways were already crowded with people getting ready for their 8:00 a.m. classes.

"Are you okay?" he asked. "You don't look so good."

"Well gee, thanks." I ran my hand through my blue and blond mess of hair. "You're one to talk, Daniels. Trying to grow a beard?"

He rubbed his stubbly jaw, turning his head from side to side. "What? I thought you liked my scruffy look."

Actually, I did. It looked incredibly sexy on him, but right now, he did not need his ego fed. "You're looking more like a rock star every day." I smiled and pulled open the door to one of the three practice rooms in Victor Hall. I pushed the piano bench up against the wall so I could lean back and prop my iPad on my knees.

"How was your party last night?" he asked.

"After I talked to you, some sleazeball hit on me and I convinced Sarah to leave. I wasn't in the party mood."

Three tiny creases appeared between his brows, a telltale sign that he was worried. "Did the sleazeball hurt you?"

"No. But I wasn't so good last night. Like I said before, starting classes this week sucked."

"Your eyes are swollen," he commented. "You spent the whole night crying, didn't you?" He would know. He'd been with me on countless nights like last night.

"I did."

"Bean, you need to call Dr. Hoffman."

"I'm fine, Griff. When Sarah and I got back to the dorm, I talked to her. I told her what happened to Mom and Dad."

Griffin bit his bottom lip and rubbed his chin as he contemplated his response. "How do you feel?" he asked cautiously.

I took a deep breath. "Better."

"Really?" He was skeptical. "I don't want you to start hurting yourself again."

"I'm not. The thought never even crossed my mind. It actually felt good to open up to Sarah. She's amazing."

Griffin's dark eyes sparkled when he smiled. "I'm so proud of you, Jillibean. That took a lot of fucking courage to let her in."

"Thanks." I didn't think I had any more tears left, but they welled up in my eyes nonetheless.

"But, I still think you should call Dr. Hoffman. I worry that you're not meeting with her on a regular basis. College is stressful."

"If things get crazy, I promise to call her."

He exhaled, shrugging off his anxiety at the same time. "Okay."

"What are you doing up this early? Didn't you have a show last night?" I asked, trying to change the subject.

"The guys and I have a meeting with a producer this morning. But I'm not sure how that's going to work. Fucking Adam broke his wrist at the show last night. We didn't even play the full set."

"Whoa, back up a minute. A producer?"

"Yeah, the day I got back from taking you to school I got a call from a guy who heard Mine Shaft play about a month ago. He was interested in our sound and wants to meet with us."

I straightened up on the bench, grabbing my iPad in excitement. "Are you kidding?" I squealed. "Griffin, that's awesome. Why didn't you tell me?" I was so proud of him, yet a small pang of sadness hit me when I realized he hadn't called me when he'd gotten the news.

"I was going to tell you, but things have been so busy. And now all this shit with Adam." Griffin rolled his dark brown eyes. "Besides, I knew you were starting school this week and I didn't want to distract you."

"That's bullshit and you know it. I always want to know what's going on with you. No matter what."

The right corner of his lips pulled up in a sheepish grin. "Forgive me?" He pressed his hands together and pouted.

God, I missed him. "Yes," I grumbled. "But you better not do it again. You better fucking call me the instant something happens." I pointed my finger at the screen, scolding him.

"Yes, ma'am." He saluted.

"You said Adam broke his wrist? How did that happen?"

"We were at the Sig Nu house last night, and according to Adam, he saw a frat boy with his hands all over Trina."

"Uh-oh," I replied.

"Yeah, Adam went ballistic. He chucked his drumstick at the guy's head and went after him. Adam said the dude had a jaw made of fucking steel. Needless to say, he couldn't finish the set and we had to pack up and leave."

"Ugh, I'm sorry."

"We can't afford to cancel the rest of our shows. And there's no way in hell I'm going to miss out on what this producer wants just because Adam can't control his fucking temper. We're going to have to replace him until he can play again."

"Anyone in mind?"

"Not off the top of my head. We'll figure something out. I don't want to talk about Adam; it just pisses me off." A wavy lock of hair hung across his forehead and he brushed it away in his frustration. "You said some jackass was hitting on you last night?" I didn't think it was possible, but his eyes got darker and the warmth disappeared.

"Yeah, but don't worry about it. He knew I was not interested."

"Hold on a second, Bean." I heard the doorbell ring again as he set his iPad down. I was left staring at his red and black bass guitar that sat in the corner of his living room. After a few seconds, the image on the screen jostled around and Griffin came back into view, sharing the screen with Erin.

"Hi, Jillian," Erin said, waving.

"Hi, Erin." A knot developed in my stomach and I suddenly felt very self-conscious. Erin's shoulder-length blond hair was straightened to perfection and her makeup was flawless. I also didn't miss her hands lightly massaging his shoulders.

"Hey, Bean, we need to get going. I'll call you later and let you know what the producer said."

"Sounds good."

"Bye, Jillian," Erin shouted over Griffin's shoulder.

"Bye, guys," I said.

"Bye, Bean." He smiled and disconnected the call.

Staring at the blank screen, I was hit with a wave of jealousy. Even though Griffin was never without a girlfriend, I was always there for him when something was important. I should have been the one going with him to see the producer, not Erin.

Chapter Seven

Standing up from the piano bench, I clutched my iPad to my chest with one hand and pounded the lower octave piano keys with my other hand before marching back to my room. I didn't know why Erin's presence irritated me so much. It wasn't like I could go with Griffin to see the producer anyway.

When I opened the door to my room, I glanced at Sarah, who was still asleep. She hadn't moved an inch since I'd been gone. I wondered if she were serious about skipping class today. I couldn't wait to get to class—anything to take my mind off of Erin's hands. And the fact that she was with him right now and I wasn't.

I looked at my alarm clock: 7:30 a.m. I didn't have class until eleven, giving me plenty of time to make it to the fitness center and work off the growing tension in my muscles.

I tossed the iPad on my bed and went to my dresser. Pulling open a drawer, I rifled through a stack of t-shirts, looking for workout pants. Not finding any, I slammed the drawer shut and pulled open another. *Where the hell did I put my workout clothes?* Not finding any in the second drawer, I slammed it shut, too.

"Jillian?" Sarah said groggily. "What are you doing?"

I turned around. "Sorry. I was just looking for something."

Sarah rolled onto her side and beat her pillow a couple of times. "You're up early."

"Griffin called." I walked over to the closet and started shuffling through my clothes. *Maybe I hung my yoga pants up when Griffin and I unpacked everything.*

"Oh, really." I noticed a lilt in her voice even through her grogginess. "What did he want?"

"Nothing." I was in no mood to talk about him…or Erin. I pushed a hanger aside and it clacked against another one. "He just called to say hi."

"Mmm-hmm," she mumbled. I glanced over my shoulder and scowled at her innuendo. She readjusted her blanket and smiled. "What are you looking for?"

I turned back around and shoved another hanger across the bar. "My workout clothes. I was going to hit the gym before class." As soon as I said the words, my eyes zeroed in on a box I'd shoved into the back of the closet. The box with my yoga pants. And pictures.

I turned around and looked at Sarah snuggled in her bed. "Do you have any yoga pants I can borrow?" I asked. After last night, I refused to open that box.

She smiled. "Bottom drawer." Her hand crept out from under the blanket and pointed in the general direction of the dresser.

I walked over and opened the bottom drawer. "Thanks." I pulled out a pair of black pants and held them up to me. Even though Sarah was a few inches taller than me her pants would work until I could get myself a couple of new pairs.

"Is everything okay?" she asked. "You seem…irritated." She shifted. I could feel her watching me.

I turned and looked her in the eye. "I'm fine." Or I would be after forty minutes on a treadmill. "Thanks for letting me borrow these." I held up the pants and walked back to my side of the room.

"Sure, no problem." Sarah rolled over and faced the wall. "But, if you want to talk about what's bothering you, I'd listen," she said.

Once again, I shuffled through my drawer, this time looking for a tank top and sports bra. "Thanks, but I'm really okay."

"Okay," she said. "I'm going back to sleep. Have fun at the gym." She pulled her long brown hair out from under her face, fanning it on the pillow.

"I will."

* * *

When I walked into the Fitness Center, it resembled a Walmart on the day after Thanksgiving. I scanned the room for an open treadmill, finally noticing one in the back corner.

Weaving my way through rows of Nautilus equipment and sweaty bodies, I plugged in my earbuds, drowning out the sounds of clanking weights and grunting meatheads. I scrolled through my playlists looking for Mine Shaft.

In a cramped, dark corner, I mounted the treadmill and pushed play, turning up the sound as loud as it would go. Moving my index finger to the treadmill's settings, I held the upward facing arrow until the soles of my feet hit the rubber mat with the same steady beat as Adam's drum intro and Griffin's driving bass riff.

With each stride, my muscles welcomed the familiar stretch, while my lungs drew in large breaths. I quickly found my rhythm and settled in, already feeling my irritation melting away.

I concentrated on my breathing. *In…out…in…out…* Griffin's husky voice filled my ears and I couldn't help the smile that spread across my face. I remembered sitting through countless Mine Shaft rehearsals. Mine Shaft was Griffin's baby. Adam, Thor, and Pauly may have been members, but Griffin was the boss. Since Griffin had started the band in high school, the guys looked to him as their artistic director, along with being the lead bassist, front man, and songwriter.

Griffin would record their songs and burn them onto CDs. He'd use the recordings to hear the band's sound as a whole and fix the parts he wasn't happy with. When he didn't need the CDs anymore, I'd take them and download the music onto my iPod. Griffin hated that. He made me promise never to let anyone hear those shitty recordings. I always told him they weren't shitty, but he never agreed. Along with all the other hats he wore, he was also their worst critic.

I wondered how his meeting was going. If something happened, he'd call. I increased the speed, hoping to outrun the little voice in the back of my head telling me that Erin was with him and he didn't need me.

* * *

After my forty-minute workout, I went back to the dorm, showered, and got ready for class, taking care to put a few pink streaks of chalk in my long blond hair. I grabbed my backpack from the closet and glanced at Sarah still snuggled in her blankets. "Sarah?" I said, moving toward her bed. "Sarah." I tapped her shoulder.

"Hmm?" she answered.

"Are you sure you're not going to class today?"

She lifted her head off the pillow and looked at me. "Ugh," she moaned. "What time is it?"

"It's ten o'clock."

Sarah sat up, wrapping her blanket around her shoulders. "I suppose it would be really bad if I didn't go, huh?" A diffident smile spread across her face.

I nodded. "Yeah. What time is your class?"

"Eleven."

"You can make it, then," I added.

"All right," she groaned. She threw her blankets off and got up. "Where are you headed?"

"I was on my way to the dining hall."

Sarah frowned. "I'd love to go with you, but I don't think I'll have time."

"That's okay." I smiled. "I'm sure we'll have plenty of opportunities to eat at the dining hall together."

"I'll see you after class, okay?" she said.

"Yep." I walked toward the door and stopped. Turning around, I said, "Thanks for last night."

She pulled her hair through a ponytail holder and smiled. "Anytime."

* * *

I pushed through the doors of Victor Hall and walked down the hill toward the dining hall. I had an hour to kill before my three-hour Design and Draw class, and Lucky Charms and coffee were calling my name.

The dining hall was crowded, but not like the fitness center. I picked up a tray and a bowl, found my cereal of choice, and went to sit down at one of the few open tables. Before I dug into my breakfast, I checked my phone, worried that I might have missed a call from Griffin.

No missed calls. No new texts.

I stared into the bowl and watched the dehydrated marshmallows soak up the half and half I'd substituted for milk. Pushing my spoon around, I gathered a sticky clump together and took a bite. While I chewed, I calculated how long Griffin had been in his meeting. If his meeting started at 7:30, surely he'd know something after two and a half hours, right?

He probably forgot to call because he and Erin are out celebrating some awesome news. The little voice in my head was getting pretty damn noisy. He'd call. He just couldn't right now.

I ate fast and gathered my things. Keeping busy was the only way I could ignore all the potentially terrible reasons why he hadn't called yet. I hoped class would serve as a distraction, too.

By the time I arrived at the studio, the western sky swirled with ominous storm clouds resembling giant bruises. The wind picked up and tossed my pink streaked hair into my face as I pulled the door open. Thunder rumbled in the distance.

The halls of the studio were busy, students hustling to get to their classes on time. I had twenty minutes until class started. I shuffled down the hallway, searching for lecture hall 104c. When I found it, I took a seat near the back, pulling my iPad from my bag. I connected the keyboard and sat back, waiting for class to start. *Waiting for Griffin to call,* my inner voice corrected.

I checked my phone again. Nothing.

The lecture hall filled up and Professor Vine walked in a few minutes before eleven.

"Good morning," she said, setting her briefcase on the desk. She opened it and pulled out a large stack of paper. "This is your syllabus for the semester. Please don't lose it; important dates and information regarding the Spring Showcase are detailed inside." Professor Vine handed the stack to a girl that sat in the front row.

While the syllabi circulated through the room, Professor Vine's lecture commenced with a laundry list of projects that would need to be completed for finals in December and then for the Spring Showcase in May. When the stack got to me, I took one and passed the rest. My eyes glazed over as I paged through the nine-page catalog of assignments. *Was I cut out for this?* I glanced around the room, trying to gauge the reactions of my classmates as they leafed through the syllabus. From where I sat, none of them looked as daunted as I felt.

The pretty girl next to me dutifully took notes and appeared to be highlighting key words and phrases as Professor Vine spoke. Seriously? Damn, she wielded a highlighter like Thor swung his hammer. I looked at my stark white syllabus and rubbed my temples, feeling very overwhelmed.

Professor Vine continued to address our small group. "If you have any questions regarding the information in your syllabus, please don't hesitate to schedule a meeting with me. I also have a couple of TAs who would be more than willing to help, should a problem arise. For the remainder of our time, I'd like to see what kind of talent I'll be working with this year. Please take out a sketch pad and pencils."

When I leaned over to pull out my vellum sketch pad, a loud crack of thunder rattled the windows and the lights flickered. I looked to the windows, at the storm raging outside. I hoped it would pass before class ended since I'd left my umbrella in my room.

"I'd like you to sketch some female figures, each depicting styles from different eras. I'll be walking around the room observing your progress," Professor Vine said.

I went to work drawing my pencil across the empty page. In no time at all I had the beginnings of an eighteenth-century woman I envisioned wearing a layered gown with Juliette sleeves.

When it came time for me to add the sleeve, I started at the curve of the shoulder and tapered the sleeve as it came down the figure's arm.

A shadow fell over my paper and I looked up. Professor Vine stood beside my chair. "May I see your progress?" she asked, holding out her hand.

"Sure." I handed her my sketch pad.

She peered over her glasses, looking at me. "And what is your name?"

"Jillian Lawson."

"Well, Jillian, this part here," she pointed to my sketch. "It isn't proportional." She tilted the pad toward me and slid her finger to the shoulder area. "You need to tighten up your design and try again." She handed the sketch pad back to me and pushed her glasses up.

"Okay." I erased my sorry attempt while Professor Vine went on to praise the girl next to me. When Professor Vine asked the girl her name, she said it was Chandra. I didn't know Chandra, but from the sketches I saw, I could tell she was talented. Apparently Professor Vine thought so, too.

Turning my attention back to my offensive sleeve, I set the eraser down and gave it another try.

Geez, what is my problem? This design is shit. Each freshly drawn line of the full shoulders and narrow forearms ended in sleeves that resembled balloons. People generally didn't want to wear balloons on their shoulders. Maybe I was better suited to designing costumes for the circus.

Out of the corner of my eye, I glanced at Chandra's sketch. The contents of her mind flowed fluidly from her brain to her pencil's tip. Her pencil scarred the vellum with each flick of her wrist. I watched, mesmerized, as her pencil bled beautiful marks onto the page. I wondered why I couldn't make my pencil bleed that way. Chandra looked up from her drawing and smiled at me. Embarrassed that I'd gotten caught staring, I returned her smile and went back to drawing my crap. According to Professor Vine, Chandra's scars were beautiful...mine were just disfiguring. Professor Vine had no idea how much truth her statement actually held.

Two and a half hours into class, Professor Vine grew tired of her lazy circuit around the room and perched herself on a stool behind her desk. I purged as much creativity from my pencil as humanly possible, but ended with more trash than usable designs.

"Class dismissed," Professor Vine announced. A collective sigh traveled through the entire room, as if the walls had been holding their breath for the last three hours. Pens and pencils clicked and paper crumpled as my fellow classmates packed away their belongings. I placed my mediocre creations into an accordion folder and stuffed my pencils into their case.

"Jillian?" I jumped, startled by the tap on my shoulder. Professor Vine stood behind me.

"Um…yes?" I replied.

"From the work I've seen you produce today, it seems that you're struggling with some of the simpler drawing techniques. Since the semester has just started, you might want to get a tutor to help you brush up on your technique."

A tutor? Really? I could draw. I just didn't have my best stuff today. She must have really thought I sucked. "I'm sorry. I'll keep practicing. Today was just an off day."

She smiled, but it wasn't warm. "Several faculty members spoke very highly of your portfolio when they saw it last spring. I hope that's all it is."

"Just a bad day." I gave her a reassuring smile, but inside I wasn't smiling. My stomach was in knots.

She pushed her thick Prada frames up on her nose and walked back to the front of the room.

Wanting to avoid any other cuts to my ego, I grabbed my bag and ran for the door. This year was not off to a great start. There seemed to be a slow leak in my creativity pool and I couldn't figure out how to fit the plug back into place and stop the drainage.

Standing at the door to the studio building, I watched the rain fall down in torrents. I pushed the door open and stepped into the storm.

Chapter Eight

I ran as fast as I could through the rain. By the time I got back to the dorm, I looked like I'd gone through a washing machine's spin cycle. I shook the water from my arms and wrung out my hair, making a pink puddle on the floor courtesy of my hair chalk.

My shoes squished and squeaked on the tile floor as I walked down the hall to my room. Unlocking the door, I noticed Sarah had left a message on the dry-erase board attached to our door: "With B. Be back later."

Great. Being alone wasn't really what I wanted…or needed right now.

I sighed and pushed the door open. Retrieving my phone from my drenched book bag, I went to lie down. Holding my phone up, I stared at the dark screen. He knew I was in class. That's why he hadn't called. *Yeah, that's why*, the voice whispered.

Screw the voice. I pressed the home button and the picture of Griffin giving me a piggyback ride brightened the dark room. I slid my finger across the bottom and went to my favorites. His was the only name on my list. I tapped it and waited for him to answer, listening to his ringback tone. Matt Berninger of The National sang to me until Griffin's voice told me to leave a message.

"Hey, Griff, it's me." I wanted to cry. This day had sucked even worse than yesterday and I'd only officially been in college for a grand total of two days. "I was wondering what happened with the producer this morning. Call me."

I clicked end and sat the phone down. A trickle of hot tears fell from the corners of my eyes, slid past my ears, and collected on my pillow. If I opened my eyes all the way, a gush of salt water would slide down my cheeks. My heart weighed a hundred pounds and the old self-inflicted scars on my skin tingled, reminding me that I couldn't escape my past.

With no other classes on Thursday afternoon, I pulled myself off the bed, dried my tears with my hands, and decided to do some laundry and work on my sketches. And wait for Griffin to call.

I traded my damp clothes for a pair of sweats and gathered the rest of my dirty laundry and a roll of quarters for the machines.

I dragged the sack down my hallway, a few flights of stairs, and into the basement. Pulling open the heavy steel door, scents of flowers, mountain springs, and ocean breezes assaulted my nostrils. The door slammed shut behind me with a loud thud.

The newest-looking washers and dryers were hidden in the back of the room—that's where I headed. I bent down and gave the bag a good heave and lifted it onto a washer, filling the one beside it with damp towels. I tossed in a detergent pod, closed the lid, fed the greedy machine a handful of quarters, and set the dial.

What else can I do to keep my mind off Griffin?

The pile of tissues from last night still littered my floor. I marched back up to my room and tidied up the mess. That took all of five minutes. *Now what?*

Who was I kidding? It was killing me that I hadn't heard from him.

With tears in my eyes, I dug my iPod, sketchbook, and a set of pencils from my backpack and sat down on my bed. Cranking up the volume on the classical music I liked to draw to, I let my fingers go to work smearing and rubbing, trying to bring the images in my head to life.

I flipped to my eighteenth-century figure from earlier and tried to improve upon that. It didn't take too long before I got lost in my music, letting it guide my pencil as opposed to my brain.

After several hours of drawing and running down to the laundry room, I'd lost track of time, but it felt good to turn off my head for a while and do completely mindless tasks. I'd heard from Sarah a few times; she was out with Brandon and his group of friends. She'd asked me if I wanted to come out with them, but I politely declined. I didn't feel like being around people at the moment. And if Griffin did decide to call me, I wanted to be able to actually talk to him.

Once my laundry was folded and put away, I laid my sketchbook and pencils on the desk and flopped onto my bed. Plugging my earbuds back in, I traded Mozart for Mine Shaft. If I couldn't get ahold of Griffin to talk to him, at least I could press play and listen to him sing. The smooth, deep tones of his voice resonated through my whole body, and I relaxed. I closed my eyes and tried to picture what he was doing right at this moment when the voice in my head whispered, *nothing that concerns you.*

* * *

I sat up with a start. A flash lit up the room, followed immediately by a loud crack of thunder, scaring me from a nightmare I'd already forgotten. The only reason I suspected it was a nightmare was because my heart was racing and a thin layer of sweat made my clothes stick to my skin. Because of my antidepressant, I rarely remembered my dreams. That was probably a good thing—that meant I couldn't remember my nightmares either.

I rolled off the bed and went to check my phone. I had missed two calls from Griffin and I had one new voicemail. *Damn it!* I'd waited all day to hear from him and when he'd finally called, I'd missed him. *Shit!*

I pressed play on the message. "Hey, Bean. Sorry I didn't call earlier. So much crazy shit happened today, I can't even begin to tell you over voicemail. Call me." According to the time stamp on the message, he'd called just a half hour ago, at 9:30 p.m.

Without a moment's hesitation, I called him back. Once again, I was greeted by the deep, bedroom voice of The National's lead singer. Halfway through the song "Graceless", Griffin's voicemail message clicked on.

I hated playing phone tag. "Hi, Griff. I got your message. I can't wait to hear what happened today. Please call me back." I was just about to hang up, but for some reason I couldn't. Even though it was just his voicemail, it still made me feel closer to him somehow. "I miss you." My voice wavered and I hit end.

To salvage the rest of my evening, I worked on some preliminary Spring Showcase sketches that Professor Vine outlined in her syllabus. However, as I sketched, I couldn't escape Professor Vine's disapproving words. Actually, I couldn't escape any of the voices whispering in my head. I recognized each distinctive voice: Professor Vine's, Jennifer's...and mine.

When I was little, Jennifer's voice had sounded the loudest. As I got older, her voice became backup vocals to my own.

My mind raced through the coping strategies Dr. Hoffman had taught me: *Draw. Be creative. Live in your heart...not your head.*

Talk to someone you trust.

Coping mechanism numbers one and two: Draw and be creative. That's what I would do.

I sifted through fashion magazines, determined to make a collage. I avoided pictures of actual clothing, but instead focused on peculiar pictures with unique visual qualities.

I cut a hot pink chameleon from a paint advertisement, shaping it into a handbag. The chameleon made a fabulous accessory to the metallic Keurig miniskirt I'd already glued to the pages of my sketchbook.

Creating collages was one of my favorite designing techniques. I loved the abstract quality of the figures I created when I glued a collage together. I held the creative license. Proportions and perfection didn't matter and no one could tell me I was wrong.

By the time I looked up from my nearly finished collage, the clock blinked midnight. I appraised my project and for the first time in a while, something I created made me happy. And the voices shut up.

Thank God. And my therapist.

I admired my abstract model outfitted in a metallic silver, asymmetrical miniskirt with a watermelon-colored blouse (complete with disproportionate Juliette sleeves the color of the sky). I glued the last piece of the ensemble to the paper, a hot pink handbag.

My fingers stuck to the page as I blew on the magazine print. My puckered mouth morphed into a genuine smile as I peeled my fingers from the paper, revealing my eclectic masterpiece.

I enjoyed my accomplishment in quiet solitude. Smiling, I rested my head on a crunchy pillow of gluey magazine scraps.

On the back of my eyelids, I saw Griffin's face. His disheveled, dark hair always fell in his eyes and drove me nuts. I'd give anything to be able to brush it out of his eyes right now. I wondered what he was doing…what had happened today.

With Griffin on my mind, I remembered the day I moved into my grandparents' house, permanently—the day I realized I wasn't alone in this world.

Grandpa pulled into his driveway. "We're home, girls. We're going to have to make a run for it," Grandpa said.

Through the pouring rain, I stared at the pea green siding, recalling hundreds of other visits. A trip to Grandma and Grandpa's tiny house always elicited excitement. Euphoria would propel me from the car like a bullet from a gun.

"Let's go find Grandma," Grandpa said. He hid it well, but I heard the sadness in his voice. He'd lost a daughter and son-in-law, after all.

Jenny pulled the handle on the car door and got out, bolting through the rain to the front door.

I stared at the pea green siding.

No excitement. No euphoria. Nothing. An empty barrel.

I just sat…and stared. I watched the raindrops roll down the window, gobbling up other drops on their way down.

Grandpa and Jenny went into the house figuring I'd be scared sit-

ting in a storm by myself and follow them in eventually. I wasn't scared, so I sat.

To a six-year-old, time ticks differently. I could have sat in Grandpa's car for five minutes or thirty minutes and I wouldn't have known the difference. To a six-year-old, either amount of time seems like forever.

I sat in Grandpa's car forever and wondered if the people in the house even cared that I hadn't come inside.

Probably not. They hated me.

I knew Jenny did at least.

She told me it was my fault that Mommy and Daddy didn't come home. If I hadn't asked them for a snow globe, they wouldn't have decided to meet their friend.

Tears trickled down my mottled cheeks as the back passenger door pulled open. The boy who lived next door to Grandma and Grandpa crawled in beside me and shut the door. He shook his wavy hair and raindrops splashed onto my already wet face.

Griffin and I played together whenever I visited my grandparents. He was nice. We always had fun together.

"Hey, Jillibean." He always called me that. At first I'd hated it. Mommy told me that if I ignored him, he'd stop.

He never stopped.

"Hey," I answered.

He brushed a wet curl out of his eye. "What are you doing in here?"

"Nothing." I wiped my wet face with the back of my hand.

"You want to come over and play?" he asked.

I shook my head. I didn't feel like playing.

"Okay," he said.

We were both quiet for a long time. For forever.

Griffin looked out the windows and I bit my fingernails. I didn't have a mom to tell me not to.

A loud crash of thunder shook the car and I jumped.

"Jillian," he said after a while. "I know what happened. My mom told me."

I turned my head and looked at him. If his mom had told him what happened, would he hate me too?

He scooted toward the middle seat, right next to me, and put his arm around my shoulder. "When you're sad, I'll try to make you feel better. How does that sound?"

I nodded my head and smiled. He didn't hate me. "Good."

He offered me his hand. "Come on, let's make a run for it." He smiled. "The yard's not that big, we won't get too wet. What do you say?" He raised an eyebrow and held out his hand for mine. "Give me your hand, we'll cross the distance together."

I put my hand in his and looked up at him. "Promise?"

"Forever."

Chapter Nine

Even though I was awake, I refused to start the day. I hated Mondays—my Mondays began in the dark and ended in the dark. Despite being in school for over a month, I still couldn't get used to the long hours I had to spend inside the studio labs. The fluorescent lighting was suffocating.

Outside of the door, Sarah's keys jingled and then the door pushed open. "Hey, you going to class today?" she asked, kicking the side of my bed.

"What time is it?" I groaned.

"8:30 a.m."

"I really don't have a choice." Not if I wanted to get any work done on my Spring Showcase projects. I sighed and pulled the blankets off of my legs. "You're up early."

"I made Brandon run with me today. I needed to get some shots of athletes for one of my classes, so I recruited him." After storing her bathroom necessities, she turned in my direction. "Geez, Jillian, you look like hell."

"Thanks," I replied sarcastically.

"No, seriously. Are you feeling okay?"

"Yes, I just hate Mondays." And college in general. With the exception of Sarah, college wasn't what I'd expected. My apparel classmates possessed a far superior level of talent than I'd been blessed with and each new day only reiterated that fact. And then there was Griffin. I hardly heard from him—not since Mine Shaft had signed their record deal. Our lives were moving in two different directions and I couldn't stop it. I missed him so much it hurt.

"Yeah, Mondays do suck. But, if you hurry up, we still have time to get some breakfast before class." She smiled and started humming an old Bangles song.

"I'm going, I'm going." My feet hit the floor and I moved about as fast as a download using a dial-up connection.

Thirty minutes later, I was showered, dressed and ready for another day of getting beat down in my design classes.

Sarah tossed me one of my bags and it fell with a thump at my feet. "Come on, I didn't throw it that hard." She put her hands on her hips and tilted her head, glaring at me with her big violet eyes.

I shrugged and bent to retrieve it from the floor.

Sarah locked up our room and we walked over to the dining hall. By the time we got there, lines of students hurried in and out, fueling up for a long day spent creating masterpieces.

Sarah and I grabbed our Lucky Charms and coffee and found a seat.

I took a sip of my heavily creamed coffee and made a mental list of everything I needed to accomplish today. The most pressing task was nailing down my sketches for the Spring Showcase. If I didn't figure out my collection's theme and get to work on sewing those pieces, I was going to flunk out of design school.

"Jilli, what's up with you this morning?" Sarah lightly kicked my shin underneath the table. I snapped back into reality.

"What?"

"Where are you this morning?"

"Sorry. I'm just really stressed." I sat my coffee cup down and took a bite of my soggy cereal.

"About what?" she asked.

"You name it, I can probably find some reason to stress about it," I replied.

Sarah tossed her hair over her shoulder and fished marshmallows from her bowl. "Is there anything I can do to help?" she asked, spooning the colorful charms into her mouth.

"Not really." I shook my head.

"Have you heard from Griffin lately?"

I shook my head again. "He's been really busy."

"Is he still with that Erin girl?" At the mention of her name, I felt my depression morph into bitterness.

"Yes," I grumbled. I picked at my cereal like Sarah, spooning marshmallows from the chalky colored cream, and shoveling them into my mouth.

"Oo, do I sense some hostility?" she crooned. "Are you jealous?"

Yes. "No," I snapped. "What he does with his girlfriend is his business."

"And that irritates the shit out of you." She looked me straight in the eye. "I don't get you two."

"What don't you get?"

She shook her head. "I've seen the way your face lights up when he calls you." Sarah set her spoon down and dared me to look away.

"Whatever. It does not." I looked away. "I just miss him. That's all."

"You can keep telling yourself that, but it won't make you feel any better."

Where the hell did she get off? She didn't know anything about Griffin and me. I couldn't explain why I felt so much rage all of a sudden. I looked at her and spoke through clenched teeth. "I've known Griffin since I was six. He's *just* my friend. I don't expect you to understand."

"Oh, honey, I think I do. It's you that doesn't understand." Sarah picked up her coffee cup and drained what was left.

What was that supposed to mean? I did understand. I knew what I wanted. I just couldn't have it. I didn't know how to respond. Sarah's blunt comments always caught me off guard.

Sarah wiped her mouth on a napkin. "I've got to get to class. Brandon and I are meeting here for dinner. You're welcome to join us."

I looked at her and instantly regretted the way I'd spoken to her. "Sarah," I said. "I'm sorry. I've been a complete bitch all morning. I shouldn't have talked to you like that."

Her mouth curved into a tight-lipped smile. "I'm sorry, too. You're right, I don't know what you and Griffin have and it's none of my business." She stood up and slung her messenger bag over her shoulder. "See you tonight?"

I nodded. "Yeah."

"Good." She smiled and picked up her tray. "Happy Monday," she said and walked away.

Happy Monday, Jillian. The voice in my head taunted me, not whispering anymore.

* * *

I leaned on the crash bar of the studio door, excited at the prospect of some fresh air. Outside, a cold October wind blew across my face and sent a refreshing chill down my spine. After spending an hour and fifty-five minutes sitting at an industrial-sized sewing machine, stuck under awful fluorescent lights, I felt like I was drowning.

I longed for a good run, but I didn't have time. I had fifteen minutes to enjoy the last few beams of sun before my second studio lab was scheduled to start.

I took a quick peek at the time on my phone and scrolled through some messages while I powered down a chocolate chip granola bar. Sarah texted: *I hope your day's going well.*

I sent her a quick text back: *Not too bad. Thanks.*

Just as I was about to put my phone away it vibrated with an incoming text. When I looked at the screen a genuine smile spread across my face. It was from Griffin. I quickly opened it, seeing a picture of him on stage during his show last Saturday night, along with a note about having some great news.

I wished I didn't have to go back to class. I wanted to call him and find out what his "great news" was. I texted him back: *I'll call you as soon as class gets out! Can't wait to hear about your great news!*

By the time I got back to the lab, several of my classmates had already started measuring, ironing, cutting, and folding the pieces of muslin we were assigned to work with. Our lab objective today involved draping a dress form and developing a useable pattern. It was meant to foster our measuring and sketching skills. I loved the sketching part, but I always struggled with measurements. I dropped my bag on the empty chair next to Chandra's station and went in search of a dress form.

I pulled the dress form over to my work station and laid a stack of muslin on the table top. After arranging my rulers, pens, pencils, and several pins, I figured I'd procrastinated long enough. I caught a glimpse of Chandra. Her muslin was ironed and she'd already begun to pin it to the dress form. I sighed and shook my head, wishing I possessed even an eighth of her natural talent.

After an hour of stretching, pinning, sketching, and taking breaks to breathe, my dress form began to look dressed…sort of. I scanned the room, gauging the other designers—comparing my work to theirs. Everyone had taken their muslin from the dress form and began sketching lines and measurements onto their pattern paper. Everyone but me.

I really sucked at this. With each tick of the clock, my confidence disappeared. I felt a lump rise in my throat while I continued to pinch and mark my darts, careful to measure as precisely as possible without crying. With my left thumb, I held the dart and reached for a razor blade to cut away a frayed piece of muslin. I pulled the fabric taut and slid the blade down the edge of fabric. Pinching the fabric as the blade cut away the frays, I felt the sharp edge graze my index finger, slicing the skin.

The pin between my teeth dropped from my mouth. I let go of the fabric I held in my left hand, dropped the razor in my right, and zeroed in on the line of blood blooming on my right index finger. Instantly, my body flooded with endorphins. Without thinking, I pinched my finger and made the line of blood grow. I knew what my therapist would have wanted me to do, but for the first time in a long time, it felt so good not to listen.

If this one little cut felt this good, just think how much better you'd feel if you…

Wait! What was I thinking? Instantly, I snapped out of the blood-induced trance. I grabbed a tissue from a nearby table and wrapped my finger to staunch the bleeding.

My poisonous thought and the endorphin release had scared the hell out of me. That was how I *used* to be…that wasn't me anymore. I couldn't hold the tears back. I hadn't thought about hurting myself in almost two years—when I'd promised Griffin I would get help.

I needed help now.

Chapter Ten

I grabbed my purse and coat and bolted from the room. On my way out, I thought I heard Chandra ask if I was okay, but I didn't stick around long enough to see if she had really spoken to me.

Outside, the sun had set, leaving the sky the color of dark denim. I walked around in the cold, mid-November air for a few minutes, unwrapping and rewrapping the tissue around my finger, checking to see if the cut was still there.

Peeling back the tissue for a third time, I prayed the cut might have magically disappeared, or that I'd imagined the whole incident. I stared at the inch-long gash on my finger and cringed. *Nope, it really happened.* Even though it wasn't bleeding any longer, I put the tissue back in place and continued my hurried pace down the sidewalk.

After five minutes of wandering, I came across a bench and plopped down on the cold concrete, fumbling through my purse with my uninjured hand, looking for my phone. I pulled it free, pushed his name on my contacts list, and hoped he'd answer.

"Jillibean!" he said happily.

Thank you, God! I could hear a smile in his voice. It had been at least four days since I'd talked to him. I felt a smile pulling at the corners of my mouth, but the shaking in my body erased it like an Etch-A-Sketch image.

"Jillibean?" he asked again, sounding more concerned.

Even though I wasn't crying, I still couldn't manage to spit out any words. I couldn't convince my body to do anything except listen to his voice.

"Jillian, you're scaring the shit out of me. Say something," he demanded.

"I'm…here." My voice cracked. A cold wind blew across the quad and I shivered. I balanced the phone between my ear and shoulder, holding my coat closed with both hands. I was careful to hide my injured finger beneath my good hand, as if I were afraid Griffin might see it.

"What's wrong?" he asked again.

"I just wanted to hear your voice," I whispered.

"That's bullshit. I can tell something's wrong." He paused and took a breath. "Just tell me what it is, so I can help you."

Help. That's what I'd called for. Griffin would help me. "I hurt myself." My answer was monotone. I probably sounded like a robot.

I heard him suck in a breath before he asked, "How did you hurt yourself?"

"In the studio, I was cutting fabric." I paused. "I sliced my finger."

He exhaled. In my mind, I could see him running his hands through his hair. He was probably pacing back and forth, too.

"It's okay, Bean," he said. "It was an accident, right?"

"Mmm-hmm," I mumbled.

"Is your finger all right?" he asked.

I didn't answer his question. Instead, I was compelled to tell him how it felt when the blade broken through my skin. "It felt…good, Griffin. For a split second, I thought about…" I stopped. I'd run out of words.

The other end of the line was quiet. He knew what I meant.

"Jillian, you need to call Dr. Hoffman," he said. "You promised if things got too crazy, you'd call her."

Dr. Hoffman wasn't who I wanted right now. I wanted Griffin. I wanted his strong arms around me. I wanted him to whisper reassuring words, his warm breath to replace the cold phone at my ear. I hated that he was so far away.

Tears stung my eyes. "I'm so stressed, Griff. I'm not cut out for this."

He lowered his voice, pleading. "Will you please call Dr. Hoffman? At least talk to her until I get there."

I sat up straighter and grabbed the phone from my shoulder, not quite sure I'd heard him correctly. "What? You're coming here?" I held my breath, too afraid I'd misunderstood.

"I was planning on visiting you for Thanksgiving, since I knew you weren't coming home. It was supposed to be a surprise."

"Griffin," I sighed. An answer to my prayers; he was always a step ahead of me. A blissful calm washed over me and I instantly felt better.

"But I'll only come on one condition," he interrupted me. "You have to call Dr. Hoffman. Promise me," he demanded.

A full-blown smile bloomed on my face. "I will. I promise."

"Good." He let out a sigh. He sounded relieved. "So, you're cooking me a Thanksgiving feast, right?"

"Um…no." I chuckled, then sniffled.

"Wow. You treat all of your guests like that? Or do you save your top-notch hostessing skills just for me?" he teased.

"I'm not in culinary school, Griff."

"Damn," he groaned. "And here I thought you'd be so happy to see me, I'd get a five-course feast out of the deal."

"How does pizza sound?"

Griffin's deep, rumbling laughter filled my ears. "Now that's a Thanksgiving feast I can't resist. But," he said, "none of that shitty, fancy pizza. Normal pizza, just meat and cheese."

"And pineapple," I added.

"Ugh," he moaned in disgust. "Being a sophisticated college woman hasn't refined your palate any."

"Nope." I giggled, shrugging. The line remained quiet. "Griff? You still there?" I asked.

"Yeah," he sighed. "It's just good to hear you laugh. You feel better now?" he asked softly.

I put the phone back between my ear and shoulder and pulled the makeshift bandage off of my finger, brave enough to take another look. Seeing the cut now, with a clear head, I knew I'd overreacted. "Yeah, thanks to you." I took the phone from my shoulder again and stared up at the night sky. An inexplicable heaviness pushed me down, like gravity had suddenly multiplied. "You always have a way of making everything okay."

"I promised you a long time ago that I'd always try to make you feel better," he said. "I'm just glad I still can."

The pinch in my heart reminded me that it was still there. "Forever," I said, but I doubted he heard me. The enormous amount of gravity that suddenly surrounded me had buried my voice. I cleared my throat. "I should probably get back to class."

"Don't forget to call Dr. Hoffman." Griffin spoke up. He cleared his throat, too. "I'll be there in a couple of days. Take care of yourself, do you hear me?"

"I will, I promise." My voice wavered. "'Night, Griff." I didn't want to hang up.

"'Night, Bean," he replied quietly. Then all I could hear was the soft whistle of the wind. Our brief connection had ended.

When I got back to the studio, everyone was in full clean-up mode. If I wasn't behind before, I was now. Defeated, I walked back to my station and haphazardly started tossing things into my bags.

Chandra ran up to me; a worried expression darkened her usually cheerful face. "Jillian, are you all right?"

"I'm fine. I just needed some air." I couldn't explain what had happened, but it was nice of her to ask if I was all right.

"I could help you clean up," she offered.

I started unpinning the muslin from my dress form. "Thanks, but I don't want to keep you."

Chandra's bright smile stood out against her milk chocolate skin. She had the kind of smile that exuded warmth and sincerity. "You sure? It's no problem."

"Yeah, I'm sure." I gave her a reassuring smile. "It won't take me very long." I folded the fabric and put it into my bag.

Chandra's honey-colored eyes glowed with kindness. I'd never really noticed her striking features before and I was taken aback. Despite having declined her offer, there was a small part of me that actually felt bad about it—like my refusal would somehow disappoint her.

Chandra picked up her bags, tossing them over her shoulder. "If you're sure then." She hesitated.

I nodded.

"I'll see you later." She gave me a sweet smile and walked out of the room.

* * *

On my way back to the dorm I found Dr. Hoffman's number in my contacts. Even though it was after hours, I decided to call her anyway. *And fulfill my promise to Griffin.* At the very least, I could leave a message and she would call me back.

As soon as the automated voice prompted me, I left a short message for Dr. Hoffman and quickly hung up, running back to Victor.

After jogging down the hallway toward my room, I unlocked the door and threw it open. Sarah was sprawled across her bed with several books open around her. "Well, hey there, stranger," she said, looking up.

"Hey," I said. "Are you busy?" It was obvious she was, but I had no desire to stay in. I had too much pent up excitement, anticipating Griffin's visit, and I didn't want to think about what had happened in class. I needed a distraction. "Dinner?" I suggested. "Not dining hall crap."

"Um…" She bit her lip, looking at the unfinished work that sat in front of her. "Oh, what the hell." She slammed a book shut and brushed the rest to the side, jumping up from her bed, ready to put her work on hold for me.

* * *

Inside the restaurant, the ambiance was impeccable. The beautiful green stained-glass windows by the bar cast an emerald hue over the dining room. The interior design was remarkable.

The hostess greeted us with a smile and said, "If you would please follow Mandy, she will show you ladies to your table."

The hostess handed Mandy two menus. She turned around and smiled at us. "Right this way, ladies."

We followed her to a table at the back of the restaurant. "Will this be okay?" she asked, smiling.

"Yes, thank you." Sarah and I answered in unison.

"Your server will be with you shortly." Mandy laid the menus on the table and returned to her post at the hostess's desk.

We sat down and picked up our menus. "So, what's good here?" I asked.

Sarah perused her menu and said, "Everything is divine."

All throughout dinner, Sarah and I talked about what classes we enjoyed the most and which ones sucked. Then our conversation turned toward our lives outside of school.

"I know you're not close to your sister, but what about your nephews?" she asked.

"Yeah, the twins are okay. What I love most about my nephews is that they're rowdy, messy boys, and my prissy-ass sister has to clean up after them," I chuckled. "That's karma at its best."

"What are the boys' names?"

"Michael and Mitchell," I said, taking a drink of water. Talking about home was about as enjoyable as a root canal, but I was determined to let Sarah in. In Griffin's absence, I needed someone

I could trust with all the baggage I carried. "You're an only child, right?" I asked her. I thought she'd told me that over the summer.

"Mmm-hmm." She nodded, swallowing a bite of scallops. "But I feel like I have two older brothers. Brandon's brothers have always treated me like their little sister."

"Do you have any plans for Thanksgiving?" I asked.

"One of my aforementioned big brothers lives in Cranston. I'm spending Thanksgiving break with Brandon at his brother's place. What are your plans?"

I was a little apprehensive to tell her Griffin was visiting. I knew she'd turn it around and try to make it out to be more than it was, but I was so excited to see him, I needed to tell someone the good news. "Griffin's coming." I bit my bottom lip, anticipating her tongue-in-cheek comments.

"Aw, yeah," she sang, nodding her head in approval. "Damn, I'm just sorry I'm not gonna get to meet him." She stuck out her bottom lip, pouting.

"Shut it, Sarah. I don't know how many times I have to tell you. It's not like that between us."

She sat her elbows on the table and folded her hands in front of her face. "Bullshit."

"Why do you say that?" I asked. "What makes you think there's more to our friendship? You've never even met him." I wasn't mad at her and was careful not to raise my voice. I genuinely wanted to know why she'd jumped to the conclusion that Griffin and I were more than just friends.

Sarah took a sip of her water and thought for a second. "At the mention of his name, there is a fleeting moment where all the hurt and sadness inside of you disappears. It's like you're not afraid to let him carry some of your past for you, if only for a little while, so you can breathe. There's a radiance that flashes across your eyes and the hint of secret on your lips. If just the sound of his name has that kind of power, I can only imagine what it's like when you two are actually in the same room together. If that's not love, I don't know what is."

I swallowed the lump in my throat and blinked at her, stunned.

"I'm right and you know it. Why do you fight it so hard?" She stared at me with her smooth amethyst eyes, waiting for an answer that I didn't have.

The only thing I did know was that *nothing* got past Sarah Theissen.

Chapter Eleven

I just had to stop for gas. I'll be there in about thirty minutes."

"Well, hurry up!" I shouted.

"I am." He laughed at my impatience.

I hung up the phone and tried to find something constructive to do for thirty minutes, but that proved to be an exercise in futility. Too much excited energy coursed through my veins to read a book. I'd already straightened up a hundred times, and Sarah had left to spend the weekend at Brandon's apartment.

I checked my phone again—only fifteen more minutes. Determined to wear a hole in Sarah's bright pink area rug, I paced back and forth like a neurotic house pet. If Griffin didn't get here soon, I would owe Sarah a new rug.

My phone buzzed and Griffin's picture lit up the screen. "Griff?"

"Are you going to let me in or what?" he said.

"Ahh! You're early!" I screamed. "I'm on my way down!" I practically rode the banister down the stairs, leaning into it as I skipped four or five steps at a time to get to the door. I stepped off the last step and ran full speed toward the glass doors, slamming into the crash bar. Griffin stood on the other side waving to me. A huge smile spread across his face. I pushed the door open and didn't even let him in the building before I was in his arms.

He wrapped his arms around me and I buried my face in his leather riding jacket. I breathed him in. He smelled like leather and wind…like home.

"Jillibean," he said in a low and hushed tone at my ear. "You going to let me through the door? It's freezing out here."

"Oh, sorry." I smiled sheepishly, looking up at his reflective, dark eyes. *Holy hell, I'd forgotten how tall he was.* I stepped aside and he came in, hauling his duffle bag with him.

The second he was through the door, he pulled me to his side. Despite our crazy height difference, I marveled at how well we fit together. *God, I've missed this.*

He glanced down at me, his mouth pulling into an impish grin. "Have you always been this short?" he asked. "I don't remember you being this short." I laughed and he responded by pulling me even closer to his side.

"You have no idea how happy I am to see you," I whispered.

"Oh, I'm pretty sure I do," he replied quietly.

Once we made it to the top floor, I pushed open the door to my room. Griffin let go of my shoulder, walked over to my bed, dropped his bag on the floor, and fell onto my lime green comforter. His muscular 6'4" frame swallowed my small twin bed.

"You're tired," I said, feeling completely ill at ease. During our two-month separation he'd morphed into a tried and true rock star: perfectly mussed hair, come-hither eyes, bedroom voice, and loads of charisma. I was the same old boring me. Things felt weird. I didn't know how I was supposed to act around him anymore.

He kicked his boots off and stretched his arms out to me. "Come here." His voice was low and exhausted.

I walked over to the bed and sat down on the edge. I looked at him and smiled, fidgeting with the hem of my shirt. Griffin stilled one of my hands by pulling it onto his chest. His thumb and forefinger moved slowly over the Band-Aid on my index finger. My heartbeat was jumpy and arrhythmic. *What the hell was my problem?*

Griffin slid his butt over toward the wall and tugged on my hand, pulling me down beside him. "Now I can rest," he said, folding me perfectly to his side. He closed his eyes and smiled contentedly. His chest rose and fell with each deep breath, growing steadier as he drifted off to sleep.

I closed my eyes, finally relaxing next to him. Before my heavy eyes closed, I whispered, "Me too." And for the first time in months, I slept peacefully.

* * *

Thanksgiving Day arrived with a fresh blanket of snow. Griffin and I woke up early, not wanting to waste the limited amount of time we had together. Thankfully, the awkwardness I'd felt the night before had disappeared and things felt normal between Griffin and me. Just like old times, we decided to be the first ones to leave tracks in the newly fallen snow. We bundled up and went for a walk, hoping to find an open coffee shop somewhere.

Griffin and I walked side by side, our hands shoved deep in our pockets to keep warm.

"How have things been?" His voice was serious, and I knew exactly what he was asking about.

"Good," I answered. "Now that you're here." I looked up at him with a playful smile on my lips.

"No, seriously. You scared the fuck out of me the other day. I was about to get on my bike and drive out here right then and there."

I sighed, feeling guilty for causing him to worry. "I'm sorry," I said.

"No," he replied urgently. "Don't apologize." He stopped walking and put his hands on my shoulders, turning me around to face him. "Jillian, you call me *every* time. Do you hear me?"

My eyes started to water. I wasn't sure if it was a result of the cold wind whipping around or impending tears. I nodded my head in answer to his question because I knew my voice would betray me.

Griffin pulled me to his chest and hugged me protectively. "I almost lost you once," he said. His warm breath fell over the top of my head and I shivered even though I wasn't cold. "I'll be damned if I let that happen again," he said.

Still sealed inside the warmth of his embrace, I found the courage to tell him what I'd thought. "For a split second, I thought about cutting all my stress away. But…" I trailed off.

He pulled me away, placing his hands on my shoulders, and looked me straight in the eye. "But?" he asked.

"But." I bit my lip, contemplating my motivation behind not acting on that temptation. "But, I didn't want to go back down

that road. I told myself that was the old me...not who I am now."
And I believed that. I looked him dead in the eyes because I
wanted him to believe it, too.

Griffin's lips pulled up at the corners, and the warmth of his
smile spread to his dark chocolate eyes. He brushed the back of
his hand lightly across my cheek, tucking my hair behind my ear. I
tilted my head, leaning into his hand. I craved the feel of his skin
on mine, even though I knew he didn't feel the same way. "You
amaze me every freaking day, you know that?" Running his hands
down my arms, he captured my hands between his and squeezed.
His dark eyes smoldered, and my breath hitched. "You are the
strongest woman I know," he said softly.

I blinked away the weird tension and quickly tried to think
of something to change the subject. I'd never done well with
compliments and now was no exception, especially with him
staring at me like that. "Come on, it's freezing out here." I laced
my fingers through his, pulling him along beside me. He smiled
like an idiot and squeezed my hand tighter, yanking me to his
side.

After walking in silence for a while, enjoying each other's company, we finally came across an open Starbucks. Griffin let go of my
hand and held the door open. He ushered me in, placing his hand
at the small of my back as the warm scents of coffee beans and pas-
tries greeted us. I stomped the snow from my boots and rubbed my
hands together. We walked to the counter, and I ordered my usual
venti mocha with soy and a slice of pumpkin loaf, while Griffin ordered his usual boring black coffee (minus the lid), and a blueberry
muffin.

Sitting down at a small table, we shrugged off our coats and warmed our hands on our coffee cups. I couldn't help but smile at him as he sipped his coffee.

"What?" he asked, squinting at me.

"Nothing. Just happy."

"Me too." He smiled, set his coffee down, and started peeling the paper from around his muffin.

"Tell me everything that's been going on with you." I said, picking at my pumpkin bread, too anxious to eat.

He popped a bite of muffin into his mouth and chewed before he answered. "On a whole, the band is doing great. But, I'm really glad it worked out that I could visit this weekend. I needed a fucking break." He exhaled and took a drink. "If I have to listen to Adam and Thor bitch about dropped notes and song lyrics one more time, I'm going to kill them both. I love those guys, but they bicker like two old biddies."

"Yikes." I cringed. "That sucks. But, whatever you guys are doing is paying off, right?" I smiled. "You're recording a freaking album. You're a real rock star now," I said, punching him lightly on the shoulder. I was so proud of him. "How cool is that?"

He shrugged. "Yeah, it's cool. But it's a shit load of work, not that I'm complaining." He held his hands up in a defensive gesture before tipping his chair back, seizing a stack of napkins from the counter behind him. Napkins in hand, he let the chair fall forward with a thud. "My parents are on my ass because I'm not taking enough classes, the guys don't seem to take shit as seriously as I do, and Erin bitches about me never having any free time."

Even though it probably made me a terrible person, I couldn't help the thrill that went through me when I heard that he hadn't had much time for Erin. "Well, I'm sure that when your album goes platinum, and you're booking tours, and headlining sell-out shows, people will figure out that this isn't just a hobby."

"Yeah, then I'll have the other problem." He stretched his long legs out and put his hands behind his head. "They'll all be kissing my ass when I'm some famous rocker," he scoffed.

With his arms back, I saw just a hint of the black cursive script that wound around his right bicep. *Damn, he looked good.*

"What?" Griffin said, sitting back up.

Shit, I'd gotten caught staring. "Um…what?" I said, shaking my head clear of the crazy thoughts going through my head.

"What were you thinking about?" he asked, draining his coffee cup.

"You're really going to help me with my designs while you're here?" I asked, changing the subject. He'd promised to help me work on some designs for the Spring Showcase.

"Victoria told me all of her secrets before I left." Griffin tapped his head with his finger.

"Well, shit, too bad I'm not designing a line of lingerie. And how did you get Vicky to share her secrets?" I asked, grinning.

He winked and stood up, putting on his coat. "You probably don't want to know."

I stood up and grabbed my coat from the back of my chair, shaking my head. "You're incorrigible."

He reached over and helped me with my coat. "Damn right I am."

* * *

Griffin and I sat cross-legged on the floor with a couple of pizza boxes between us. "This is the best Thanksgiving dinner I've ever had," I said, pulling off a bite of pizza with my front teeth. Griffin finished off his beer and nodded in agreement. "Although last year's dinner was pretty entertaining," I added, as highlights of last year's debacle flashed through my mind. "Do you remember Jennifer's temper tantrum?"

Griffin pulled another piece of pizza from the box and laughed. "Uh, yeah. She was so pissed you invited me, she slammed a whole platter of turkey onto the table."

"I tried so hard to stifle my laughter when Mitchell leaned over and said, 'Mommy, you have turkey in your hair,' and then proceeded to pick it out." My stomach hurt from laughing so much. I bent over, trying to compose myself.

"Uh, Bean?" Griffin said.

"Yeah?" I said, between fits of laughter. It only took one beer to make me goofy. I had no tolerance.

"Your hair is in the pizza."

I felt Griffin moving handfuls of my hair off of our Thanksgiving dinner. Sitting up, I flung my hair back and smiled at Griffin. "Oops," I giggled, running my hand through my hair.

"Wait, don't move," Griffin said urgently. His eyes widened.

I froze with my hand on top of my head. "What?"

He leaned over the pizza box and moved very slowly toward me. *Is it me, or did it just get really hot in here?* Suddenly, I wasn't feeling very silly anymore. My heart pounded in my ears. I clamped down on the urge to close the distance between us and kiss him. *Don't do it…don't do it…* an insufferable voice chanted in my head. With all my energy swallowed up by restraint, my hand dropped to my side, and Sarah's voice echoed in my head. *I can only imagine what it's like when you two are in the same room.*

"Hold very, very still," he whispered, looking me right in the eyes.

His eyes were too intense...I couldn't hold them. I glanced at his mouth, just a few inches from mine. *What was he doing? He'd already told me he didn't want this.*

I remained stone-still as his hand smoothed down the top of my head. His fingertips grazed over the sensitive skin just behind and below my ear. "There," he breathed.

What?

He pulled away, holding something in his hand. "Pepperoni," he said. Between his thumb and forefinger, he held a slice of pepperoni. "You had a little..." He pointed the piece of meat at my ear. "Behind your—"

"Ugh!" I screamed. "Griffin Daniels!" I picked up an empty paper plate and smacked him repeatedly on the shoulder. "What the hell!"

His deep, booming laugh filled my room and I couldn't help but laugh too. "I did *not* have that behind my ear," I scolded.

He put his hands up in defense. "Hey, you're the one who decided to put your head in the pie. I was just looking out for you." His well-defined cheekbones pulled up in a sinful smirk.

I shook my head and pursed my lips with chagrin. He thought he was so funny. "You just wait, Daniels," I warned, pointing a finger in his direction.

"Bring it on, Jillibean," he taunted. The smile disappeared and was replaced with a different emotion. For just a second, I thought I saw passion darkening his face, practically begging me to cross the line again. It may have been the beer clouding my vision, but then again, I'd only had just one.

And then it was gone. He sat back, took a drink of his beer, and smiled at me. "So, what is this Spring Showcase thing that has you doubting your mad skills?" he asked.

What the hell was going on? I needed another drink. And some distance from him. I got up and went to the mini-fridge to get another beer and to clear my head. Pulling open the fridge, I started explaining my task for the Spring Showcase. "Every year, the apparel design department hosts a student-led runway show. All fashion majors must design an original, themed collection to be presented at the show. Most of my classmates have already sketched their designs and have begun to put them together." I turned around and took a long pull on my beer.

"How far are you?" he asked. He stretched his long legs out and sat back against my bed. I chuckled at how ridiculous his massive black boots looked against the backdrop of Sarah's girly pink shag carpet.

"What's so funny?" he asked.

"You," I replied bluntly, pointing my beer bottle at him.

He pointed at me. "I'm cutting you off. I forgot how wacky you get when you drink." He rested his head against the mattress.

"I do not get wacky." I stuck my tongue out at him in defiance.

"I rest my case," he chuckled. "How far have you gotten on your Showcase stuff?" he asked again.

I shook my head. "Not very."

"When is the show?"

I sat back down on the carpet, pushing his ginormous feet out of the way. "Not until May, but we're required to have a minimum of five different pieces, so it takes a while to sketch the ideas and turn them into wearable clothes."

"Well, let's get on it, then." He lifted his head and clapped his hands together. "You said the collection has to be themed? What does that mean?"

I pulled at the label on the bottle while I regurgitated parts of Professor Vine's syllabus. "All the pieces must be different, yet similar enough to tell a story. There has to be something that ties all the pieces together."

Griffin pulled his legs up and rested his elbows on his knees. "Get your stuff. Let's see what you've got."

"Really, Griffin, you don't have to do this." I sighed, set my beer down, and collapsed onto my back. Shielding my eyes from the light, I threw my arm over my face. "I'm sure an up-and-coming rock star has better things to do with his time."

He nudged my side with his boot, forcing me to look at him. "Seriously, Jillian, go get your shit. I don't know one thing about designing clothes, but I can certainly watch you do it. Get up." Griffin held out his hand and I took hold. In one swift motion, he pulled me up so we sat face to face. "Where's your stuff?" he asked.

I nodded my head in the direction of my desk. "On the floor over there."

"Well, go get it." He tapped the tip of my nose lightly with his finger.

Begrudgingly, I got up, trudged over to my desk, leaned down beside it, and pulled two large duffle bags and my book bag from the floor. "I've got dozens of different fabrics and embellishments in these two bags," I said, holding them up.

"Embellishments?" Griffin's eyebrow pulled up. "What the hell is an embellishment?"

A small smile spread across my face as I tossed my bags into the center of the room. I dragged my book bag behind me as I plopped down next to the duffle bags. "I have my sketchbooks in here," I said, setting it on my lap.

"Do me a favor," he said, catching my eye. "Never mention this to the guys."

"Your secret's safe with me." I sealed my lips, pretended to lock them up, and pantomimed tossing a key over my shoulder.

Griffin pulled the purple duffle to him and unzipped it. He turned it upside down and emptied the contents onto the floor. Ribbons, beads, appliqués, yarn, patches, sequins, and countless other adornments fell into a pile between us. Griffin ran his hand through the mess and looked at me quizzically.

"What?" I asked, unzipping the other duffle bag full of fabric swatches. "You wanted to know what embellishments were... Well, there you go." I grabbed a fistful of beads and playfully tossed them at his head. His arms went up and shielded his face from the bead attack.

"I think I'm going to need another beer for this." He reached over and pulled one from the mini-fridge.

We stared at the small, sparkly hill in the center of my room. "Any ideas?" he asked, twisting the cap off his beer.

"None. I'm telling you, the second I got here, every ounce of my artistic ability disappeared."

"Fuck that." He took a drink and reached backward to set his beer on my desk. "Come on, there's got to be something in here you can use." Griffin pieced through the pile. Within seconds, he pulled out a circular lace appliqué and some tassels. "Here, what about this?" He placed the appliqué on his head and batted his eyelashes. A swell of laughter pushed its way from my core and through my lips.

"Or this," he continued, holding up each tassel to his chest, twirling them around suggestively.

"Stop...stop," I cried, punching his shoulder, laughing. His strong hands lightly pushed me backward and I fell on my back, sighing. Griffin tossed the tassels back onto the pile and sat up on his knees, smiling at me.

I laughed again and turned my head to look at him. "If the guys could see you now," I giggled.

"Uh-uh," he *tsk*ed, waving his index finger back and forth. He shuffled on his knees through the glittery mess between us and hovered over me. "You promised." Griffin pressed his calloused finger to my lips and smirked. "You locked it and threw away the key." Moving his leg over my body, he straddled me and leaned in close, pinning me to the floor with his shoulders and muscular torso. My eyes grazed the features of his face. Black waves fell onto his forehead, hanging just at his eyebrows. Something smoldered in his deep-set brown eyes, and I feared I would combust. My fingers itched to brush against his stubbled jawline. I bit my lip hard to keep from screwing up our friendship.

Griffin slid his hands down my arms, stopping when he held my sides in his firm grasp. His eyes blazed with an intensity I didn't understand, and I couldn't seem to remember how to breathe anymore. Staring at me, his shoulders moved up and down in a rapid, steady manner. Then, ever so slightly, the corners of his mouth pulled up, and his fingers started to wiggle at my sides. He tickled me mercilessly while I laughed and writhed beneath him. "You promised," he said, his voice barely a whisper at my ear.

"Okay! Okay!" I squealed, trying to wiggle out from under him. "I give!" I giggled.

Just when I thought I would pass out from laughing so hard, the door shot open. Like we'd been caught doing something inappropriate, Griffin instantly sat up and pulled me up with him.

Sarah stood in the doorway, shock written on her face. "I'm sorry…I didn't mean to interrupt," she stuttered.

"Sarah, no…it's fine," I said in between heavy breaths.

"Yeah, no problem," Griffin added, also out of breath. "Hi, I'm Griffin." He reached around me, offering Sarah his hand.

Sarah stepped closer and took his hand. "It's nice to finally meet you, Griffin. I've heard so much about you." Sarah looked from Griffin to me and smiled.

"Is everything okay?" I asked. "Aren't you staying at Brandon's brother's house?" I had a difficult time looking her in the eye. I knew what she was thinking…only because I'd been thinking the same thing most of the night.

Sarah stepped over the pile of crap on the floor and looked up at Griffin, who was standing in front of her dresser. "Excuse me." She smiled.

"Oh, sorry." Griffin took one giant step and went to sit on my bed, running his hand through his hair.

"No, no, it's fine," she said, pulling open one of her dresser drawers. "I just forgot…something." She looked at me from over her shoulder and smirked.

I cleared my throat. "How was your Thanksgiving?" I asked, trying to ease the awkward tension in the room.

She claimed her forgotten item and stood up, pushing the drawer shut with her foot. "Good," she drawled. "But, apparently, the party is here tonight." Her eyes scanned the mess on the floor and then the two of us.

"Griffin was just—"

"Helping Jillian find her muse," he interrupted.

"I can see that," she intoned, giving me a dubious stare. "Well, Brandon's waiting in the car," she said, walking to the door. "Good luck finding your muse," she giggled.

"Good night, Sarah," I groaned. "I'll talk to you tomorrow." I pushed her toward the door, hoping she'd give up on the innuendos.

"Good night. Nice to meet you, Griffin," she called over my shoulder.

"You too, Sarah," Griffin called from the bed.

I shut the door and turned around. "Well," I sighed. "That was weird."

Griffin nodded, running his hand through his already messy hair. "Yeah." He stretched his long legs out in front of him, still fussing with his hair. A telltale sign that Griffin felt the awkward strain between us, too. "Sooo," he drawled.

Ugh. There was no way Sarah would let this go. I'd have to have some kind of explanation when she returned. But what? He'd been flirty all night. Why?

What is happening between us?

I stared at him, desperate to understand.

"Back to work?" he asked, averting his eyes.

No! Not back to work! What the hell is going on, Griffin! I wanted to yell. *You're confusing the shit out of me!*

Instead, I walked over to the bed and fell face down behind him. "It's late and my head feels fuzzy. I need to go to bed." Maybe sleep would bring the answers I needed.

Griffin pushed me closer to the wall. "Scoot over." He kicked his boots off and lay down too.

I tried to relax beside him, regulating my breathing, burying the feelings drudged up by the odd foreplay earlier. *He came here to help you…to be supportive. Nothing more, nothing less.* I sighed. "Thanks for putting up with me."

Griffin stretched his arm over me and pulled me to his side. I turned my head to look at him, using his shoulder as a pillow.

With his other hand, he smoothed my hair away from my face. "Jillibean, I will always be here for you," he said, tucking a strand of hair behind my ears. He kissed my forehead and my eyes slid closed.

Hmm…what would those lips feel like moving down my neck…over my breasts…my stomach… I shivered and my eyes sprang open. *Not going there, Jillian.*

He tensed. "Cold?" He rolled over, squashing me beneath him.

Taking advantage of the situation, I inhaled. *Bad idea. Oh, god, he smells good. Not helping, Griffin.*

Falling back beside me, he drew a blanket over us, taking care to tuck me in. "There. Better?"

Yes…no…

"Hmm…" I settled in next to him like I'd done a million times before. But it was difficult to keep my thoughts friendly, especially with his muscled body pressed so close to mine. The safety of his arms had always helped me breathe a little easier. Now, they stole my breath away.

Chapter Twelve

On Friday, Griffin and I spent most of the day Christmas shopping, but sadly the day passed too quickly and Saturday morning arrived like an unwelcome house guest.

Feeling the cold absence of Griffin's warmth beside me, I threw the pillow off my head and sat up. He was kneeling on the floor, stuffing his clothes into a small bag.

I frowned.

I propped my head on my elbow like a kickstand and watched him roll his clothes into tight cylindrical noodles. "You know what I'd love to have right now?" I said.

Now aware that I'd woken up, he looked at me and smiled. "What's that?"

"A bright blue police box that can transport me back to Tuesday night," I sighed.

Griffin left the last of his belongings on the floor and stood up. Walking over to the bed, he pushed me over and flopped down next to me. I rolled onto my side, sandwiched between the wall and Griffin, and buried my hands under the pillow. He rolled onto his side too, so our faces were only a few inches apart. The corner of his mouth pulled up, but the smile didn't touch his eyes. He smoothed my hair away from my face. "All you've ever talked about was getting the hell out of Jennifer's house and going to design school. But…" he said, burrowing his hands under the pillow, too. His fingers curved over my hands, holding them tightly. "Now you're sad all the time. Is this still what you want?"

I shook my head. I didn't know what I wanted. But I did know that I hated being away from him. He was the one part of my past I wasn't willing to run away from. "I feel like a failure here. Everything feels…forced." My words fell flat. "Except for these last few days." My eyes searched his face, but I couldn't keep looking at him if I wanted to get through another good-bye.

I averted my gaze and concentrated on the barely visible, slanted dark lines of the tattoo circling his bicep. A deep-seeded need to touch him washed over me, and without any hesitation, I pulled one of my hands free of the pillow. I brushed his shirtsleeve up, revealing the masculine cursive script, winding around his arm. I remembered when he'd gotten it. Five years ago…right after my accident. I'd seen it a million times since then, but now, for some inexplicable reason, the ink was like a magnet, and my fingers couldn't escape its pull. I lightly traced the curved lines, flowing from one letter to the next. At my touch, I felt Griffin shudder infinitesimally.

I stopped tracing for a moment and reached for the blanket, sealing us into a fleece cocoon.

"Can I tell you something?" he said in a low and gravelly voice.

Beneath the covers, I continued brushing my finger along his arm, loving the feel of his warm, smooth skin stretched over his taut bicep. I looked into his dark eyes, and my heart fluttered. Why did his eyes hold so much heat? They consumed me. When it came to Griffin, my willpower was burning away fast. With each new day, I wanted him more and more. "What?" I asked.

"I feel the same way." His voice rumbled low in his throat.

My fingers wrapped around his bicep, holding as much of the artwork as I could in the palm of my hand. "You do?"

"'Forced' is the perfect way to describe everything." He tightened his grip around my hand that was still under the pillow.

I was taken aback by his response. I knew the band was keeping him crazy busy and he was stressed. But I knew he loved every minute of it. I had no idea he was feeling the same way I did. I scrunched my face into a questioning look and said, "The same can be said for you. You're following your dream. The band's doing well and…" I trailed off, thinking of Erin. As much as I didn't want to admit it, he had her, too. "You've got Erin," I whispered. A sharp pain stabbed my heart. I wanted so badly to be the one he wanted. But I wasn't, and I had to live with that. "What's not right?"

Griffin released my hand and drew his out from beneath the pillow. With his long fingers, he smoothed the creases between my eyes. "None of the band's success feels right without you there to share it with. And Erin…" He paused. "She's not who I want."

I drew in a quick breath, my heart and lungs constricting at the same time. What was he saying? I gripped his arm harder, not wanting to let go. "Who do you want?" I choked.

Griffin used his thumb and wiped my falling tears from my cheek. Then a loud beeping sound blared from his pocket, scaring the shit out of me. Griffin cursed under his breath and shot up, digging his phone out of his pocket. At the same time, I sat up, feeling like he'd just been ripped from my side. I wiped my eyes with my hand and sniffled. "Who is it?"

He gave the screen a quick glance, pressed a button to silence the beeping, and returned his attention to me. "It's Ren. I've got her car."

"Oh," I said. My throat was scratchy and my voice came out all garbled.

Griffin held his hand out to me. I placed mine in his upturned palm and he yanked me into an all-consuming hug. I wrapped my arms around his waist, and buried my head between his arms and chest, refusing to let go.

Something was changing between us and I wasn't sure who was more scared: me, because he'd rejected me once, and I was afraid to let those feelings return; or him, because he knew I wasn't someone he could fit into his "love 'em and leave 'em" lifestyle.

* * *

"Jillian, I'm back," Sarah called before she opened the door.

I rolled my eyes. She was ridiculous. "You don't need to announce your arrival, Sarah. Griffin's gone," I said, looking up from the sketchbook on my lap.

She opened the door and poked her head around. "Well, I didn't want to interrupt anything...again." She grinned, pushing the door open wider.

"For the hundredth time, you didn't interrupt anything. You know Griffin is only a friend." *Or is he?* I was so confused. I lowered my eyes back to my mediocre sketches, trying to ignore the I-told-you-so vibes radiating off of her.

"Yeah, that's what you *say*." She sat her overnight bag on the bed and started unpacking.

"Whatever," I said. I was annoyed, but not at Sarah and her comments. I was annoyed because ever since Griffin left yesterday morning, I felt we had more distance between us than just the thousand miles of road.

Seeing I was in no mood to joke around, Sarah busied herself unpacking and organizing her drawers in between trips to the laundry room. After Griffin had left at the butt crack of dawn on Saturday, I'd spent the whole day and all of today finishing my laundry and cleaning up the mess we'd made in the room. With all of my housekeeping finished, I reserved tonight to catch up on some projects and study for my upcoming finals.

* * *

I was trudging through the snow on my way to the science building with my head crammed in a notebook filled with chemical formulas from my Chemistry of Pigment class. I took advantage of the long trek from one end of campus to the other just to get a few more minutes to study for my final. When I reached the lecture hall, Professor Royson stood at the door ready to greet each student personally by handing them their test as they walked in. "Good morning, Miss Lawson," he said, shoving a test in my face.

I closed my notebook and stowed it under my arm, smiling up at him. "Morning." I took the test from his hand and walked into the lecture hall.

"Even though you're early, you may take a seat and begin. You will have until 12:30 p.m. to finish your final; after that, I will collect them. If you finish before the allotted amount of time, you are free to leave."

I turned around to acknowledge his instructions. "Thank you."

The empty hall had me wondering how early I actually was. As I climbed my way to the top row, I pulled out my phone to check the time: 10:15 a.m. I was only fifteen minutes early. Shoving my phone back in my pocket, I sat down with my test.

I immediately dove into a sea of elements, molecular bonds, and unbalanced chemical equations. I really didn't see how a chemistry background would enhance my designs, but it was refreshing to study something with actual right and wrong answers as opposed to being graded on something completely subjective.

As the clock ticked closer to 12:15, I balanced my last equation and checked one more final off of my list. I was now officially half-way finished with my first semester of college, and two finals away from heading home. I was ready for a break, despite returning to my sister's house. Hopefully, Jennifer and I would fall back into our wary dance of avoidance; otherwise, it would be a very long month. I was excited to see the twins, though; I missed them. But most of all, I couldn't wait to see Griffin. I felt my cheeks flush at the thought. Since he'd left almost three weeks ago, every time he called, I couldn't escape the jittery anxiety I felt.

I placed my test on the stack with the others and headed for the door. When I walked into the hallway, my phone buzzed in my pocket. I pulled it free, seeing a FaceTime call from Griffin.

I still didn't know how to interpret Griffin's flirty behavior at Thanksgiving, and what he'd meant when he said Erin wasn't who he wanted. The few times we'd talked since then, my imagination always got the better of me, and I turned into a bumbling, nervous mess. I'd even spoken to Dr. Hoffman a couple of times about how confused I was. I couldn't reconcile my feelings with the words Griffin had spoken last year, and what his actions had hinted at weeks ago. *Had he changed his mind?* In the end, Dr. Hoffman posed a question to me: "What do you want, Jillian?" She didn't want me to answer, but to think about it, and when I knew, to be brave enough to follow my heart and own my decision. She also told me she wanted to see me over winter break. Even though our little phone sessions didn't help clear any of the fog from my brain, it was still really nice to hear her voice.

A kaleidoscope of butterflies turned over in my stomach when I slid my finger over the screen. Griffin smiled back at me as my picture shrank into the letterbox in the corner. "Hi, Griffin," I said, smiling back.

"Hi, Bean," he said. "I can't talk long, we're filming a scene for our music video, but I wanted to wish you luck on your finals."

The deep timbre of his voice made my cheeks burn. I took a deep, focused breath before I replied. "Thanks. I've only got two more and then I'm outta here. But, wow, a music video?"

"Yeah. You'll be home on Sunday, right?" He ran his hand through his hair—something he did when he was nervous. *Hmm, was he feeling the same way I was?*

"Yeah." I nodded.

"Cool. I'll see you on Sunday, then. I gotta go, Bean," he said, directing his thumb over his shoulder. "They're ready to start filming."

"Have fun. See you soon."

"Not soon enough." He winked at me and the screen went dark.

I couldn't agree more. A giddy smile spread across my face and the butterflies in my core fluttered with hope.

Chapter Thirteen

*O*ne more day. One more day. One more day...

All I had to do was get through today and then I would get to go home. Not home as in Jennifer's house, but home as in Illinois...where Griffin was.

Two finals stood between me and where I wanted to be. I'd breeze through one, but the other had the potential to kill me.

I walked into the classroom just minutes before my teacher. As Ms. Halestrom passed out her History of Costume Design test, nervous energy poured from my fingertips. I tapped my pencil on the desktop and bounced my legs up and down waiting to get started on my final.

Ms. Halestrom slid a stapled stack of papers onto my desk, and I quickly got to work. I read each question carefully and filled the bubbles with graphite. After forty-five minutes, I penciled in the last circle and sealed my fate.

Handing in the test, I made a quick dash to the dining hall. I hoped to find a secluded table near the back of the room, grab a bite to eat, and review my presentation for my last final—Apparel Design Studio I—a.k.a. The Dream Crusher.

Luckily, I had missed the lunch rush. Grabbing a tray, I went through the line and found a small table near the back of the room. I sat down with my turkey sub and pulled out my portfolio for one final review.

I pored over the designs I'd made after Griffin's Thanksgiving visit. Listening to him talk about Mine Shaft during those couple of days got the wheels turning in my head. When Griffin had started the band in high school, the guys had decided on the name Mine Shaft in order to pay homage to the historic coal mining industry of our city. It felt right that I should also take inspiration from those old abandoned mines for my Spring Showcase Collection.

Taking a bite of my sandwich, I flipped through the pages of my portfolio and admired the sketches of my *Diamond in the Rough* collection. I envisioned models traveling up and down the catwalk sporting platinum blonde wigs with very urban styles: blunt cut bangs, short bobs, and uber-straight long hair. The models represented the "diamonds," and the "rough" part would be conveyed through the coal black attire they modeled.

In my preliminary sketches, I tried to keep my designs dark and edgy, with a hint of femininity. I limited my color scheme to silver, black, and white in an attempt to remain true to my collection's name.

As I turned over the last page of my portfolio, I finished my sandwich and smiled. My pulse quickened with anticipation. It was time for me to get in front of my peers and show them what I was made of…that I did have the savvy to make it as a designer. I brushed a hand over my portfolio, feeling pride in my accomplishments. I'd done it.

I stowed my portfolio in my bag, cleaned up my mess, and then speed-walked to the door. Picking up my pace through the quad, I made it to the studio building with ten minutes to spare.

Breathless, I collapsed in my seat. I closed my eyes and focused on regaining a normal breathing pattern before I needed to present my collection. Luckily, I had the alphabet on my side. Being an "L" meant three other presenters would go before I bared my soul.

Professor Vine stood before us and explained how she would evaluate our final presentations. Each student was required to introduce their collection for the Spring Showcase through a virtual runway show on the school's design software. Along with the virtual runway presentation, we needed a finished piece that would be used in the Showcase in May. The final portion of our grade focused on marketing—we had to sell our brand. If our fellow classmates weren't "sold" on the designs and our presentation, our final grade would reflect a significant reduction.

When Professor Vine finished her monologue, I felt sick to my stomach. Heavy self-doubt sat on my confidence and squelched the small amount of bravery I'd felt in the dining hall. I hated that part of my grade rested in the hands of my classmates. Small beads of sweat formed along my forehead even though I felt cold and clammy.

By the time two of my classmates had finished their presentations I breathed a sigh of relief...until Professor Vine called Chandra to the front.

Our collections were required to have five different pieces, and our overall theme was to remain present throughout the entire presentation. Chandra's collection featured seven different pieces—two of which were already completed. As I listened to her pitch, my stomach twisted into a giant knot.

Chandra finished her presentation with two mannequins adorned in artfully created cocktail dresses. One dress was the color of dark chocolate, and the other was called raspberry souf-flé—aptly named for her *Just Desserts* theme. The class gave a thundering round of applause as she pushed the mannequins into line with the others. Graciously taking her final bow, she smiled and walked back to her seat.

Now it was my turn.

Before Professor Vine called me forward, my phone vibrated in my pocket. I pulled it free and saw a text from Griffin. *You're going to knock their fucking socks off!*

When my name was called, I stowed my phone and smiled, walking to the front of the classroom. While I set up for my presentation, Professor Vine thanked Chandra for her outstanding performance and turned the floor over to me. "Jillian, are you ready?"

I took a deep breath and nodded. "Yes."

Standing before my peers, I decided to take Griffin's advice. I opened my mouth, and the words flowed from me perfectly as I presented my virtual runway show. I explained the inspiration behind my collection and ended with a mannequin dressed in my signature piece: a black satin tank top with a thin white stripe separating the flowing ruffles that cascaded down the length of the left side. Sheer silver chiffon overlaid each shoulder strap. I paired the tank with low-rise black denim jeans, coated in shimmering silver glitter, and accented with white spandex pockets.

Adorning the mannequin's waistline was a slim, black patent leather belt with a silver loop at the navel. Black strappy, heeled sandals completed the outfit, tying the whole ensemble together. My mannequin looked ready for a night of clubbing, just as I'd intended.

When I finished, I looked over the crowd and then to Professor Vine. Smiling, she joined me at the front of the room. My classmates applauded and Professor Vine thanked me for my hard work. Like Chandra, I pushed my mannequin into line, and took my seat. Professor Vine called up the next student and I breathed for the first time since I'd gotten to class. I was finished.

After thirteen presentations, class was dismissed. I gave myself permission to celebrate the small victory over my final, but I knew I was far from finished. I still needed five perfect ensembles for the Spring Showcase. I sighed, shrugging off my daunting second semester. I didn't want to think about that right now. Pushing open the doors of the studio building, I sent Griffin a text: *There were fucking socks flying everywhere!*

Walking into Victor Hall, I encountered corridors filled with blaring music, laughter, and an overabundance of dresser drawers slamming shut—a good indication that we were all parting ways for an extended period of time. As I turned down the hall toward my room, Sarah came running up behind me. "Hey, Roomie, how did it go?" she asked, slinging her arm over my shoulder.

My lips pulled into a smile. "I think I did really well."

Sarah threw her other arm around me, giving me a quick hug. "See, I told you so. One of these days, you're going to start listening to me. I know what I'm talking about." She winked.

Walking down the hall to our room, I fished my keys from my

purse and unlocked the door. "Yes, but I wouldn't want to be responsible for your head getting too big." I smirked.

I followed Sarah into the room, dropped my bags next to the closet, and staggered to my bed. She walked to her side of the room and did the same. "When do you leave?" she asked.

"As soon as the sun wakes up tomorrow." I turned my head in her direction. "What about you?"

"I fly out tonight. My parents got a cheap flight for me on the red eye." She glanced at me and shrugged.

I didn't like the fact that she insisted on flying. Just thinking about her on a plane made my stomach twist up like a pretzel. I couldn't bear the thought of anyone I loved being in or near any mode of transportation that left the ground.

Overcome by fear, I launched myself off the bed. Startled, Sarah jumped from her bed. "Shit, you scared me!" she screeched.

I stepped closer and wrapped her in a tight hug. I contemplated never letting her go. "I don't care what time it is when you land. You better call or text me."

Even though her arms were pinned underneath mine, she still managed to lift them enough to pat my back. "I promise. I'll call you before I even let my parents know I've landed."

"You better," I said, still holding onto her. She didn't say a word, but only nodded her head in agreement. She wiggled her shoulders, trying to pull away, but I wouldn't let go.

"Jillian, honey," she said, patting me on the shoulder. "Um…"

"You see, I have a plan," I muttered. "If I don't let go, then you can't pack. If you don't get packed, you'll be late for your… You get the idea?"

Without warning, she went limp in my arms. As she dropped to the ground, I fell with her and lost my grip. Shock and worry was smeared across my face while she was doubled over in a fit of laughter.

"That got your attention," she laughed.

I swatted her arm. "You scared the shit out of me!" I shrieked. "I thought you passed out."

Laughing hysterically, she reached over to her bed and grabbed a pillow. "You wouldn't let go." She reared back and swatted me with the pillow, giggling. "I'll be fine. Don't worry."

I tried to pull the pillow away, but her grip was too strong. "Just call me, okay?"

She gave me a reassuring smile and said, "I promise." Getting up, she smacked me over the head one more time. "I've got to start packing."

* * *

By late evening, Sarah had left for the airport, I was packed, and the rest of the dorm grew quiet as more people left for winter break. Lying on my bed, bored out of my mind, I called Griffin. I realized it was a Friday night and he probably had a show, but I tried anyway.

"Jillibean?" he answered.

"Holy shit, you answered." I was shocked. "Don't you have a show tonight?"

"Nope. We have the night off." He was quiet. *Uh-oh.* He sounded distracted. I probably interrupted something. *Shit!*

"Uh…can you talk?" I cringed, hoping he and Erin weren't taking advantage of his free time.

"To you? Fuck yeah. What kind of question is that?" he chided.

"Oh, well, you just sounded busy. I didn't want to interrupt anything." I laughed humorlessly. "You're not hanging with Erin tonight? I thought she'd be all over your down time." I cringed at the thought.

"We broke up," he said nonchalantly. "And Thor has a date, so he most likely won't be home before sunrise."

Did I hear him correctly? "You broke up?" I asked, trying not to sound too hopeful.

"Yeah." He didn't sound too broken up about it, so I took that as a good sign.

"What happened?"

"Nothing really. We just weren't that into each other." He didn't offer any more of an explanation. And he was so quiet.

"Is everything all right?" I didn't really need to ask. I could tell something besides his breakup with Erin was on his mind. I was used to Griffin's introspective moods. He'd stew about something for weeks and get really quiet while he formulated an answer. He wasn't the kind of person that liked to talk about his feelings; he'd much rather put them into a new song. When he got like this, he wrote the best songs.

"Mmm-hmm," he mumbled. "Just working on..." He paused for a beat. "...a new song. We have a gig on New Year's Eve, and I want it ready for that night."

I knew it! A beatific smile spread across my face. "That's awesome, Grif. Where's the show?"

"At The Pageant." He said it so casually; it was as if they were playing a show at the mall. The Pageant was a big damn deal. Huge artists played there, and now Mine Shaft was among them. Pride welled inside me.

"What?" I shouted. "That's huge! Why aren't you more excited?"

"I guess I'm just a little nervous. I don't want any fuck-ups."

"Griffin!" I cheered. "I'm so proud of you! You guys are great, you have nothing to worry about."

"You'll be there, right?" he asked. I detected a hint of trepidation in his voice.

"Uh...yeah. What? You think I'd miss your biggest gig yet?" I retorted. "Someone would have to chain me to a cinderblock wall to keep me away."

"Good," he sighed, relieved.

"Will you sing me the song you're working on?" I asked. His voice always melted over me like warm, sweet syrup on a pancake. Instant comfort.

I waited.

"Please, Griff?" I asked again, pouring on some sweetness of my own.

"All right, but if I'm going to do this, I need to play it, too," he said. "Hang up, and we can FaceTime. I'll test what I've got out on you. Sound good?"

"Hell, yeah." I sat up, excited.

A low chuckle resonated through the receiver. "I'll get my shit together here, and I'll call you right back. Give me a minute."

"Okay," I said, and then the line went dead.

I reached behind me and pulled my iPad off the desk, resting it on my lap while I twisted my body around to fluff the pillows at my back. I ran my fingers through my hair a couple of times, letting it fall onto the pillow. Then I waited.

I snuggled into the covers and drew up my knees, using them to prop my iPad.

Then it rang.

A giddy smile pulled at my lips, my heart dropped into my stomach, and a fan-girly squee escaped as I tapped the screen, answering the call.

"Okay, I'm set up here," he said, coming into view on the screen. "Can you hear me all right?"

I nodded my head, wearing a ridiculous smile. "Perfectly."

His smile was just as big as mine. "It's good to see you, Bean."

"Ditto," I said, exhaling.

Griffin smiled back at me for a second more, then looked down at the acoustic guitar in his hands. He strummed a couple of slow, steady chords and then looked back to me. His simmering gaze sent goose bumps across my skin. I felt the meticulously constructed wall around my heart burning to the ground with each scorching glance. A couple of dark waves of hair fell into his eyes as he got ready to sing. I'd give anything to sweep them away…to run my fingers through his hair.

When he opened his mouth, a deep sexy baritone voice filtered through the speakers of my iPad. I watched him intently, taking in everything from the sway of his body when he played his guitar, to the way his mouth moved, remembering the way it had felt oh-so-briefly on mine. I watched in blissful silence, soaking up the rich sounds of Griffin's song melting into my ears.

I was so ready to go home…to him.

Chapter Fourteen

I sat quietly at Jennifer's table, sliding some saucy concoction around my plate with a fork. I glanced at the clock and wondered how Griffin's recording session was going. Since I'd gotten home four days ago, he'd called me whenever he could, but that was about it.

Mine Shaft's record label had some big plans in the works—first and foremost, to finish up Mine Shaft's debut album. Without school to interfere, Griffin spent every waking moment laying down tracks, which meant I hadn't gotten to see him at all. The record company had pretty strict rules about friends tagging along, so I was forced to spend some *quality* time with my sister. *Yeah, right!* Whenever possible, I retreated to my old sanctuary—the fabric store I used to work at while I was in high school.

Jennifer's shrill voice brought me back to the present. "Matthew," she said icily. "You're doing the dishes." Jennifer looked at her husband with about as much affection as a person would use to admire a dung beetle. I swore the woman's heart was surrounded by a glacier. Over the years, the glacier had migrated northward, now visible in her frozen blue eyes. I watched Jennifer and Matt's interactions, knowing full well that I did *not* want a relationship like theirs. Ever.

"Matthew!" she shrieked again. "Did you hear me?"

Matt looked up from his phone, a clueless expression on his face. "What?" he asked with a hint of annoyance in his voice.

I didn't want to listen to either of them anymore, and since I had nothing better to do, I offered. "I'll take care of them, Jenny," I said softly.

The twins sat silently, looking from their mom to me. Michael's face scrunched in confusion. "Mommy, your name is Jenny?" he asked.

She glanced at her son, then turned her frosty glare on me. "Don't call me that." Even her voice was cold.

"I like Jenny, Mommy." Mitchell smiled up at his mom, shoveling a spoonful of food into his mouth.

I returned her glare, biting my tongue to keep from laughing at my nephews' comments. The twins always provided a much-needed dose of comic relief in this household. I placed my fork down on the plate with a clink, challenging her. The few months I'd spent on my own had strengthened my resolve when it came to dealing with her shit. "Do you want my help or not."

Pushing his chair back with a loud screech, Matthew stood up. "Sounds good, Jill." He clapped a hand on my shoulder, then stretched his hands above his head. "I've got some work to do in the office." Without another word, he turned around and walked out of the kitchen.

Jennifer sighed and looked at me. "Do what you want." She got up and took her plate with her. "Boys, give me your plates." They put their forks down and handed them to their mother. Jennifer went to the trash can, scraped the remaining food into the receptacle, and deposited all three plates in the sink before summoning the boys to follow her out of the kitchen.

Wow. I offer to do something nice for her and she acts like a complete bitch. I shook my head and got up, taking my plate and Matthew's to the sink.

I went to work on the dishes in relative quiet. Occasionally, I'd hear one of the boys squeal from the next room, followed by Jennifer shouting at them to "use their inside voices." I leaned over and did some creative rearranging on the lower tray of the dishwasher, so I could fit Jennifer's large mixing bowl and serving platter in the same load. With enough room for both, I reached into the sink and pulled out the platter, rinsing it under a stream of lukewarm water. Rinsed clean, I was just about to put it into the dishwasher when it slipped from my fingers and crashed to the floor, shattering into a thousand pieces. "Oh, fuck," I hissed.

"What did you do?" Jennifer's accusatory whisper filled the kitchen. *Damn, she's fast.*

I turned around, seeing her standing in the doorway. The pure, unadulterated hatred radiating from her made me want to run and hide.

"Jennifer, I'm so sorry," I said timidly. "I didn't mean to..." My eyes stung. With just one incensed look from my sister, all of my newfound mettle disappeared, and I felt like was six years old again.

"Shut up!" Jennifer yelled, holding her hands up to cut me off. "Just shut up." She stomped into the kitchen and went straight to the utility room. When she reemerged, she held a broom and dust-pan.

"Here," I said, holding out my hand. "I'll clean up the mess."

"You've done enough." Jennifer wouldn't even look at me, but instead went right to work sweeping up the broken glass. "I'm so *sick* of you ruining things for me," she said cruelly.

That was all it took. I couldn't keep the tears at bay now. "What's that supposed to mean?" I choked.

She lifted her head up and pierced me with her gaze. "I'm sure you can figure it out."

I stared at her, not knowing what else to say. Sobbing, I fled the room.

On my way upstairs, I stepped around the twins playing with their toy cars on the living room floor and went up to the guest room. Shutting the door behind me, I plopped down on the bed and sent Griffin a text. *Are you busy tonight? I REALLY want to see you.*

Jillibean, I'm so sorry. I can't come over tonight. I'm at the studio until late.

The heaviness in my chest threatened to crush me. The screen blurred through my tears while I thumbed back a canned response. *No problem. I miss you.*

I know. I miss you, too. I'm sorry.

Don't be sorry. I'm proud of you!

Thanks, Bean. I'll talk to you later.

Later. When was later? I sent a smiley face back and wiped the tears from my cheek. Lying back on the bed I stared at the ceiling. I needed to talk to someone. *Who could I talk to?* Considering that Griffin and Sarah were my only friends, my only other option was Dr. Hoffman.

I picked up my phone and found her number. *Why did my breakdowns always happen after hours?* After the robotic voice prompted me to leave a message, I told Dr. H. I was back in town, and I really needed to speak with her. I hoped she'd get me in tomorrow. I couldn't take much more of my sister's malevolence.

Now, with nothing to do, and no one to talk to, I was at a loss. The hateful voices in my head decided to keep me company, and I'd do anything to quiet them.

I reached over to the nightstand and pulled my earbuds from the drawer. I slipped them in and turned the music up loud enough to drown out every possible noise.

I reveled in the release of tears even though I could think of a better way to cut the hurt away. I forced myself to enjoy the tears just as much. I cried until my tears formed a gluey substance over my eyelids, making them too sticky and heavy for me to hold open any longer.

***

"I will, Mom," I mumbled, trying to roll over. Something heavy weighed me down.

"Aunt Jillian, who are you talking to?"

A raspy voice was right at my ear. I pulled open one eye and screamed. Sitting bolt upright in bed, I stared into four pale blue eyes. "What the fu…" I stopped myself from saying anything more. All I needed was for the twins to tell their mother that I'd taught them that word. I flopped back down with the twins still sitting on top of me. "What are you two doing in my bed?" I sighed.

"We were bored," Mitchell said. "You almost said a naughty word." He pointed at me and giggled.

I lifted my head up and gave Mitchell the eye. "I did not."

"Yes, you did," Michael chimed in.

"Whatever." I flopped back onto the pillow, blowing air out of my mouth. I was screwed. "So, was it fun watching me sleep? Are you still bored?" I asked.

"Yes, we're still bored. You're a boring sleeper. Come on, Mitchell, let's go bother Mommy until she lets us go outside."

As soon as the boys were gone, I threw my arm over my eyes and tried to go back to sleep. But the early morning light, filtering in through the shades, put a monkey wrench in my plan. The room was way too bright. *So much for sleep.*

I huffed, throwing the covers back, willing myself to get up, when my phone started vibrating beneath my leg. The phone must have gotten lost in my bed covers when I fell asleep last night. I pulled it out from underneath me and saw Dr. Hoffman's name displayed across the screen. *Thank God.* I breathed a sigh of relief and pressed answer.

After a brief conversation with Dr. H.'s receptionist, I had an appointment scheduled later that morning. I got dressed in a hurry, and was out the door in record time. I was eager to speak with her. Phone sessions were okay, but I craved the serenity of her office. I'd always felt safe there.

Dr. Hoffman's office was small and quaint. It was in the rural part of the city, surrounded by a huge, beautifully manicured lawn, pristine walking path, and small koi pond. Sometimes Dr. Hoffman liked to take her patients outside for "walking sessions," and her facility certainly provided patients with a peaceful and safe atmosphere. I'd been on dozens of walking sessions with Dr. Hoffman, but today I knew we'd spend our time in her cozy therapy room since it was freezing outside.

When I pulled open the door, the receptionist greeted me with a smile and asked for my name. "Jillian Lawson."

She wrote my name down and looked back to me. "Dr. Hoffman is wrapping up with a patient now. She'll be with you shortly. May I get you a bottle of water while you wait?"

"No, thank you," I said, walking toward one of the two oversized plush chairs in the waiting area.

"We'll call you soon." She smiled and went back to the paperwork in front of her.

I looked back over my shoulder and said, "Thank you."

Flopping into one of the chairs, I leaned my head on the high cushioned back. Piped over a sound system was some generic station that specialized in instrumental versions of pop music; I recognized the current song as a close approximation of Madonna's *Lucky Star*. Humming along, I pulled my phone out, double checking to see if I'd missed any messages from Griffin.

None. Damn, he wasn't joking when he'd said he had no free time. Who knew being a rock star was a full-time job?

"Jillian?"

I looked up from my phone and saw Dr. Hoffman standing in the doorway. I quickly jumped to my feet. "Hi," I said, giving her a small wave.

"It's good to see you, Jillian." She extended her hand in greeting, and I shook it lightly. "Why don't you come in?" She stepped aside and ushered me through the door. "Can I have Suzy get you anything?" she asked, referring to her receptionist.

"No, thank you. I'm good."

Dr. Hoffman nodded with a warm smile. She pointed me to a chair and took a seat right across from me. "It's so good to see you," she said again.

"It's good to see you, too." I set my purse down on the floor and shrugged off my coat, getting comfortable.

"So, Jillian, how have things been since the last time we talked?" She rested her iPad on her lap, sliding her finger across the screen.

In my head, I tried to remember how long it had been since I'd talked to her on the phone. Maybe a little over a week? "Okay, I guess," I answered.

Her brows pulled together, scrutinizing my words and body language. "What do you mean, 'you guess?'"

A heavy breath fell from my lips. "Just an argument with my sister." I shrugged.

"Did this argument make you want to harm yourself?" she asked.

I shook my head. "No, not last night. But there were a few times during the semester that I thought about it," I admitted.

"Well, I'm glad that last night's incident didn't cause you any setbacks. You've done remarkably well, Jillian. You should be very proud of your progress," she said, smiling. "And, even with the thoughts of wanting to hurt yourself, you didn't act on them, and that's a huge accomplishment. But I am concerned about you falling back into old habits when things become too stressful."

"I'm worried about next semester. It's going to be tough," I confided.

"Have you thought about ways you can minimize your stress level?" Dr. Hoffman typed on her iPad and looked up at me.

"Running helps. And talking to Griffin," I replied confidently. Sarah popped into my head, too. "I have a really great roommate. She doesn't know about my inclination to self-harm, but I could talk to her if I needed."

She nodded and clicked on something. "Good. Those are all healthy ways to manage stress." Dr. Hoffman considered me for a moment, tilting her head to the side, before she asked her next question. "I'm curious, since we don't meet on a regular basis any longer, and you're so far from home, how do you cope with seeing the scars, now that you're so far away from your support network? I remembered from some of our previous sessions, when you mentioned how much you hated to look at them. We used to talk about your scars all the time."

I looked away, feeling ashamed. I still hated them. They represented every ugly truth about my past. My torso was a cross-hatched mess of raised and puckered skin. I didn't answer, but instead focused on the hem of my shirt, memorizing the pattern of the double needle straight stitch, and the feel of the thread holding my hem together. After a beat, I shook my head. "I try my hardest not to look at them. Shower quickly…get dressed in the dark…and I never touch them," I mumbled.

"Jillian," Dr. Hoffman said, trying to regain my attention. I sighed and met her eyes. "I want you to remember that those scars are just superficial marks. They don't represent you and you don't need to be ashamed of them. The kind, imaginative, talented, beautiful Jillian lies far deeper than any of those scars. She's safe and protected and loved, and no blade can cut deep enough to get to her. That's the Jillian who has been making it on her own."

She fixed her gaze on me and clicked her iPad off. "I have a question for you." She set her iPad on the table beside her chair and leaned forward. Her intense hazel eyes had the capability to see through all my defenses. Only one other person had that kind of super power.

I uncrossed my legs and pulled them onto the chair, hugging my arms around my knees. My chest felt tight, like someone had plunged their hand through my skin and was squeezing the life out of my heart. Under her scrutinizing gaze, I fidgeted with the bottom of my shirt again. "What?" My voice rasped.

"It kind of goes along with the question I asked you when we talked over the phone. I still want you to visualize your life five years from now. Where do you see yourself? But, in the short term, answer this question: Are you cheating yourself out of happiness?"

Huh? Cheating myself out of happiness? What the hell is that supposed to mean? "I'm not sure I understand."

Dr. Hoffman pressed her elbows into her thighs and rested her head on her folded hands. "You deserve to be happy, Jillian, and no amount of hateful words, glances, or scars will ever change that. You *deserve* happiness. Don't cheat yourself out of something you deserve because of lies others, or even yourself, have convinced you are true."

My eyes welled up with tears, and I bit my bottom lip to keep from letting them fall.

Dr. Hoffman continued. "Do you think this is what your parents wanted for you? Do you think they wanted you to spend your life running, and hiding, and crying all the time?"

"No," I whimpered. Dr. Hoffman's words triggered a memory of my mom.

I was five. I'd been chosen to sing a solo in my kindergarten musi-

cal. The night of the performance, I was so scared, she came backstage. She fixed my hair, put a little blush and lip gloss on me, and helped me into my rainbow costume. Right before I was supposed to go on-stage, I started crying uncontrollably. Mom took me in her arms, the best she could, because of my awkward costume, and asked why I was crying.

I told her I was scared. What if I messed up? What if everyone thought I was terrible?

She smiled and wiped my eyes. "Jillian, I want you to go out there and sing for you." She pointed to my heart. "All that matters is that you try your best. It takes guts to go out there and sing in front of strangers. But, you're brave. I know you can do it." She tried to hug me, but pinched my cheeks instead. "Now, no more crying, you've got a song to sing, let 'em hear it."

"Jillian? Is everything okay?" Dr. Hoffman asked, pulling me from my memory.

I shifted in the chair and nodded. "Yeah, sorry. Something you said reminded me of my mom."

"Really?" she asked.

"Yeah. A long time ago she told me to stop crying, and let them hear me sing," I said, sucking up my tears.

"That's good advice." She reached across the space between us, offering me a tissue box. I took the box, clutching it to my chest like a lifesaver. "Isn't happiness worth taking risks for, Jillian?" Dr. Hoffman added.

I didn't want to cheat myself out of anything, but I was scared as hell to let my voice be heard. In my experience, hatred and rejection cut just as deep as a blade, and I didn't know if bravery was a strong enough armor to protect my soul.

Chapter Fifteen

Boys, don't open them yet," Jennifer scolded. "I've got to get the camera."

I sat curled up at the end of the couch and watched as Michael and Mitchell resisted their instincts to rip into the presents that sat beneath the tree. They practically salivated while they waited for their mom to return.

Matt sat on the other end of the couch with his nose shoved into his iPhone, completely ignoring his sons.

I kept my eyes on the boys. They were good for about five minutes. *What the hell was Jennifer doing?* At the six-minute mark, Michael and Mitchell were done being patient with their mother's pretentious hang-ups. The boys were off of the floor and inching their way toward the tree.

They each worked their way through the absurd mountain of presents, shaking boxes until they rattled. When they tired of a box, they'd toss it over their shoulders and reach for a new one. I found their complete disregard of their mother's command very funny. They had inadvertently managed to make my Christmas morning somewhat enjoyable.

"Michael! Mitchell!" Jennifer shouted, walking back into the room with a large and very expensive-looking camera. "Matthew, what are you doing? Why aren't you watching them?"

"Oh, sorry." He looked up from his phone and over at the boys. "I had to change my fantasy football line-up."

"Boys," Jennifer barked. "Put those gifts back where you found them! Pictures first, then presents." Jennifer knelt down and helped the twins put all the boxes back under the tree. How she expected two five-year-old boys to sit still and stare at a Christmas tree on Christmas morning, and *not* touch the presents was beyond me, but that was Jennifer—everything was always about her.

I pulled my legs up to my chest and buried my smiling face between my knees. I would have stopped them, but Jennifer hated when I corrected the boys.

"Matthew, I could use some help," Jennifer barked.

Having regained my composure, I lifted my head, not wanting to miss a minute of Jennifer and Matt's loathsome glances. Rolling his eyes, Matt stood up from the end of the couch and palmed a few gifts, chucking them back under the tree.

"Matt, be gentle, please! What if it's breakable?" Jennifer commanded.

Matt glared at her. "I'm sure the boys took care of it already."

Jennifer pursed her lips and began strategically rearranging the gifts under the tree. I felt sorry for Santa; after people saw the Barrett Family Christmas photos, they would think he was an anal-retentive jolly ol' elf.

While Matt gathered the remaining presents and Jennifer

meticulously arranged them, the boys quietly sat on the ottoman. To amuse themselves they unclipped their cherry red bowties, untucked their shirts, and started working on the buttons. My shoulders shook with laughter as I watched them undress. Their mother was going to blow a gasket.

"Okay," Jennifer sang as she stood up from her tree-rearranging. The second she turned around and got a glimpse of the boys she screamed. "Ugh! Boys! What are you doing?"

"This shirt is itchy, Mommy," Mitchell complained.

"And this…" Michael held his bowtie up to her with a look of utter contempt. "Is awful."

Jennifer turned around and glared at me. Her face glowed bright red. "You couldn't have stopped them?" she said through clenched teeth.

"When I step in, you tell me not to. Make up your mind," I replied.

"She's got a point, Jennifer," Matt said, handing a gift to Michael.

Jennifer's eyes shot pure hatred at me before she turned around to tend to the boys. She didn't even acknowledge Matt's comment. He shrugged and plopped down on the couch again. If he held his phone any closer, he'd run the risk of accidentally swallowing it.

Through my quiet observation of Jennifer and her family, I began to understand what Dr. Hoffman had said about happiness. Neither Jennifer nor Matt was happy. They both suffered silently, trapped under the weight of their hatred for each other. Would things be any different if they opened their mouths and were brave enough to tell the other person how they felt? I wondered.

Jennifer knelt down in front of Mitchell and began tugging and tucking his shirt back into place. She scowled instead of returning the smile that was on her baby's face. I didn't think Jennifer had the capacity to feel real love, even if it bit her in the ass. For a split second, I actually felt sorry for her.

"Jillian," Jennifer snapped.

I blinked reality back into focus. "Hmm?"

"Make yourself useful for once and take our picture." She pushed the camera in my direction. I unfolded myself from the couch and took the camera from her hands. "Matthew, I need you," she screeched.

Matt mimicked my apathetic rise from the couch and trudged over to stand next to his wife. He stretched an arm around her waist, leaving about a foot of distance between them. Luckily, Michael and Mitchell filled the awkward gap. I peered through the viewfinder. "Say 'Merry Christmas,'" I said.

"Merry Kissmiss!" Michael and Mitchell said in unison. Jennifer and Matt painted on their practiced toothy grins, and I snapped their "happy" holiday picture.

Handing the camera back to Jennifer, I fell right back onto the couch and curled myself up at the end.

"Matthew!" Jennifer shouted. "Would you be Santa, please? It's time for presents."

"Yay! Presents!" The boys jumped up and down. Mitchell, in an unbridled moment of pure joy, plucked his bowtie from his neck and sent it sailing into the tree. I couldn't help the smile that grew on my face.

"Mitchell Barrett, go get that tie this instant!" Jennifer bellowed.

After all these years, I began to see Jennifer for what she really was: a woman consumed by her own grief. It had never dawned on me before, but Jenny had been just a little girl when Mom and Dad died, too. Both of us had built walls around our hearts, afraid to ever feel that kind of pain again. For Jenny, I guess it was easier to be miserable and push everyone away; at least then she wouldn't have to contend with the agony that would follow if something happened to a loved one again.

I watched Mitchell walk over to the tree and pick his tie from one of the branches. He brought it back to his mother, holding it out to her. She took the tie, tossed it onto the coffee table, and picked him up, setting Mitchell on her lap as Matthew passed out gifts. Jennifer and I never mourned our parents together. We never shared our pain with each other, and that weighed on my heart, because if there was anyone who knew how I felt, it was her.

"Jillian, this one's for you," Matt said, shaking me out of my thoughts. He reached across the coffee table and handed me a rectangular package.

The tag read, "To: Aunt Jillian, From: The Twins" just like every Christmas gift I'd gotten for the last five years—ever since the twins were born. Before Michael and Mitchell the tag always read, "To: Jillian, From: The Barretts," and before Matthew it said, "From: Jennifer Lawson." I'd be willing to bet I could pinpoint the exact Christmas I started getting gifts from "Jennifer Lawson"—twelve years ago.

Twelve years ago my sister's heart broke…just like mine.

I turned the gift over in my hands and looked down at Michael and Mitchell, "Thank you, boys."

Peeling the tape from the corners, I gently tore through the Grinch's too-small heart. A zebra print, 8"x10" spiral bound sketch book revealed itself as I removed the last pieces of the Whoville Christmas tree. "Aw, I love it. Thank you, Michael." I got up from my seat and wrapped my arm around him. "Thank you, Mitchell." I pulled him in with the other arm. Both boys were oblivious to my thankfulness, never taking their eyes from the toy cars they *va-roomed* on the floor.

Matt passed out the rest of the gifts and I watched them open one after the other. On the couch cushion next to me my phone vibrated. *Merry Christmas, Bean!* Griffin texted.

I texted him back: *Merry Christmas, Griff! Please say I get to see you tonight?* I crossed my fingers. We'd only been able to hang out twice since I'd gotten home more than two weeks ago, and both times were as awkward as hell. At some point, it seemed our friendship had crossed that line again, but this time, it seemed Griffin had crossed it with me...I hoped. Regardless, I was a hot mess of emotions, and I didn't know how to make sense of any of them.

He replied, *You bet your ass, it's Christmas.*

Remind me to thank baby Jesus for giving you a reason to hang with me! A goofy smile spread across my lips.

Damn, that's harsh. I'll see you later! he texted.

Tears instantly sprang to my eyes when our texting conversation ended. I wasn't sad or upset; I was happy. It felt good to be happy. I deserved to be happy.

* * *

Besides the photo fiasco this morning, the rest of the day was blissfully uneventful. After the gifts were all unwrapped, Jennifer put Matt to work assembling the twins' new train set and commanded me to clean up the wrapping paper mess in the living room.

I disposed of the overflowing thirty gallon trash bag in the garage and retreated to my old room with my new sketchbook in hand.

I stacked the exorbitant amount of throw pillows against the headboard and leaned back. Jennifer certainly hadn't waited long to redecorate my old room. I sighed and propped my new sketchbook on my lap, plugged in my earbuds, and cranked Mine Shaft up to earsplitting decibels. Listening to Griffin's low and seductive voice hum through the speakers, I let his song guide my pencil.

I started with his unruly hair, using the side of my pencil to create the dark waves he always drove his hands through. With Griffin's voice in my ears, my fingers went to work smearing and rubbing, trying to bring him to life on my paper.

Slowly, I slid my pencil down, forming his thick jawline and neck, with his Adam's apple shadowed in right beneath his chin. My fingers trailed over the planes of his face and neck, and I wished it was more than paper beneath my fingertips.

Needing to change positions, I tossed the sketchbook to the foot of the bed and crawled onto my stomach. I stretched out and brought my drawing closer, ready to work on his arms and chest, paying special attention to his insanely hot tattoos.

My hand composed the bulges of his upper and lower arms, adding contrast and depth to his physique. On his right bicep, I reproduced the cursive writing that curled around the entire circumference of his muscle. Then I traveled downward to his chest, taking care to accentuate the lines of his well-defined abdomen, before I went to work on the broken bass guitar spanning from his right ribcage, across his chest, and ending at the top of his left shoulder. Despite being gorgeous in his own right, the artwork on his arm, chest, and back were masculine and exquisite. He was beautiful. Griffin always had the bad boy thing going for him.

Exhaling, I swiped my arm across my brow, and picked up my work up for inspection. I shifted the book to the right and left, viewing it at different angles, trying to gain more perspective. It was a good start, but I wasn't anywhere near finished.

I placed the book on the bed and went back to work, singing along with him. As Griffin's body slowly took shape on the page before me, I smoothed the pencil down his waistline, creating the v-shaped cut in his abdomen. Dipping lower on his body I formed his legs, before using my imagination to complete the rest of his anatomy. I was also well aware that the temperature of the room felt as though it had gone up several degrees, and I had a thin sheen of sweat across my forehead. My eyes fell over the drawing and a hundred dirty thoughts raced through my head. I was most certainly starting to figure out what I wanted. I just needed to find the courage to tell him.

Bringing my eyes back up to less blush-inducing regions, I tried to clear my head and focus on filling in the features of his face: his expressive dark eyes, a sinful smirk, angular cheekbones, the tiny creases on the sides of his eyes when he smiled…my list of details could go on for centuries.

I set the tip of my pencil to the paper, and as if it had a mind of its own, it trailed slightly across his face, outlining the curves of his eyes. At the same time, my mattress shifted. Startled, I quickly turned my head and saw Griffin lying right beside me. It was like he'd leapt off the page and materialized on the bed.

I rolled onto my side and rested my head on my arm. He

brought his hand up and brushed away a few stray strands of hair from my face, holding my gaze. My heart forgot how to beat for a millisecond, and my lungs couldn't remember if they were supposed to breathe in or out. Griffin's warm breath filled the space between us. I leaned in, dangerously close to crossing that line again. I wanted my lips on his.

Then I remembered the open sketchbook lying right under my arm, and my face flushed with embarrassment. If I moved, he'd see that I'd drawn a very detailed nude image of him. *Holy shit! This is bad. He cannot know that I was drawing a naked picture of him.*

My heart beat in time with the driving bass line of the song thumping in my ears. Trying to play it cool, I inched my hand, the one that lay between us, closer to my armpit, hoping to burrow my fingers underneath my other arm and push the sketchbook onto the floor. Some of my pencils fell off the bed and rolled away. Without saying a word, Griffin grabbed my arm and pulled me closer, wrapping his arm around my waist. With only an inch or two between our bodies, heat exploded through mine. I still hadn't recovered from my naughty art project and now I was in jeopardy of spontaneously combusting.

He lifted his arm from my waist and rested his fingers on my neck. Trailing them up my jaw and toward my ear, he pulled on the wires, and popped my earbuds free. He smirked, then put his hand back at my waist. "Whatcha drawing?" he whispered.

Sprinkles of sweat broke out along my forehead. *Dear, sweet Jesus!* I couldn't remember how to talk, or breathe, or function like a rational human being.

"Jillibean?" Griffin brought his elbow up and rested his chin on his fist. "You okay?" he asked.

Suddenly, all my synapses fired at once. In one quick motion I jumped from the bed, making sure my sketchbook fell to the floor, joining the pencils. "What? Yeah…fine. I'm fine," I stuttered.

He gave me a quizzical look and ran a palm through his hair, then rubbed his hand over his face a few times. He exhaled and stretched over the side of the bed, looking to the floor. Still unable to make my body function, I watched as he reached for my book. "Let's see what masterpiece you've created today," he said. *Oh, it's a masterpiece all right.*

His fingers were relentless. They touched the spirals…the pages…trying to grab it from the floor. If I just showed him, I could spill my guts, and tell him what I wanted.

But that took bravery. And I wasn't brave enough to feel his rejection again.

Griffin was just about to bring the picture around his head, ready to get a good look. I lunged forward and smacked the book from his hand. My sketchbook went sailing to the other side of the room, landing almost in front of the door, a few feet away.

"What the fuck!" he shouted. "Why'd you do that?" He sat up on the bed, shock written all over his face.

"I…I'm sorry." I tripped over my words, shaking my head because I didn't have a better answer.

Griffin pulled his feet up and rolled all the way to other side, planting his feet on the ground. Standing up, he took a step in my direction. He lightly pinched my chin between his thumb and forefinger and drew my head up, forcing me to look him in the eye.

"You better start talking. What's wrong?" His baritone voice rumbled through his core and into mine.

I stared into his probing gaze, waiting for the right words to tumble out. But I didn't have any "right" words…at least none I was brave enough to say.

Not pressing me for an answer, he just brought me to his chest. He always knew what I needed. Sometimes better than I did.

"Come on, get changed. We've got somewhere to be," he said, pulling away from me, smirking.

Chapter Sixteen

Griffin slowed my car and pulled into a long, gravel driveway. Three years ago, his parents had bought an old farmhouse just outside of the city limits and spent all their free time fixing it up—it had always been one of Mrs. Daniels's dreams. In that time, she'd managed to transform the dingy, rundown, twelve-room home into something palatial and radiant.

Killing the engine, Griffin pulled the keys out and smirked at me. "They've been dying to see you." He pushed opened the door and looked over his shoulder. "You coming?"

"Yeah." I smiled. I tugged on the latch and swung the door out wide. Stepping onto the driveway, I took in the grand estate. The front door was surrounded by two large pillars on both sides. A balcony, accessible from the master bedroom on the second floor, was directly above the main entrance. All the other rooms were recessed on both sides of the beautiful entryway.

Griffin came around the car, holding his hand out for mine. He pulled me up the walk and we went right inside. Awesomesauce, Griffin's parents' French bulldog, came scampering down the stairs, barking gruffly. "Hey, buddy," Griffin crooned, bending over to scratch behind the dog's ears. Last year, Griffin's bandmate Pauly had been forced to give up the dog or be kicked out of his apartment for possession of an illegal pet. Griffin had talked his parents into adopting Awesomesauce. At first, Mrs. Daniels wanted no part in a dog, but once she saw the blond, pointy-eared ball of cuteness, she couldn't say no. She had wanted to change his name, but Griffin wouldn't hear of it. Mrs. Daniels still refused to call the dog by his name, only referring to him as Mr. A.

Awesomesauce rolled over onto his back, begging Griffin to scratch his belly. "Come on, boy. Let's go see what that amazing smell is."

When Griffin talked to animals or babies it always brought a smile to my face. His low, deep timbre softened and made my heart melt instantly. Griffin looked at me and smiled, nodding his head in the direction of the kitchen.

Standing in the foyer, I drew in a large breath, taking in the scents of turkey and apple pie. It smelled divine. My stomach rumbled in anticipation. "Everything smells heavenly," I said blissfully.

Griffin tapped his leg, encouraging Awesomesauce to follow along as we started for the kitchen. "Mom insisted we have a late Christmas dinner, so I could pick you up." Griffin said, looking over his shoulder at me.

Mr. and Mrs. Daniels had always been like surrogate parents to me. If it hadn't been for them, I probably wouldn't have met Dr. Hoffman and gotten the help I needed.

"Mom, we're here," Griffin called, walking down the hallway.

His boots clomped on the shiny floor and Awesomesauce trotted at his heels. "Mom?" he called again.

"I'll be down in a minute!" Mrs. Daniels hollered from somewhere upstairs.

Griffin turned around and shrugged.

Following behind, I stepped lightly on the shiny, cherrywood floors. On our way, we passed by a stream of evergreen garland wrapped around the grand staircase, illuminated by sparkling, clear Christmas lights. It looked like a scene right out of a Norman Rockwell painting.

Whenever we came into the kitchen, I always marveled at its size. The house I grew up in could practically fit inside this kitchen.

Griffin went to the oven and pulled it open, peeking inside. He hummed, inhaling a giant whiff of turkey. "Now that's what I'm talking about," he said, closing the oven door and turning around.

"Thank you," I said, feeling overwhelmingly happy.

Griffin lowered his brow. "For what?" he asked, walking back to me. He took my purse and set it on the floor beside him, returning his hands to my shoulders. Slowly, he pushed my coat back, dragging his hands down my arms as my coat slipped off. "I'll put these up for you," he said with a wink, picking up my purse.

"Jillian!" a sweet voice sang from behind me.

I turned around and saw Mrs. Daniels in the doorway. "Mrs. Daniels," I said, walking over to greet her. Her lips pressed together in a thin smile, holding her arms open wide, she brought me close. Compared to all the freakishly tall people I spent my time with, it was nice to be at eye level with someone for a change.

"It's so good to see you, sweetie." She rocked me back and forth. "We've missed you so much."

"I've missed you, too."

She pulled away but didn't let me go. Her thin smile touched her dark eyes, the ones she'd given Griffin. Slipping her arm through mine, she patted my hand and led me toward the island in the center of the kitchen, stepping around Griffin and the dog. As we walked by, I caught Griffin's eye and he shook his head, grinning.

"Hey, Ma, remember me? Your son?" Griffin tapped her on the shoulder.

"Oh, shoo." She waved her free hand, brushing Griffin out of the way. "You're here at least three times a week raiding my refrigerator." She smiled at him, and he stepped out of her way.

"I don't know," he crooned. "I've always suspected you liked her better than me."

"Well, duh," Mrs. Daniels joked back. "She's much easier on the eyes."

"I can't disagree with you there, Ma."

I giggled, feeling my cheeks redden. It was nice to watch them lovingly jab at one another. Griffin had always gotten along really well with all of his family members. The Daniels family were a tight-knit clan that would drop everything at a moment's notice if a loved one was in need. I'd seen it happen when I was bleeding to death on Jennifer's bathroom floor two years ago. When Griffin found me, it was the Daniels who stood vigil at my bedside, not Jennifer.

Mrs. Daniels pulled out a bar stool for me to sit, while she went to work chopping the fresh vegetables that were spread out on the countertop.

"I'm gonna go find Pop," Griffin said on his way to the living room. "Don't talk about me too much while I'm gone."

Mrs. Daniels picked up a small piece of broccoli and tossed it at Griffin's head. "Didn't I tell you to shoo?" Awesomesauce waddled over, sniffing the fallen vegetable, and turned his nose up at it.

"I'm shooing!" Griffin held his hands up, trying to block any other flying vegetables.

"Let me help you with that," I said, reaching for the extra knife lying on the counter.

Mrs. Daniels gently laid her hand on mine and shook her head. "Nonsense. You're on vacation. You sit, relax, and tell me all about school."

Although she'd never admit it, ever since my accident, Mrs. Daniels always tried her best to keep sharp objects out of my reach. Steak night at the Daniels' household was highly entertaining. It was laughable watching everyone try to cut their steaks with butter knives, because Mrs. Daniels wanted to make sure I didn't hurt myself with the steak knife. I didn't mind that she babied me; she was the closest person I had to a mother, and she was amazing.

I watched her chop away at the stalks of broccoli, arranging the florets into a decorative pattern. "School's good," I said. "Hard, but I'm learning."

"It's good to be challenged. You need to talk some sense into that boy of mine. I can't get him to take more than one or two classes a semester." She shook her head, disgusted.

I loved Mrs. Daniels, but my loyalties were always with Griffin. I'd defend him with my dying breath if I had to. "Yeah, but Mine Shaft is doing so well right now. I know he's having a hard time juggling all of his commitments."

She peered at me from under her heavy eyelids and smirked. Griffin looked exactly like her when he did that…well…except for the sexy as hell "I haven't shaved in three days scruff" he always sported. I was sure Mrs. Daniels couldn't pull that off the way Griffin did.

"I just wish he'd take school more seriously. He's so bright. He could be anything if he put his mind to it." Her motherly concern was evident.

"No disrespect, Mrs. Daniels, but Griffin is doing what he wants. He's put his mind to being a musician, and he's good at it. It may not be what you want for him, but he's choosing his own path."

Mrs. Daniels shook her head and smiled. "Well, in my defense, you're probably not the best person to voice my concerns to. Griffin could be one of those people who advertise pizza by flipping a sign on the roadside, and you'd still have stars in your eyes when you talk about him."

My cheeks warmed in response to her knowing stare, and I had to avert my gaze.

Mrs. Daniels chuckled and transitioned to her carrots.

The back door pulled open and Awesomesauce barked, running to greet whoever was about to come inside. Griffin's sister Ren pushed open the door.

Ren wasn't nearly as tall as her brother—then again, who was—but she was taller than most girls, standing at five-eleven. She and Griffin both had their mother's olive complexion, dark hair, and eyes, but their height came from their dad. Mrs. Daniels was as short as I was.

The last time I'd seen Ren, about a week before I left for school, she'd had really long, curly hair. But now it was cut into a short pixie.

"Jillian!" she sang, dropping her purse and gift bags onto the dog and running at me with open arms. "When did you get back?" she asked, enveloping me in a hug.

"About two and a half weeks ago," I said. "Your hair is so cute. When did you cut it?"

She pulled back and ran her hand over some of the spikey pieces. "Oh, about a month ago. I was in the mood for something different. And there's a lady at work whose daughter was diagnosed with cancer. A bunch of us in the office decided to donate our hair to Locks of Love in honor of her daughter."

"That's really cool. And it looks great." I hadn't only missed Griffin, I'd missed the whole Daniels family.

"I'm so glad you're back." She beamed. "Maybe now Griffin won't be such a moody dickhead."

"Renata Daniels, watch your mouth!" Mrs. Daniels scolded.

She looked at her mom. "What? He has been." She scowled before turning her attention back to me. "Jillian, since you left, Griffin's been impossible to be around."

Huh. I let her comment swirl around in my head. I'd try to decipher its meaning later. For now, I was happy just spending Christmas evening with my family.

* * *

Mr. Daniels carved the turkey while everyone passed around the side dishes. Once our plates were filled to capacity, Mr. Daniels said grace and we dug in.

For the first few minutes, we ate in comfortable silence, enjoying the feast Mrs. Daniels had prepared. "This is great, Mom,"

Griffin said. The rest of us nodded in agreement, adding our compliments to Griffin's.

"Thank you, thank you," she replied. "I'm just glad to have all of my kids back, safe and under one roof."

My heart skipped a beat, knowing she counted me as one of her children. Griffin gave me a close-lipped smile in between mouthfuls of food.

"Jillian," Mr. Daniels said, "Griffin mentioned that you have a big project coming up this semester."

"Yeah, I do," I responded. "Fashion majors are required to do a runway show at the end of the year. I'm excited about it, but it's going to be a stressful semester."

Mr. Daniels waved his hand in jest. "Nonsense. You'll do fine. I may not know anything about designing clothes, but I do know you are talented."

"Thanks," I said, smiling. Griffin patted my leg affectionately. "Speaking of 'talented,' though, Griffin's the one doing well." I bumped him playfully with my shoulder.

"Yeah, who would have thought my goony little brother would become the front man of a hot new band?" Ren teased.

"I have never been 'goony.'" Griffin shot her a look, pretending to be offended.

"Oh, really? Should I get out the photo albums?" Ren countered.

"Shhh, Ren." Griffin held his pointer finger to his lips. "Don't mention those in front of Mom, or she'll never let us leave," he said in an affected whisper.

"Ha, ha. Very funny." Mrs. Daniels smirked.

"I don't know, Griff. You were pretty goony," Mr. Daniels chimed in. "What was your nickname in middle school?"

"Oh, I know," I laughed, raising my hand. "Bird Boy." I got right in his face when I said it, too. "Because you were so freakishly tall and skinny, everyone said you had bird legs."

Griffin threw his hands up in surrender. "I give up. But, just so you know, you all suck." He pointed to each of us. Even though he sounded hurt, the megawatt smile on his face told a different story.

I couldn't help but laugh. Griffin's family had always thrived on giving each other crap. It was one of the many ways they showed their affection.

* * *

By the time Griffin and I got ready to leave, it was well after midnight. Ren had left an hour ago and Mr. Daniels was fast asleep in his recliner, snoring louder than a jackhammer plowing through concrete. Awesomesauce was curled up on Mr. Daniels's lap, and refused to move, even to see us off.

Mrs. Daniels walked us to the door, and I gave her hug goodbye, knowing it would be summer before I saw her again. Griffin's parents enjoyed spending the first few months of the year in Phoenix, something they had done ever since Ren and Griffin moved out on their own.

"'Bye, Ma," Griffin said, kissing her cheek. "You and Dad take it easy driving out there."

"We will, Baby Boy." Mrs. Daniels hugged her son. She looked so tiny in his arms. She had always called him Baby Boy, but seeing him hulking over her, it didn't seem possible that she'd once carried him in her arms. "You two be careful. I love you." She held onto Griffin just a moment more and then let go.

Griffin stepped back to my side, and draped his arm around my shoulder. "We will. I love you, too." Griffin drew me closer and I noticed Mrs. Daniels's smile widen in response to the way he touched me.

"You take care of her, Griffin," his mothered ordered sweetly.

Griffin looked down at me, and his face softened. "I always try, Ma."

Griffin and I walked to the car and got in. Mrs. Daniels watched from the doorway as we pulled out of the driveway.

"Thank you, Griffin. That was exactly what I needed." I said, relaxing back into the seat. I was emotionally sated.

Griffin glanced at me and smiled, laying his hand on my leg again. But this time, it wasn't a quick pat. This time he left it there, trailing his fingers up and down. The friction between his fingertips and my jeans made every nerve cell in my body stand at attention. Occasionally, he'd squeeze my leg at the top of his north/south journey, and I had to bite my lip to keep from straddling him and planting my mouth on his. *Is that what he wants? Am I ready to try again?*

Every so often, he'd turn his head and look at me—almost daring me to make the next move. I wanted to, but a tiny barb of apprehension was still stuck in my heart, and I couldn't figure out how to remove it, and tell him how I felt.

I was pulled from my thoughts when Griffin removed his hand from my leg and sat up straighter in the seat. Outside the window, a line of traffic inched along—very odd, considering how late it was.

Griffin concentrated on the road and I craned my neck, trying to see beyond the cars in front of us. Red and blue strobes pulsed and spun, an ominous glow penetrating the darkness. A stationary emergency vehicle flashed an arrow, shifting oncoming traffic to the outer lane. As we approached the sight of the accident, a motorcycle was being loaded onto a tow truck.

My stomach sank. "Did you get a helmet yet?" I asked.

"Not yet," he said guiltily.

"WHAT?" I roared. "You haven't gotten a fucking helmet yet?" My temper went from zero to ballistic in point-three seconds.

"I haven't really had time. I eat and breathe Mine Shaft right now."

"Ugggh!" I growled. "I am so pissed at you right now!" I crossed my arms over my chest, fighting off the urge to throw something. Fury quickened my heart rate, and my pulse beat in my ears.

Griffin had turned left, heading through town toward Jennifer's house, when it dawned on me that he had met me at Jennifer's, which meant his bike was still there. He was planning on driving that thing back to his apartment without a goddamned helmet. *Urrgh!* "Where are you going?" I asked indignantly.

"To Jennifer's?" He cut a quick look at me, confused by my question.

"Uh-uh." I shook my head. "Go to your place. I'll drop you off and drive myself back to Jennifer's," I said.

"Jillian, that's ridiculous. I'm not leaving my bike parked at your sister's house." He argued.

"All right," I challenged, turning my whole body around to face him. "We'll go get your bike, but I'm following you home." I pursed my lips and dared him to argue with me anymore.

He peeked at me and shook his head, but kept his mouth shut.

When he pulled into Jennifer's driveway, I waited for the car to come to a complete stop before I jumped out and walked around to the driver's side door.

Griffin pushed the door open and stepped out, leaving the car running. "Bean—"

"Don't," I interrupted. "I'm following you home, and you're not going to change my mind."

The look on my face must have told him there was no point in arguing. "I'll see you at my place, then." He sighed and walked to his bike while I got in my car.

It didn't take more than ten minutes for us to get to his place. Griffin pulled into the back parking lot, and I followed. I parked in a space next to him and turned off the ignition before Griffin quieted his bike. The loud rumble of the Triumph rattled my car's windows.

I stepped out of my car and Griff killed the bike's engine. "It's late, Bean. Why don't you just stay?" he asked, swinging his leg off the motorcycle.

I shook my head. "I've got to go." I was still too mad at him.

I was just about to climb back into the car when he said, "Jillian, wait!" His voice boomed, amplified by the quiet of the early hour. I expected to see lights flipping on throughout the complex, but thankfully, none did.

Against my better judgment, I halted. Griffin walked over and met me at my car door, pressing his hands to my shoulders.

Remorse softened his features. "I'm really sorry, Bean." He sounded contrite, but I was still fuming. "I've just been so busy."

"Since September!" I spat.

He cringed. "Will you go with me to get one?" His lower lip turned down in a frown, waiting for my answer.

I nodded. "I'm still pissed at you, though." He ran his finger lightly along the side of my face. "I should go," I sighed.

"You sure?" he asked, cupping my face in his hand.

No. I wasn't sure about anything anymore, except that his hand on my face had extinguished my fury and lit a different kind of fire within me.

Chapter Seventeen

Jillian, call me, dammit!

By the sixth text I finally gave in and dialed her number. Sarah had been trying to get a hold of me for a few days, and I'd put her off as long as I could. Ever since my argument with Griffin, I hadn't been in the mood to talk to anyone—including him. He'd called between rehearsals a dozen times in the past week, but I let his calls go to voicemail. When I left his place Christmas night, I knew what I wanted. The hard part was I just couldn't figure out how to tell him. And I was pissed at myself for spoiling the moment and driving away…running away.

I sighed and picked up the phone, giving Sarah a call. It was time I snapped out of my reclusive mindset and rejoined society. I'd moped for too long.

After two rings, Sarah screamed in my ear. "Jesus H. Christ, Jillian! Where the hell have you been? I've been trying to get a hold of you for days."

I drew the phone away from my ear during her tirade. When

she finished, it was my turn to apologize. "I'm sorry, Sarah. I just haven't felt much like talking."

"Uh-oh. What happened?" she asked worriedly.

"I've just had a lot of shit to sort through, but I think I've got it all worked out." I smiled, confident that my words weren't just an empty placation for Sarah, or myself. "So, what's new with you?" I asked, redirecting the conversation to her.

"Oh, well…" she drawled for dramatic effect. "Brandon asked me to move in with him." I could practically hear her smiling.

"What? Sarah, that's awesome!" I cheered. "Are you going to?" I pulled my bottom lip between my teeth, worried I'd have a stranger moving into my room back at school.

"Yeah, but not until summer. My parents aren't too hip with the idea, and my mom begged me to 'think' about it for a few months."

I exhaled a silent sigh of relief. "So, I'm going to have to find a new roommate next year, huh?"

"Sorry," she replied sheepishly.

"Don't be ridiculous," I reassured her. "You and Brandon have been together for a long time. This was inevitable."

"Thanks." She sounded relieved. "I was worried you'd be upset with me."

"Not at all. I'm happy for you, Sarah," I said.

"Do you have plans for New Year's Eve?" she asked.

"Yeah, I'm going to a Mine Shaft concert tonight," I bragged. "What about you?"

"That's cool," she said. "Brandon and I are going over to a friend's house. Nothing too exciting."

"You live in New York, and you're not going to watch the ball drop?" I teased.

"Hell no!" she laughed. "I'm not going anywhere near Times Square tonight. I'll watch the ball drop on television, thank you."

"Well, you have fun staying in tonight," I said.

"Have fun at Griffin's concert," she sang.

After we hung up, I lay in bed thinking about how happy Sarah seemed about moving in with Brandon. I wanted that kind of happiness, too, but I would have to stop running from my past long enough to find it. I was tired of watching my life pass by in a blur because I was too busy running away. I'd missed so much already, and I'd be damned if I missed out on any more.

I needed to tell Griffin how I felt…how I'd felt since last year.

* * *

I showered quickly and threw my hair into a messy bun on top my head. My checklist of things to accomplish before the Mine Shaft concert steadily grew. Thankfully, I hadn't wasted the last week. I had used my solitude and gotten my ass in gear, pooling all my resources to create another piece for my *Diamond in the Rough* collection. I needed to pick up a few items at the fabric store before my newest creation was complete. My plan was to wear an original Jillian Lawson at the concert tonight.

I skipped down the stairs and into the kitchen. Jennifer stood at the sink preparing breakfast for the twins, who were playing with their train set in the living room. I fetched my car keys from the shelf, hanging next to the door to the garage. Jennifer didn't acknowledge my presence, as if I were invisible—a ghost. Typically, I would have pretended to be a ghost and left it alone, but I wanted to put forth a concerted effort and make things better.

I mustered up all the confidence I could and stepped right up behind her. I stretched my arms out wide and wrapped them around the tops of hers, pinning them to her sides.

Jennifer froze. The knife in her hand hovered mid-chop over a green pepper. For a split second I wondered if I'd live to see the New Year, but then her hand released the knife and it clattered to the counter. I laid my head on her back, between her shoulder blades, and closed my eyes. I couldn't remember ever willingly hugging my sister. It was the strangest and most liberating thing I'd ever done.

I drew in a large, soul-cleansing breath, squeezed Jennifer a little tighter, and let go. Spinning on my heels, I clung tightly to my keys and the strap of my purse, making my way down the hall, toward the front door. A wide smile tried to bloom across my face, but I pressed my lips together in a tight line. Like a shaken can of soda, if I allowed my lips to spread into the smile they so desperately wanted to, I would explode with bubbles of laughter and joy. Damn, it felt good to let go of some of that hurt.

After ten minutes of scraping and defrosting my car windows, I headed to the fabric store. My dress was almost complete except for the white faux-leather straps that would intersect at various points across my bust, midsection, and waist. I also needed to pick up some fishnet tights and find the perfect pair of black, knee-high heeled boots. I wanted to look my best tonight, because for the first time, I didn't feel like hiding.

When I pulled into Sew Good's parking lot, it was evident they weren't expecting many patrons. The lot remained a snowy mess. I parked and killed the engine. Getting out, I crunched my way through the lot and stepped into my rainbow-colored sanctuary.

In high school, I'd worked at Sew Good. It was peaceful being surrounded by bolts of fabric, yards of ribbon, and bobbles of every shape and size. Those few hours of work quieted all the negativity in my head, and I could imagine becoming a designer one day.

"May I help you?" a voice called from behind the counter, at the back of the store.

"No, thank you. I'm just going to look around," I answered. The woman at the counter was new; I didn't know her.

She picked up a book and smiled. "Let me know if you need anything."

"I will. Thanks."

The willowy woman went back to reading her romance novel. I walked down the small aisle, which was stacked from floor to ceiling with bolts of various colors of cotton, polyester, rayon, satin...the list went on and on. My hand trailed along the edges of the folded fabrics. The tips of my fingers registered the differences in textures as they bumped from one bolt to another. My imagination ran ahead of me down the aisle, gathering a plethora of ideas and liberating my stifled creativity. Unfortunately, time forced me to rein in my creative spirit. I needed to focus and find what I'd come for.

A few aisles over, I found spools of two-inch, shiny, white faux leather belting—exactly what I needed to finish my dress. I pulled two spools from the rack and took them to the lady reading at the counter.

"I'd like to get a yard and a half of this please," I said, passing over the spools.

"Sure." She set her book down and took the spools from my hand. Her long bony fingers pulled the stretchy material over the yard stick built into the table. She snipped it at a yard and repeated the process one more time, before she folded and pinned the belting into a neat loop. I handed her the cash for my purchase and bundled up before I went back out into the snowy parking lot.

* * *

By the time I found my boots and tights, the day had disappeared. I was in a hurry to get back to Jennifer's (hey, there's a first time for everything) and finish my dress. Before I pulled out of the parking space at the shoe store, I sent Griffin a quick text: *Good luck tonight! I know you'll rock their fucking socks off! :)*

We hadn't spoken in the last week. He'd been really busy prepping for the concert, and I'd been too busy trying to figure things out. Needless to say, Griffin still didn't have a helmet, but as soon as this concert was over we were going to remedy that problem.

Thx! You're coming tonight, right? He wrote back.

Butterflies danced in my stomach as I replied. *I can't wait to have my socks rocked off!*

My phone buzzed. *Oh, that won't be a problem…I'm THAT good!*

Cocky much? I wrote, smiling at the screen. Yep, I was ready. Tonight, after his set, I was going to be brave and tell him how I felt. By the way he'd acted around me the last couple months, I was confident he felt something, too; I just couldn't figure out why he hadn't acted on it. Whatever the reason was, I didn't plan on waiting for him to figure it out. I was in love with him and it was time he knew it.

Griffin texted, *I can be cocky. I've got the goods to back it up!*

Promise? was all I wrote in reply, waiting for his usual response.

Griffin's message popped up: *FOREVER*. My heart skipped a couple of beats and my cheeks warmed. I was so ready.

I had one more stop before I went back to Jennifer's. My chest thumped harder the closer I got, but I had to do it. They'd told me good-bye; it was time I did the same.

I turned the car onto the narrow street and climbed over several hills before I pulled over. Stepping out of the car, I threw my hood up and trudged through the wind and snow flurries, shivering from the cold. Or just from being here.

Stopping a few feet from the road, I knelt down and brushed the snow from the marble plaque in the ground. "Hi, Mom. Hi, Dad," I whispered, even though I knew they weren't physically buried there. My grandparents had insisted on the marker, so Jennifer and I would have a place to talk to them. I'd only come here a handful of times, because it hurt too much knowing they weren't *really* here. But now I finally understood my grandparents' reasoning—it was a reminder that they existed, that they'd left a mark on this world and would never be forgotten.

I ran my finger over the engraved letters, hearing the last words my parents had ever spoken. Even though I'd only listened to that recording once, their words were seared permanently into my memory, just like the words etched into the stone beneath my fingers.

"My sweet, baby girls," Mom choked. *I could hear that she was crying, but she tried to push her tears away with a chuckle for us. "Daddy and I wanted to tell you how much we love you." She cried.*

Dad came on the line. "I love you, girls." He was crying, too.

"Daddy and I don't have a lot of time." Mom's voice sounded

rough. "Something's happened…"She paused, overcome with tears. Taking a deep breath, she continued. "We need you both to be strong," she said forcefully, pushing through her sadness to get the words out. "And take care of each other and listen to Grandma and Grandpa."

"Girls," Dad interrupted, sounding very serious. "We love you both so much," he stressed. His voice was low and scratchy. "Jenny, I wish more than anything, we could have one more tickle fight. I can hear your honeyed belly laughs as I speak." He chuckled at the memory. "And Jillian, what I wouldn't give for one more fashion show in the living room." He tried to stifle a sob. "I love you, girls. You're always with me. Take care of each other."

Mom came back. "I love you, Jenny. I love you, Jillian." She said our names bravely. "I'm so, so proud of you both. You're the best parts of my life, and I'm not ready to say good-bye." She broke down. A heavy crackling sound filled the line along with her sobs. Working through the tears, she spoke firmly this time. "I won't be there for all the important things, but here's my advice for you: Believe in yourself, and listen when life's trying to tell you something." She sniffled and went on. "We're family. We may not be together anymore, but we're always a part of each other. Bye, Loves."

"Bye, Mom," I said quietly, answering the memory. "I just needed to tell you that." My eyes watered. "I miss you both so much. I love you. And Dad, I know you'll be watching my show from up there." I looked toward the sky. Tiny snowflakes tickled my face and I smiled, knowing I was going to be all right.

Chapter Eighteen

Since Mine Shaft was headlining the New Year's event at The Pageant, their set wasn't scheduled to begin until 10:30 p.m. That gave me plenty of time to finish my dress, color my hair, and calm my nerves. At 7:30, I sewed the last button in place and admired my one-of-a-kind creation.

I ran to the bathroom, got cleaned up, and was ready to get dressed. I pulled the ensemble over my head and smoothed it down over the curves of my hips. The black spandex clung tightly to my body, accentuating my usually non-existent bust line. The white, faux leather straps traveled vertically from each shoulder to the peek-a-boo hemline with intersecting straps across my bust, waist and hips. The dress ended just higher than mid-thigh and blended perfectly with my fishnet tights.

Sitting down on the bed, I pulled a long shiny boot over each of my calves and stared at my transformed self in the mirror. I reached for my phone and snapped a couple of shots. I sent Sarah a Snapchat, knowing she'd want to see my new dress.

I dropped my phone back onto the bed and stared at the pseudo-voluptuous blond with hot red streaks of hair chalk. I twisted from side to side in order to get the full effect.

My phone buzzed. Sarah sent back a selfie with a caption that read, *Damn! Who is that hottie?*

As soon as the picture expired I sent her a close-up of me rolling my eyes and sticking my tongue out. *Do you approve?* I asked.

Hells yeah! She wrote back, giving me a thumbs-up and a silly grin.

I'm off to the concert. I wrote in response.

Opening her Snapchat, she sent a picture of herself, kissing the screen along with the caption, *Have fun, Jilli!*

I kissed her back. *Thanks! Happy New Year!*

* * *

I sent Griffin a quick text, letting him know I'd made it to the venue. *Hey Griff, I'm here. Headed for the dance floor.*

His response came back quickly. *Be careful down there. I hate that you're alone.*

I'm fine. Don't worry about me, I wrote back.

I always worry about you, Bean. Go to the main bar area, I left a VIP pass for you.

I thumbed my reply. *Thanks! Can't wait for the show!*

I weaved through throngs of people toward the bar. It didn't surprise me that the entire bi-state area's twenty-something population had come out for Griffin's show tonight; Mine Shaft was amazing.

By the time I got to the bar, I'd worked up a sweat. I stood, waiting for the bartender to finish with the couple at the other end. Spinning around, I took in the stage. A single spotlight was trained on the center microphone while various pinks and blues lit the floor.

"What'll it be, beautiful?" A male voice said behind me.

I spun around and focused my attention on the bartender. He didn't seem much older than me, and he was hot. Hello, biceps. The black t-shirt he wore was under a serious amount of strain. I could appreciate the beauty in other people, but in my eyes he didn't hold a candle to Griffin.

"I'll have a Schlafly Oatmeal Stout, please." I dug through my purse in search of my fake ID and some cash.

"You got it." He took a few steps down the bar and returned with my beer.

"Thanks," I said, handing over the money to pay for my drink. "Griffin Daniels said he left a VIP pass for me. I'm supposed to pick it up."

"What's the name?" he asked.

"Jillian Lawson," I shouted over the crowd.

He tapped the bar with his hand and said, "I'll go check."

While he was gone, I turned around and saw a couple of roadies doing sound checks on the stage. A quick glance at my phone confirmed I had about ten minutes to get down to the floor. I wondered what was taking Mr. Biceps so long.

"Jillibean Lawson?" he asked, strutting back toward me.

My smile widened at the sound of my nickname. "Yeah, that's me."

"There's also a note here that says your drinks are covered for the night." He held the VIP credentials out to me.

"What?" I reached for the badge, not really sure I'd heard him correctly.

"Being with the band has its perks, beautiful." He winked at me, handing my cash back. "You better get down there; the show's about to start."

I hesitantly took the money. "Thanks." I smiled. When Mr. Biceps went on to the next customer, I left a few dollars on the bar for his tip, and shoved my way closer to the stage.

Moments before the start of the show, my phone vibrated. I pulled it from the confines of my clutch and read the text message from Griffin. *Bean, I don't like that you're on the floor alone. Come backstage for the show. You can watch from the wings.*

My hands were full, and there were hundreds of people packed in around me, but I managed to type a quick response. *I'm fine. Stop worrying and start your show!*

Seconds after I sent my text, the lights dimmed and the opening bass chords reverberated throughout the room. The crowd went insane when Adam came on stage. He mounted the drum set, gave it a few dry humps, and added a steady beat to the echoing bass filling the room. Adam's pelvic thrusts sent the women in the crowd into loud convulsions.

One by one, the members of Mine Shaft entered the stage and added their specialty instrument to the steady beat Adam supplied. Finally, it was Griffin's turn. Being the front man came with some serious responsibilities, one of which was the ability to ooze sex appeal. Squeals and catcalls threatened to drown out the heavy bass guitar riff he strummed. I stood in awe, watching him do what he loved best. Griffin always put on a great show, but this was on a whole other level. He wasn't the guy I'd just had Christmas dinner with a week ago. He was a hot, sexy rock god whose sensual voice sent every female in the room into a tizzy.

Griffin moved toward the microphone and belted the opening lyrics to one of their older and more popular songs, "Silent Trauma." With every growl and grunt, the crowd went wild. His command of the microphone pushed the females in the crowd over the edge and they screamed their appreciation.

The crowd on the dance floor got into the music and danced, while singing along, shouting Griffin's name, along with professions of their undying love. He'd done it. All the hard work, being so busy all the time—this was why.

I was so proud of him. I wanted to throw my arms around his neck and kiss him with everything I had. I wanted that kiss to convey everything that I couldn't articulate.

Halfway through Griffin's set, I was dying of thirst. I pushed my way back to the bar and found Mr. Biceps again.

"Another stout?" he asked, remembering my drink.

"No thank you. Just water, please." It was too hot on the dance floor to even consider drinking. I'd abandoned my last drink shortly after the show had begun. He nodded and disappeared down the bar.

I turned around, leaning on the bar, watching as Griffin adjusted the mic to accommodate him sitting on a stool. "We're going to slow it down a bit," he breathed into the mic.

"I love you, Griffin!" A random fangirl cried from the balcony.

Griffin smiled and laughed, ever the consummate showman. "Well, I love you too," he replied in a bedroom voice.

Several whistles and catcalls fell over the crowd. Griffin adjusted his stool and pulled his acoustic guitar over his shoulder. "This song is our brand new single, debuting tonight. It's called 'About Time.'" He strummed a few chords, adjusting the tuning knobs until the strings fell into the right key. The crowd bellowed in anticipation. I could see how much he enjoyed torturing them; he was in his element.

"Here you go, Jillibean," Mr. Biceps said. It sounded strange hearing my nickname come out of anyone's mouth but Griffin's.

"Thanks." I gulped the bottle of water.

Instead of fighting the crowd on the floor, I decided to stay at the bar. Even though I couldn't see the expressions on his face when he sang, there was something strangely intimate about watching him from afar. I moved to the center of the bar, positioning myself in a straight line from him to me. When he started strumming the chords, he looked up and pressed his mouth close to the mic.

> *Once upon a time I pushed you away*
> *Looked into your heart and begged you to stay*
> *I sang of words I couldn't speak*
> *You tried to taste them, but I was too weak*

Griffin closed his eyes, taking a deep breath and continued to bare his soul to the hundreds of people in the room.

> *And it's about time I bury the lie*
> *Speak the words and let them fly*
> *Grab hold and pull you close*
> *It's always been you I needed the most*

Pulled in every direction, but never near you
I thought this would be easy, it's time I got a clue
My words run dry, my song unsung
My actions a lie, and I know they stung

Listening to Griffin's song stirred something in my heart. The words brought back memories of the night I'd kissed him. He'd written this song for me.

I'll fight like hell, and make up for the past
A kiss to break the lie, I want to make this last
Taste the words on my lips
It's about time I let the truth slip

And it's about time I bury the lie
Speak the words and let them fly
Grab hold and pull you close
It's always been you I needed the most
It's always been you I needed the most

The crowd remained still and quiet as the last guitar chord melted away. Griffin's sexy voice and soulful lyrics cast a spell over the mass of people. No one dared a sound, not wanting to take responsibility for breaking his spell.

I let the words soak into my heart. I needed to tell him how much that song meant to me, now that I knew what he really felt. I put my fingers to my mouth and gave a whistle I hoped he could hear on stage.

There was a small beat before the crowd erupted into thunderous applause, torrents of screams, and whistles. Griffin stood from the stool and bowed with his guitar. He pointed at the crowd, and then ran off stage. In my heart I knew he meant to point at me, publicly confirming the love he'd felt all along.

Chapter Nineteen

Mine Shaft played for another half hour before they started the countdown right before midnight. With each passing second Griffin strummed his guitar and shouted into the microphone. "Five…four…three…two…one…Happy New Year!" he screamed. The band instantly broke into a rock version of *Auld Lang Syne*.

The dance floor looked like a living, breathing creature. It undulated up and down feeding off of drunken energy, and the drive of the music. From the bar, I watched hundreds of revelers ring in the New Year without a care in the world. However, I was still stuck in the last half hour. I wanted to talk to him so badly.

"You need anything else, Jillibean?"

I took my eyes from the crowd when I heard my name, giving Mr. Biceps my full attention. I didn't like hearing him say my name; it didn't have the right amount of emotion behind it. Coming out of his mouth it sounded stupid and juvenile.

"The name's Jillian. And no; I'm good, thanks." I smiled at him and turned my attention back toward the stage. Griffin and the guys started playing their closer. I dug in my purse and pulled out a twenty, sliding it onto the bar. Even though Griffin had made sure my drinks were on the house, I felt bad not tipping Mr. Biceps; he'd been good to me.

Again, I worked my way through the crowd, heading to the left side of the stage. Security was tight at the venue. Standing between me and backstage was a monstrously huge bouncer. Seriously. The guy looked like he could be Hagrid's twin brother.

"Um, I'm supposed to meet Griffin Daniels backstage?" I said meekly.

"That's what they all say, girlie." His deep voice was like a sonic boom over the roar of the crowd. "Do you have credentials?"

"I have this?" I held up the VIP pass that hung around my neck.

The bouncer held it close to his face, trying to decipher the words in the darkness.

"That'll work." He stepped aside and held the door open, allowing me to pass.

I climbed the stairs toward the side of the stage. The band was still improvising on stage, something they liked to do at the end of every concert. Griffin had once told me that improv was Mine Shaft's muse. When they were playing off of one another and messing around, their best material developed. I smiled, watching Griffin do what he loved. He was so comfortable on the stage; he radiated confidence…something I was trying to learn.

"Happy New Year, St. Louis!" Griffin shouted right before he ran off the stage. The crowd roared like a hungry beast, begging for more food. But I could tell the concert was over when Grif exchanged his guitar for a towel one of the roadies supplied.

I stood at the bottom of the stage, near the back, careful not to get in the way of people who had work to do. Griffin ran the towel over his face and neck, drying off. Sweat soaked the front of his shirt. Saturated pieces of dark hair clung to the sides of his face and a few curls hung in his eyes.

I raised my hand and shouted his name, "Griffin!"

He didn't hear me. It was so loud backstage.

"Griffin!" I tried again.

Recognition lit up his face when he heard his name, but he still couldn't find where it originated. I saw him look around, so I raised my hands above my head. Thankful my boots made me taller. I waved and called his name again. "Griffin, over here!"

Then everything froze when I saw Erin walk toward him. My heart twisted in a knot. Unable to pull my eyes away, I watched as she leaned in and gave him a hug. When they pulled apart, Griffin kept his hands on her shoulders and smiled. I felt sick. In the few days I'd locked myself in Jennifer's guest bedroom, Erin and Griffin must have gotten back together.

Instinct kicked in—fight or flight sent me running for the nearest exit. I turned around and sprinted, pushing people out of my way as I went. Tears streaked down my face and dripped off my cheeks as I sped toward the red exit sign. I was desperate to get away…desperate to start this year all over again.

Desperate to cut away the pain.

I slammed my car door shut and broke down. My head slumped against the steering wheel while my body shook uncontrollably. I thought of what Dr. Hoffman had said: Would my parents want me to cry all the time? I tried to command myself to stop. I had no right to cry over someone that wasn't mine. I was so stupid.

My phone lay on the passenger's seat, repeatedly playing Griffin's text tone. Occasionally, it would play his ring tone. I couldn't listen to his voice. I'd let myself hope that Griffin was *the one*, but I was wrong.

By 12:30 a.m. I had cried myself numb and started the car. When I got home, I parked in my usual spot on the street.

Jennifer's house was lit up like a beacon. That meant that Jennifer or Matt was still awake. I stole a peek at my reflection to assess the tear-stained damage to my face. I looked like I'd taken a jog on a manual treadmill in Hell. I hoped whoever was up would just let me go to bed. I was in no mood to talk, or argue.

Flinging open the car door, I took a very different kind of walk of shame up the paving stones to the front door. After I unlocked the door and let myself in, I was greeted by the shrill voices of overly caffeinated five-year-old twins.

"Mommy!" Mitchell shouted. "Jillian's home!"

"Aunt Jillian!" Michael launched himself onto my leg and held on for dear life.

"Hi, boys. Aren't you supposed to be in bed?" My voice felt like cotton. I cleared my throat, but that didn't help.

"Mommy said we get to stay up until next year."

"Yeah! I'm never going to bed!" Mitchell sang as he flung himself off my leg. In his wake, I threw my arms out to the sides and balanced my teetering body against the wall so I wouldn't fall.

The boys took off down the hall, chanting, "Never going to bed! Never going to bed! Never going to bed!" at the tops of their lungs.

It was entirely too late…or too early, for their five-year-old energy. I had started up the stairs when Matt came around the corner.

"Jennifer went to bed about ten minutes ago. She wants to see you before you turn in for the night."

"Thanks for the message," I said dejectedly.

I trudged up the stairs and directly to my room. All I wanted to do was collapse on the bed, but I had to find out what Jennifer wanted.

I pulled my dress over my head and tossed it in a heap on a chair in the corner of the room. I threw on my favorite two-sizes-too-big sweat pants and a tank top before I padded my way to the bathroom. After pulling my hair into a ponytail, I brushed my teeth and washed my face before gracing Jennifer's doorway.

I knocked two times and then pushed the door open. Jennifer was folded so tightly beneath the sheet and comforter there was no way she could have done it herself; I wouldn't have been surprised if she made Matt tuck her into bed. She lowered her book and stared at me with her dark brown eyes…eerily like my own. We both had Dad's eyes.

"Matt said you wanted to see me?" I asked.

"Griffin called on the landline several times tonight. Did you forget your phone?"

Griffin knew better than to call Jennifer's landline. Why wouldn't he just leave me be? "My phone died before the concert ended. I'm sure he just called to see if I made it back okay," I lied.

"Oh. Okay then." She glanced down at her book, clearly uncomfortable talking to me any longer than necessary.

"Okay then. Good night, Jennifer. Happy New Year." I stepped away from the doorframe, and was just about to close the door when I heard Jennifer say something. I poked my head back around. "Did you say something?"

"Happy New Year," she replied stiffly.

Even though she sounded like a robot, I appreciated the sentiment. I knew how difficult it was for her to say that to me. I gave her a halfhearted smile and closed the door. Who knew my hugs were capable of melting Ice Queens?

Once I shut the door to the guest room, I had no plans of leaving until I left for school. I pulled the comforter up to my chin and burrowed into its downy warmth. All the happiness and love that had filled me earlier was consumed by the urge to find something sharp.

I just needed a tiny release.

My mind cataloged all the sharp, pointy objects contained in my sewing kit: scissors, straight pins, seam rippers, an X-ACTO knife. It wouldn't hurt if I just…. I'd feel better.

Over and over, my mind cycled through the list of bloodletters until my eyes closed, and I fell into oblivion.

* * *

"Bean…" A breathy whisper tickled across my ear like a feather. I lifted a heavy arm and swiped at the feather with my hands.

"Jillibean, time to wakey-wakey," his voice rumbled.

"Ugh…" I pulled the comforter over my head and rolled to the other side. "No," I growled.

The bed shifted and I realized I wasn't alone anymore. A strong, tattooed arm squeezed my middle, pulling me closer. God, this hurt. Why was he here anyway?

"You awake?" he asked.

I nodded.

"You gonna to talk to me?" He squeezed my waist again.

I shook my head no.

"Okay, then." He kicked off his boots, pulled the comforter from under his butt, and threw it over the top of him. "Might as well make myself comfortable then."

For what seemed like an eternity, I listened to the rhythmic in and out of Griffin's breaths. His fingers gently stroked my hair. What was there to say?

Obviously nothing.

"Red, huh? I like it," he said, pulling a red streak from the blond rat's nest that was my hair. "I bet there was no shortage of guys trying to get with you last night."

At least my head still knew how to communicate, shaking left and right.

"Please, Bean. Talk to me. I've tried reaching you all day. You probably have fifty text messages from me by now."

With his arm still draped over me, I rolled onto my side to face him. The space between our noses probably measured just over two inches. My eyes roamed over the planes of his face, avoiding his eyes, and the rejection I was sure to find there.

Griffin's hand shifted from my waist to my arm. His fingertips pressed lightly on my skin as his hand traveled toward my shoulder...my neck...my cheek. In the wake of his fingertips, a trail of heat flared on my skin, sending need through my body. *Why is he doing this? What about Erin?*

I pulled my hand from beneath the covers and stilled his thumb from circling across my cheek. My heavy eyes couldn't resist the pull from his penetrating gaze any longer.

I looked at him.

Griffin's pupils eclipsed the brown of his irises. His stare communicated a lifetime of unspoken words…not the rejection I'd expected.

I didn't want to *think* anymore. I wanted to feel. I mentally snipped the thread that led to my brain and decided to listen to what my heart wanted instead.

I moved my hand to his chin. He hadn't shaved. The stubble scratched against my fingertips, leaving a tingling sensation behind. Griffin closed his eyes and let out a breath. He didn't stop me.

My fingers continued their trail up his face until my hand firmly rested against his cheek. He exhaled again like it was the first time he'd ever been given the chance.

With my heart in full control, I closed the two-inch gap between us and pressed my lips to his. I froze, remembering what had happened last time.

Griffin grabbed my shoulders and my heart thumped, preparing for another onslaught of pain. But in the span of two seconds, he pressed me onto my back and pinned me beneath him.

Griffin slowly lowered his body onto mine, leaving no space between us. He took my breath away…literally. Not being able to breathe was the most glorious feeling in the world. My heart knocked against my rib cage so hard I was sure Griffin could feel it, too.

I never wanted to come up for air…ever. I nipped at his lip and a low groan fell from his mouth. Our lips moved together at a frenzied pace, and I wrapped my legs around his, pinning him closer to me…and yet, not close enough.

His hands roamed through my hair, down my sides, and rested

where my tank top met the top of my sweat pants. Griffin's hand slipped beneath the hem of my tank while he moved his lips to my neck.

Hands on my waist...hands on my skin...this was when I usually slammed on the brakes. I never wanted anyone to see the cracks...feel the scars. But Griffin's hands felt different...like they belonged there. I knew I was safe in his hands. I would willingly give my broken heart, my fractured soul, and scarred body to him if he wanted it.

Chapter Twenty

Still wrapped in Griffin's arms, I felt him brush my hair away from my face. "It's about fucking time," he whispered, smiling at me. "I could kiss you forever."

"Promise?"

"Forever." He kissed me again, proving the statement's validity.

When our lungs forced us to come up for air, we snuggled closer together. I stared at him, trying to read the expression on his face. Over the years, I'd witnessed so many different emotions move over the planes of his features. But the expression he wore in this moment was new: devotion and happiness, and a hint of melancholy.

"What's this?" I asked, touching the fine creases at the side of his eye.

"What do you mean?" he asked, running his fingers through my hair.

"You're sad about something. I can see it right here." My thumb tried to smooth the tiny lines.

"You know me so well," he whispered.

I brushed a curl from his forehead and looked into his eyes. "What's the matter?"

"Did you hear my song last night?" he asked.

"Yes." I nodded.

"I wrote that for you." He brushed his hand over my forehead, pushing my hair aside. "And you ran away."

"Griff," I said, running my fingers over his cheek and through his hair. I never wanted to stop touching him.

"No, Jillian, wait. I need to say this." He sat up on the bed and crossed his legs in front of him. I did the same so we sat face to face. "I've waited a lifetime to say so much to you that I don't know where to start. Last year when you kissed me, it scared the hell out of me. I freaked and pushed you away because I didn't know what else to do." Nervously, he ran his hands through his hair. "When we were kids, you were my best friend. Because I was older, I felt like your protector. I loved that." He reached across my lap and squeezed my hands tightly between his. "Do you remember when we got caught drawing fake tattoos on each other's arms?"

"Mm-hmm," I nodded, recollecting the memory. "My grandma wouldn't let us near each other for a month. She thought you were a bad influence on me. Body art was definitely not her thing. What was I? Twelve?"

"And I was fifteen," Griffin added. "Do you remember what I wanted you to draw on my arm?" he asked. I thought about that day.

A multi-hued pack of Sharpie pens lay scattered between us on the concrete. Griffin bent over my arm working methodically on the rainbow I wanted inked onto my wiry bicep. He'd tried talking me into something more meaningful, but I insisted on a rainbow.

By the time he'd finished with my "tattoo," Grandma walked out onto the porch and nearly had a heart attack. She didn't approve of the temporary marks I'd made to my body and she certainly didn't like the fact that a teenage boy had his hands on me. Once he'd turned thirteen, her rules had changed. At the time I didn't understand. He was just Griffin. Grandma knew something I hadn't yet figured out.

"I don't remember, Griff. By the time you finished with that rainbow on my arm, Grandma found us and started throwing an old lady tantrum." Griffin's eyes brightened and a burgeoning smile grew on his lips from thinking about my grandma and her tantrums. Seriously, they were legendary.

"I wanted you to write 'Jillibean.'" His low, melodic voice whispered my name like a lullaby.

I felt terrible that I couldn't remember something that obviously meant so much to him. I shook my head. "I'm sorry, I don't remember."

"I knew even back then how special you are, how much having you in my life meant."

"How? We were so young."

"I knew because when I asked you to ink your name onto me, I was prepared to defend you and protect you from *anything*. But every time I looked in your eyes I could see things I couldn't protect you from. The way you blamed yourself for your parents' death, the heartache you wore like a second skin. You'd put a wall up, and I was trapped on the outside. But I still wanted to save you from all that." His eyes searched mine, hoping I understood.

I had built a wall. I'd built it around my heart; to protect it from all those damn voices.

Griffin continued, "There was no light in your eyes anymore. I told myself all the time that I'd be there for you, to hold your hand in the storm. I'd always be your friend. It was the best way I could think to protect you. I prayed that one day the storm would pass, and that light in your eyes would come back."

"Griffin," I breathed.

"Bean, please. I'm getting my chance now. Let me finish."

I nodded for him to go on.

"In high school, you were in no shape to be in a relationship, and I knew that. And then you kissed me last year." He paused, organizing his thoughts. "I got scared. Don't get me wrong, I wanted it…*god*, I wanted it." He leaned in and pressed his forehead to mine, cradling my head in his palms. "But, I didn't want to hurt you. You were doing so well, and finally getting your chance at a new life, doing what you wanted. That overwhelming urge to protect kicked in, and I pushed you away. I didn't want to stand in your way, and I didn't want to add any more stress to your life."

"So what changed?" I asked. "Why is *now* okay?"

"Being without you fucking hurts," he whispered, pulling away to hold my hands in his lap. "All these years, a day never passed that I didn't get to see you. But man, these last few months, not seeing your face every day…It was like part of me was missing."

I nodded. "I know what you mean."

"I know it's selfish, but I need you. I know you're leaving for school again, and we're going to be apart, but I can't let you go back believing a lie. I love you so damn much, Jillian." He brought his hand up to my face and lightly brushed his fingers over my cheek.

My breath caught in my throat, and my insides melted. A burning desire spread like wildfire through my core. I loved him, too.

Griffin reached for my arms, gently trailing his fingers toward my shoulders. The skimpy tank top I wore did nothing to hide the few scars below my collarbone. Once he reached my neck, his fingers trailed down, touching the top of a scar peeking out of the top of my tank. He lowered his head and placed a kiss on the barely visible scar. I let him.

While his finger continued to rub the raised line of skin, his eyes settled back onto mine. "Jillian, why did you run last night?"

It took me half a minute to register his words. My thoughts had moved elsewhere. "Uh...I was backstage watching you finish up. When you came off the stage..." I couldn't meet his eyes while pictures of Erin drifted through my head. "Erin was there."

"Seriously?" His voice dropped. "She was just saying hi, and she wished me a Happy New Year." He chuckled, gripping my chin between his thumb and forefinger. He lifted his hand, forcing me to look at him. "She broke up with me, Jillian. She knew I was in love with you. She was the one that told me to get my head out of my ass and tell you how I felt."

"Really?" I muttered. "Since I hadn't seen you in a few days, I just thought..."

"Well." He kissed my neck. "You." And then my jaw. "Thought." And my cheek. "Wrong." Finally, he pressed his lips to mine and pushed me onto my back. "I will *never* get tired of doing this." His voice rumbled in his chest and sent shivers through mine.

"Me neither." I kissed him again.

We spent the next ten minutes allowing our lips and hands to explore the landscape of each other. My fingers didn't waste any time traveling beneath Griffin's t-shirt. By the time my hands moved to his shoulders, I pulled the t-shirt over his head and tossed it on the floor. He sealed his lips back onto mine and flipped us around, so I was straddled atop his gorgeous body.

I pulled my head away from his mouth to give his body the full attention it deserved. I'd seen Griffin without a shirt countless times, but now was so much better. Griffin's sculpted torso was a beautiful work of art, and I fully intended to admire it whenever I had the opportunity.

My hands trailed over his shoulders and down his biceps. Griffin shivered beneath my hands, closing his eyes. "This feels fucking awesome," he whispered.

His eyes remained closed while I traced every inked line of his skin. I loved his tattoos; they were indelibly him. The cursive script on his right bicep read: *Always protects. Always trusts. Always hopes. Always perseveres. Never fails.* I punctuated each statement with a kiss before I moved onto the rest of his canvas.

He'd adorned his chest with the image of his bass guitar, broken in half and bleeding. The drops of blood were titles of songs he'd written when he started Mine Shaft.

My fingers traced the tuning heads of the guitar, where his jeans met his waist. Occasionally, my fingers would slide just past his jeans, and I'd hear tiny gasps escape from Griffin's mouth. Moving diagonally across his chest, I pressed lightly on each string, working my hand toward the body of the guitar. Griffin breathed heavier every time my lips touched his skin. When I'd worked my way to the point where the instrument ripped open, right over his heart, I placed a kiss on each lyrical droplet. I started with the largest at his navel, then worked my way up to his torso, savoring the taste of him on my lips. The last droplet hadn't yet fallen from the guitar, still clinging to the fracture. My eyes drank in the tiny single word refusing to let go…*Jillibean.*

I kissed my name and looked for his eyes. "When?" I asked, sliding my body along the side of his. He shifted, so I could rest my head on his arm.

He turned his head to look at me. "When I got back from taking you to school. I told you, it felt like a part of me was missing. I had to do something."

"Thank you," I whispered.

"For what?" His fingers trailed from my shoulder to my elbow. My senses were hyperaware of even the slightest touches.

"For never giving up on me. For *always* being there for me. For everything."

"Ditto." He smiled, pulling me closer.

I leaned in and tasted his lips with mine.

With our lips together, he spoke softly. "Kissing you makes me want to write a song."

"Sing to me."

And he did.

* * *

The last week flew by in a whirlwind of activity. Griffin and I spent every moment we could together, but his recording schedule was extremely demanding. Before I knew it, I only had one day of vacation left. If I was going to make it back to school by the time classes started on the thirteenth, I would need to leave tomorrow. That left Griffin and me with only today to take care of the shopping trip he'd promised. "I'm happy now," I sang, practically skipping toward the door.

"See? I was just waiting until I had you with me." Griffin held the door of the motorcycle shop open for me.

"You should have gotten one when you bought the damn bike." I looked over my shoulder and gave him a baleful stare.

Griffin punched the key fob and unlocked the doors of my car. He stepped around me and threw open the backseat door, tossing his helmet onto the seat. A second later he slammed the door shut, grabbed me around the waist, and pinned me between him and the car. He didn't waste a moment before he kissed me.

With firm lips he parted mine and slipped his tongue beyond the border of my mouth. A jolt of electricity jump-started my heart, making it beat faster.

I threw my arms around his neck and he leaned all of his weight onto me, snaking one arm around my waist and the other around my neck. Once again, I found it gloriously hard to breathe. The cold metal of the car at my back and the heat of our embrace ignited a fire inside me. I worked my hands to his hair, clutching fistfuls of dark strands as our tongues slid over each other. While our mouths played, our bodies begged to be closer.

Griffin's hand slid down my thigh and wrapped around the back, then up, cupping my ass. He drew me closer and I cursed the jeans I wore. Why hadn't I chosen a skirt?

Breathless, we both pulled away, resting our foreheads together.

"But then I wouldn't have gotten to do that," he breathed. "Thor was with me when I bought the bike. I don't think he would have appreciated that." He winked and pecked my lips one more time.

"I don't know," I drawled. "You're really good at it." Smirking, I ducked under his arm.

He pulled my door open, and just before I climbed in, smacked my backside. "Just good?" he asked, wounded.

I smiled up at him. "I wouldn't want you to get a big head." I sat down and he closed my door, shaking his head.

Walking around to the driver's side, Griffin pulled open the door and got in. "Then I'm just going to have to practice more." He stared at me while starting the car.

"It's about time, Daniels." I was enjoying our playful spontaneity.

"Hey, isn't that the name of a song?" he asked, looking over his shoulder while he backed out of the parking space.

"There's a song?" I asked, playing dumb.

"I think so." He put the car in drive, and we were off. "From what I hear, it's fucking brilliant." He shrugged.

"Brilliant, huh?"

"A real chart topper," he answered confidently.

"I'll be sure to download that one," I said, smiling. "Or, I could just ask the artist to give me a private concert."

He turned his head and smiled sinfully. "Any time, Bean," he crooned.

On the drive back to Griffin's apartment, our conversation flowed easily from one topic to the next. Griffin was curious about my Spring Showcase project, and I happily filled him in on my progress.

He reached across the seat and took my hand in his, kissing my knuckles. "I am so proud of you, Bean."

"Thanks," I said, smiling at him. He laced his fingers through mine and dropped our entwined hands onto my lap. "If it hadn't been for your visit at Thanksgiving, I don't think I would have come up with anything good enough to present."

"I know that's not true," he scoffed. "I didn't do shit. Whatever you came up with was all you."

I made sure he saw me roll my eyes right before he pulled into the parking lot of his apartment complex. Griffin led the way to his door as we trudged through the ankle-deep snow. Unlocking the door, he kicked it open and let me pass before he stepped in from the cold.

"Hey, dude," Thor said, staring at the enormous flat screen TV. He was lying on the black leather sofa wearing nothing but a pair of boxers.

"Shit, man. Go put some fucking clothes on," Griffin said, stepping around me.

Thor looked away from the TV and noticed that Griffin wasn't alone. "Jill, hey," he said, standing up.

"Hi, Thor." I waved, trying not to stare. It was difficult; his body was amazing. Not as amazing as Griffin's, but beautiful nonetheless. All the guys in Mine Shaft looked fabulous. Couple awesome music with hot guys, and the record label had a recipe for making money hand over fist.

Griffin shrugged his leather jacket off and flipped it onto the couch, and I did the same with mine.

Thor scratched his head, running his palm over his short, buzzed hair. "You finally talk him into getting a brain bucket, Jill?" he asked.

"Yes," I replied soundly, giving Griffin a stern look.

"You going out tonight, man?" Griffin asked.

Thor walked around the coffee table, toward the hall, on his way to the kitchen. "Yeah," he said, calling over his shoulder. "Got a date."

Griffin held his hand out to me and I walked over to him. We followed Thor into the kitchen. "You want anything to drink, Bean?" Griffin asked.

"No thanks."

Griffin walked over and stood next to Thor at the fridge. "Pass me a beer, will you?"

Thor shuffled things around and pulled out a bottle, holding it up for Griffin. "Thanks, man," Griffin said. "Are you coming back tonight?"

Thor clinked together some other items in the fridge, settling on a beer. He closed the door and leaned back on it, twisting off the cap. "Depends," he said, taking a drink. "Harper's different than most girls I've dated," he said.

"What?" I teased. "The infamous Thor is taking it slow with a lady?"

He shrugged and took another drink. But there was a look on his face, and I knew he'd brought the beer to his mouth to hide a growing smile.

Griffin chimed in and said, "I don't know, Thor. There has been a change in you since you've started dating her." He punched Thor's arm playfully.

"If she can tame 'The Hammer,' she must be pretty special," I said.

"She does have a point, dude," Griffin added. "When do we get to meet this chick?"

"I actually want to keep this one around, Griff." Thor scowled. "Not scare her away."

I pressed my hands to my chested and gasped. "I'm offended," I mocked. "I would do no such thing."

Thor waved me off. "Not you, Jill. She's not ready for the guys yet."

I smiled. "I can't wait to meet her. I'm sure she's great."

"Come on, Bean," Griffin said, heading toward the steps. "As much as I love hanging out with my barely clad roommate, I'd much prefer spending my time with you."

I let Griffin lead me up the stairs. "It was nice to see you, Thor. Good luck with Harper," I called over my shoulder.

"Thanks, Jill. I miss seeing you here all the time. Griffin's a cantankerous motherfucker when you're not around!" he shouted from the kitchen.

When Griffin and I got to the top of the steps, he let go of my hand to open the door to his room. Inside, his king-size bed took up most of the space, but there was still room for a floor-to-ceiling bookcase. Griffin had always loved to read.

As kids, he and I used to spend hours hanging out in each other's bedrooms. He would sit down with a book and not move until he finished. I wasn't ever much of a reader, but I would slip away into a fantasy world of my own—a place where my drawings would come to life. I would pop back to reality when I heard the snap of his book. He'd look up at me through a messy crop of dark tangles and smile, ready to tell me all about the world he'd just visited.

I stepped over piles of clothes and scribbled-on papers as I walked to the bookcase. "Read anything good lately?" I asked, brushing the spines of the books with my fingers on my way to the bed.

"I just started *Gardens of the Moon*. Great book so far," he said, flopping onto the bed, kicking his boots off. He patted the bed, silently asking me to join him. "I've been thinking."

"Uh-oh," I joked, scooting closer to him.

He lifted his arm and I snuggled in. "I know. Scary, right?"

"Thinking about what?" I looked up at him.

"When you're home from school, you should stay here." His face was serious, all signs of joking gone.

"Griffin…" I balked.

"Don't 'Griffin' me," he interrupted. "You don't have an excuse now. When you're home on breaks, you can stay with me, and summers, too."

"Okay." I gave in without an argument. Griffin was right; the only excuse I'd had for not taking him up on his countless offers to move in with him was the fact that he'd always had a girlfriend.

Besides, living with my sister served a purpose. I'd endured Jennifer all these years for two reasons: one, it allowed me the luxury of saving most of what I earned during the summers, when I worked at Sew Good; and two, I had nowhere else to go. It didn't make any sense for me to pay for an apartment in Illinois when I would be living in Rhode Island for most of the year.

"Okay? Really?" He jerked around, pulling his arm from behind my head.

"Ouch!" I yelled, rubbing the back of my head after it smacked against the headboard.

"Oh, shit! Bean, I'm so sorry." He pushed my hand to the side and rubbed the injury with his gentle hand.

I laughed and let him baby me. "Yes, I'll stay here."

Still rubbing my head, a wide smile split his face in half. "I can't believe you didn't put up a fight. You always put up a fight." He gently laid my head back onto the pillow, and planted his hands at my hips, pulling me slowly down the bed, before he straddled me. "You're always so stubborn." He smirked, dropping his voice an octave.

I sucked in a deep breath, and held it for a second. Griffin's hands gripped my waist. I felt the heat from his charcoal eyes as they roamed over my face, down my neck, over the swell of my chest, until they rested at his hands on my body. "Sometimes you make things so hard," he whispered, locking his gaze back onto mine.

"Oh, really?" I rocked my hips back and forth, slowly.

One of his eyebrows pulled up as he lowered his head to my ear and spoke softly, "Most definitely." He wrapped his muscled arms around me, pressing our bodies so close, I could feel exactly how hard I made him. *Damn that's hot.*

His breath caused my body to quake with pleasure, and I closed my eyes, savoring each reaction.

His lips pressed lightly against the skin just behind my ear, working their way unhurriedly down my neck. I tilted my head and arched my back, giving him better access. When his lips met the collar of my bulky sweater, he sat up brusquely. My skin felt cold in his absence.

"This damn thing has to go." His voice rumbled low and deep in his chest. Without a second thought, the hem of my sweater was in his hands and he was yanking it over my head.

I flopped back onto the bed wearing only a sheer, lacy cami on top...and no bra. It left little to the imagination. With each breath, my breasts swelled over the tops of the plunging neckline. Griffin's eyes flashed, drinking me in.

"Better," he whispered, admiring me beneath him. With one hand at my waist, he trailed his palm over the curve of my chest with the other, bringing it to rest on the other side of my waist.

His hands continued their languid path to my hips as he bent down, trailing his nose along the same line he'd just kissed. "You smell so good," he murmured, inhaling. "Like flowers...and the ocean."

I was ready to strip off every shred of clothing between us. My chest rose and fell rapidly, begging for his touch.

Unwilling to wait any longer, I had lifted my hands up, ready to tear his shirt away, when he grabbed my wrists and pinned them over my head. A wanton smile lingered on his face just before he lowered his body onto mine, claiming my mouth with his.

A low growl resonated in his chest as our lips pushed and pulled against one another. He kissed me hard and swept his tongue into my mouth.

His kiss was like a bolt of lightning crashing into me. The electric current spread through my body so quickly, I felt as if I were going to combust. My heart thundered in my chest. *God I want him.*

Griffin let go of my wrists and sat up just a little, never taking his mouth from mine. He slid his hands down the length of my arms, skimming over the scar that trailed down the underside of upper forearm to the crook of my arm...the place where I'd cut myself so badly it almost ended my life. But, here I was...living...feeling...wanting.

When his hands continued downward, stopping on my breasts,

I gasped. "Griffin," I moaned, licking his lips as I slid my tongue into his mouth. He tasted so good.

He made his way to the hem of my cami, working his hands beneath the material. I was sure he could feel every one of my imperfections, but he didn't seem to care. My usual self-consciousness melted away with his touch, leaving my body screaming for a level of intimacy I'd never wanted before...not until him.

I longed to run my fingers over his sculpted body. Greedily, I moved my hands to the bottom of his shirt, not wasting any time pulling at the fabric that stood in my way. My hands smoothed up the ridges of his abdomen, gathering the t-shirt as I went. A deep growl resonated in his chest and he sat up. Reaching behind his back, he yanked the shirt over his head and fell back on top of me, slamming his mouth back to mine.

I dug my fingernails deeper into the wings of the griffin on his shoulder blades each time he plunged his tongue into my mouth. My brain ceased to function, reducing me to a jumble of fiery nerve endings and desire. "Griffin," I breathed at his ear. "I want you."

His mouth left mine and kissed up my neck, his breath hot on my skin. "Yes," he groaned into my ear, before he caught my earlobe between his teeth and bit.

Holy hell.

My body trembled. I couldn't breathe. His hands made quick work, moving toward the waistband of my jeans. He easily flicked the button open and slowly drew the zipper down. With his tongue wildly caressing mine, I was just a body consumed by the sensations this beautiful man evoked from me.

I dragged my hands down his massive shoulders, to his lower

back, then cupped his ass in my hands. That was all the motivation he needed when he pushed his hand into my unfastened pants.

I gasped. The need for him to touch me reached a fever pitch. His hand circled over the outside of my panties, particularly his thumb. I raised my hips, needing more.

"Jillian," he said against my mouth. "You're so wet."

"Griffin," I moaned. "Touch me…please."

His fingers stilled their relentless movement and he growled and pulled away, rolling off of me.

What the fucking hell?

Panting, I sat up on my elbows and looked at him. He was lying on his back, his arm thrown over his eyes, trying to slow his breathing. A small pang of rejection threatened to put a dent in the armor guarding my heart. "Uhh…" I trailed off, not knowing what else to say.

Griffin pushed himself onto his elbows, giving me a guilty smile. "Damn," he exhaled. "I'm sorry, Bean. I got carried away."

I scrunched my eyes in confusion. In my opinion, we hadn't gotten carried *far enough* away. "What's that supposed to mean?" I asked defensively, the dent in my armor becoming more pronounced.

Hearing the indignation in my voice, Griffin pulled himself all the way up, and took my hands, forcing me to do the same. Situating himself so he sat directly across from me, he kept hold of my hands and looked me in the eye. "Jillian, you have always been the most important person in my life. It would destroy me if I did something to hurt you." Tenderly, he placed both of his hands on my face. His penetrating stare didn't just dent the armor guarding my heart, it hacked it to pieces. With just a look, he was obliterating my heart's only defense. "I'm not going to rush this." He shook his head.

I nodded, speechless.

Griffin smiled reverently and leaned his forehead to mine. "You and me," he breathed. "I'm not going to mess us up. We're forever. And when the time is right, I plan on being with you in every way possible. And that's a promise."

I smiled and happily took that promise, wrapping it around my vulnerable heart.

Chapter Twenty-One

My eyes opened. Sunlight streamed through the window and glared off the white walls, making it far too bright to sleep. I glanced to my side and saw Griffin still peacefully zonked. The rhythmic in and out of his breathing made me smile. Once I had agreed to stay with him during my time away from school, he'd insisted that our living together begin immediately. I couldn't tell him no on the last night of my break, even though I had none of my things. Regardless, there was no other way I wanted to spend my last night of Winter Break.

I lightly brushed my hand across his forehead, returning a wayward strand of hair to the side of his face. Watching him sleep, I saw traces of the little boy I'd grown up with, but time had turned him into the man that held my heart. Stubble shadowed his strong jawline and I fought the urge to run my fingers over his face. I didn't want to wake him.

I glanced at the clock on his bedside table: 7:30 a.m. Why was I up? After Griffin's honorable stance, we'd slowed things down and eventually ended up talking well past three in the morning. I couldn't even remember the topic of our conversation before we both passed out in his bed. Our first night of cohabitation hadn't ended in any fireworks, but it had been perfect nonetheless.

Before climbing out of bed, I pressed a soft kiss to his forehead. He stirred and rolled onto his side, giving me the perfect time to slip from beneath the covers. His room was freezing. Even though Griffin's t-shirt resembled a muumuu on me, it did little in the way of providing warmth. I tiptoe-ran across the hall and into the bathroom, hoping Thor hadn't come home last night. The cold linoleum beneath my feet sent shivers through my body, and I hurriedly finished my business, running back to the bedroom. Griffin hadn't budged.

My clothes from yesterday lay crumpled in a heap on the floor. I dressed in haste, slipping on my jeans and sweater, desperate for warmth. If eighteen hours of interstate hadn't been staring me in the face, I would have slipped back under the covers and made Griffin keep me warm. Our timing really sucked. Not taking into account our twelve-year friendship, our relationship was technically only nine days old. We still had so much to learn, and we'd have to do it with 1,124 miles between us. I prayed the semester went by quickly; summer couldn't get here fast enough.

With a heavy heart, I walked around the bed and knelt in front of him. "Griffin," I whispered. "Griff." I brushed his cheek with my fingertips, and he roused.

"Hmm," he replied groggily, rolling onto his back. Even though I was too far away to make out the words, my eyes zeroed in on his tattoo, specifically the tiny drop bearing my name. A thrill went through my body, knowing I was a permanent fixture on his.

I hopped back into bed beside him and kissed his forehead. "Good morning."

"What time is it?" he groaned, kicking the blanket from his legs.

"Quarter to eight," I replied.

Griffin sat up and had his arms around me in an instant. "Good morning," he said, kissing the top of my head.

His warm body felt marvelous. "You're making it very difficult to leave."

"Don't. Go back tomorrow," he said, holding me tighter.

"I can't," I groaned. "It's going to take me two days as it is, and classes start on Monday." I ran my hand along the planes of his chest.

"This fucking sucks." He sighed, leaning his head back against the headboard.

"Tell you what," I said, patting my name. "Why don't I get packed up at Jennifer's, and I'll come back here before I head out? You can get cleaned up. I'll be back in an hour, and we can say good-bye then."

"It's better than having to say good-bye now, I guess." He kissed my hair again.

I turned and stretched to give him a quick kiss, but Griffin pulled me on top of him, leaving our bodies flush. His lips pressed hard against mine while he tangled his hands in my hair. I felt his tongue brush against my lips, and I opened my mouth a little wider, inviting him in. My hands moved from the stubble of his chin, up his neck, and into his hair.

Griffin's hands slid down my back and cupped my backside forcefully. A small gasp fell from my lips, and I shimmied in his hands. He moaned, guiding my body in rhythm with his hands and mouth. I could feel his need growing stronger. Then he slowed down, moving his hands up to my neck, kissing me softly before he pulled away.

I opened my eyes. "Something wrong?" I teased, out of breath.

His chest moved up and down rapidly. "Oh, trust me," he smiled wickedly. "Nothing's wrong." He held my head between his hands and kissed me lightly, one more time. "Promise me something," he asked.

"Anything," I said, sitting back up.

Griffin rested his hands on the tops of my thighs, moving his hands up and down their length. "That you'll wake me up like that every morning."

Still straddling him, and still feeling how much he wanted me, I shimmied. "I'll do better than that," I promised.

Griffin growled and pulled me back down, kissing me hard one more time before he rolled on top of me and stood up, leaving me panting on the bed. "I've got a cold shower I need to take," he said, staring at me. "Go get your stuff from Jennifer's house, and get your ass back here. I don't want you making most of that trip in the dark." He held his hand out for me, and I grabbed hold while he yanked me off the bed.

"All right," I groaned. I retrieved my purse from the floor and headed for Griffin's bedroom door. Griffin opened the door and I followed him out.

Once we were downstairs, Griffin wrapped his arms around me, holding my back to his chest. He traced feather-light kisses from my shoulder all the way up my neck. His warm breath tickled my ear and it took every ounce of my restraint not to turn around and push him onto the couch.

"'Bye, Bean," he whispered in my ear. My body shivered in response. "See you soon."

I turned around and faced him. His features burned with desire, making him look even hotter. "See you soon," I said quietly.

* * *

Jennifer's house was still quiet, which meant the twins were still asleep. I went to my room and pulled a clean pair of jeans and a hoodie from my suitcase. I zipped down the hall for a quick shower before I packed up my things.

Packing was quick and easy. I stuffed some pajamas into the suitcase, not even bothering to fold them. My art supplies, portfolio, and new sketchbook were safely stored in my messenger bag. My duffle bag was full of leftover scraps from my New Year's dress.

I carried the three bags out to the car and went back in the house. I felt like I needed to tell Jennifer I was leaving—not that she cared—but it made me feel better.

I found her in the kitchen standing over the stove. She spent most of her time cooking. I wondered if cooking was her way of coping with stress…or pain…or sadness. I really knew nothing about my sister. There was a small tug at my heart. I wished we were closer. "Um, Jennifer?" I said, stepping farther into the kitchen.

"Mm-hmm," she intoned, not even turning around.

"I'm heading back to school now." That got her attention. She looked over her shoulder, in my general direction.

"Is the room put back the way I had it?" she asked, concerned.

The sound of the sautéing vegetables nearly drowned out her voice. "Yeah. I've got all of my things out."

"Good." She looked back to her pan, moving the food around with a spatula.

I looked down at the keys in my hand, flipping them around on my index finger. "I won't be staying here anymore, Jennifer."

She sat the spatula down on the counter and turned around. "Really?"

"Yeah. I'm going to stay with Griffin."

She scrutinized my face. "Griffin's begged you to stay with him for two years. What changed your mind?" It was a fair question, but what floored me was how genuine she sounded. Maybe the hug I'd given her last week really had worked some magic.

"I…uh," I stuttered, unsure of how to answer her question. "I didn't want to invade his privacy. And I didn't have the funds to help with rent."

"And you do now? Have the funds, I mean," she asked.

"Not really." I shook my head. "Honestly, you know more about my finances than I do." She was the custodian of my trust account, after all.

"True." Her perpetually groomed eyebrows pulled up in thought. I could see her running through numbers and calculating what the bottom line of my account totaled at the moment.

Mom and Dad had played the stock market well. They'd invested wisely and made sure that Jennifer and I were taken care of in the event that something unforeseen happened to them. Little did they know that would be the case. By the time Jennifer had been old enough to reap the benefits of her trust, she had a very sizable sum of money. When Grandma had taken ill and gone into the nursing home, Jennifer became the custodian of my account. It was her responsibility to monitor the fluctuations in the market and do what was in the best interest of my trust, so it continued to grow. Knowing Jennifer, there was no way in hell she would allow my trust to grow beyond what she collected. I'd asked on several occasions to see the balance of my account but she refused. There was no telling what I would get when I turned twenty-one. I just prayed I'd have enough to support myself when I got out of college.

Jennifer's voice brought me back to our present conversation. "So he's between girlfriends right now? What happens when he finds another?"

"Um…well, I don't think that's going to happen," I said timidly.

"Why?" Her brown eyes bored into me.

"Because I'm his girlfriend," I said, for lack of a better word.

"So you're moving in with him then." She blinked. Not a single emotion registered on her face.

"I really wouldn't consider it 'moving in together.' I'm just staying with him whenever I have a break from school. Just like I did here."

In the last ten minutes I'd spoken more words to my sister than I probably had all of last year. Her attitude floored me; she was actually being civil toward me for once.

"I just thought I'd let you know…and thank you for letting me stay here."

"Yes…well." She was at a loss for words. Jennifer never handled sentiment well; I guess thank yous fell under that umbrella, too. "I only did it because Mom and Dad told me to take care of you. Thank you for putting the room back the way you found it."

My keys swung from my index finger one more time before I

clasped them shut within my palm. With nothing more to say, I let out a low whistle and turned down the hallway toward the front door.

"Um, Jillian?" Jennifer called, coming around the corner.

I spun around, stunned to see she had followed after me. "Yeah?"

"Call me when you turn twenty-one. We'll get the paperwork squared away and you can have your money from Mom and Dad."

"Thanks, Jenny," I said. She cringed when I used the nickname Mom and Dad used to call her.

"Don't push it," she said sternly.

"Right." I saluted and raced toward the door. For the first time since Mom and Dad had died, I felt like Jennifer and I had bonded…the only way we knew how.

On my way to Griffin's apartment, I broke several traffic laws. I was dying to see him, and I was anxious to get on the road. My unexpected conversation with Jennifer had me running late.

I pulled into his apartment complex and parked next to Griffin's bike.

Griffin opened the door as I walked up the sidewalk. The second I was close enough, he pulled me into the living room, and before I could open my mouth to greet him, he opened it for me…with his. His arms snaked around me, securing me flush against his body. His lips roamed over my jaw and neck, giving me the opportunity to inhale his freshly showered, masculine scent. If I had ever thought it would be weird to have Griffin's lips on my body, I was sorely mistaken. It was the most natural and best feeling in the world.

"Do you have any idea how long I've wanted to greet you like this?" His breath tickled over the sensitive skin below my ear as he trailed kisses down my neck.

"I can imagine," I whispered. "Is Thor here?" I asked, hoping we wouldn't be caught making out in the living room.

"No. I haven't seen him," he said, pushing my coat to the side, giving him better access to my neck. Electricity shot through my body with each kiss. "Why?" he asked. His hands moved down my arms until he found my hands, lacing his fingers between mine. He pulled back and smirked at me like we'd just gotten away with something illicit.

I shook my head and cringed. "I don't know…It would just be awkward if he walked in and saw us all over each other."

"I've seen him all over plenty of girls. Payback's a bitch." He laughed against the corner of my lip.

I pulled back and smacked his arm. "Watch it, Daniels. I'm not just any girl."

Griffin's eyes widened and his face turned serious. "Damn straight, you're not." His deep voice resonated in the space between us. He leaned close, pressing his forehead to mine. Letting go of my hands, he cupped my cheeks in his large palms and sucked in a breath.

And then he kissed me with everything he had. He made sure this kiss would last us until May.

"I've really got to go, Griff," I said breathlessly.

"Damn it," he growled. "I hate that you have to make the trip alone. Anything could happen." His need to protect me was always at the forefront.

I leaned my forehead against his. "I'll be all right," I said, trying to reassure him.

"I know, but I still worry." His voice was low and husky.

"I'll check in every hour. It's too late for me to drive straight through, so I'll get a room."

"That makes me feel a little better." He brought me against his chest, refusing to let go.

My head rested over his heart and I tried to commit its rhythm to memory; I planned to remember it whenever I felt the stress of school weighing on my shoulders. I kissed him there, right over his heart…right where he carried me.

Griffin walked me to my car and kissed me one last time before shutting the door. It physically hurt leaving for school this time. My stomach was in a knot, and my heart ached as I watched Griffin disappear in my rearview mirror.

Chapter Twenty-Two

Jillian!" The door crashed open and Sarah rushed me like a line-backer. "I missed you!" she shouted, enveloping me in a hug.

"I missed you too!" I said, hugging her back.

"How was your vacation?" she asked, pulling away.

"Oh, pretty good, I guess." I bit my bottom lip and tried to rein in the huge grin spreading across my face.

"What?" Her eyes sparkled. I could see bubbles of excitement ready to explode from her as she waited with bated breath for whatever news I was about to tell her.

"I have a boyfriend." I said it very matter-of-factly, like it was the most common, mundane, everyday announcement.

"Okay?" Her voice turned up at the end. "Do I know him?"

I nodded my head. "Griffin," I said, smiling.

"Ahh!" she screamed. Then, out of nowhere, she smacked me upside the head.

"Ow. What was that for?" I rubbed my head as I screwed my face into a glare aimed in her direction.

"It's about damn time!" she yelled, even though a beaming smile lit up her face. "One of these days you're going to listen to me."

"You were right," I conceded. "You were right about everything."

* * *

Sunday disappeared in a blur of unpacking, laundry, and preparations for classes the next morning, which dawned bright and early when my alarm blared to life at 5:30 a.m. I smacked the clock and hid under the blanket, but I knew I couldn't be late for my first class.

Sarah's sleeping body taunted me, all snuggled up under her comforter. It seemed photography majors were given preferential treatment when it came to scheduling. I sighed and dragged my tired ass to the showers.

I dressed quickly, pulling on a well-loved pair of jeans and a sweatshirt featuring the school's seal. I didn't fuss too much with my makeup, but I did take the time to add a little color to my hair. As I pulled the purple chalk through my tresses, my phone played a few strums of Griffin's newest song…my song. I'd recorded him playing it before I left so I could listen to it whenever I wanted. It was also pretty cool to have the song before everyone else in the world. Right now it still felt like mine, and I wasn't ready to share it yet.

I picked up the phone and read his text: *I love you, Bean. Kick ass in class!*

A smile warmed my face and I sent back a reply. *I love you, too, Dr. Seuss.*

Griffin's response came right back. *He's my idol.*

I know, I typed.

I miss you, he said.

I missed him too. *Ditto.*

I love you, Bean, he wrote.

Promise? I asked.

Forever.

Happy, I tossed my phone into my bag, threw a few more strands of purple in my hair, and rushed out the door for a cup of coffee before class.

The coffee shop overflowed with art students of all kinds. Our return to campus was heralded with the warm scents of coffee, chocolate, and freshly baked confections. Several of the people that stood ahead of me in line were fashion students. Chandra was one of them. I guess we all hoped a good dose of caffeine would breathe life into our vacation-weary bodies. All I knew was if I didn't get some coffee soon, I wouldn't make it through a four-hour class today.

"Hi, Jillian," Chandra said. She'd gotten her order and was heading toward the door when she stopped to talk.

"Hey, Chandra. Did you have a nice break?" I asked.

"Yeah. Wasn't long enough, though. Spending Christmas in France makes it very difficult to come back here."

"France? Wow."

"Yeah, I applied for a short internship, and they accepted me over the break. I was working on a couture line at a small fashion house in Paris."

"That's amazing. What a fabulous opportunity," I added. I tossed my hair over my shoulder and shuffled up in line.

"How was your vacation?" she asked, smiling.

"The majority of it sucked ass, but the last week was paradise. I had a difficult time coming back, too," I admitted.

"Well, at least we've got the Spring Showcase to look forward to. I'm sure we'll all be so busy after today we won't have time to bitch about being back," she said with a shrug.

"I'm sure we'll just bitch about how much work we have to do," I countered with a smile.

"You're probably right," she laughed. "I'll see you in class. Design Studio II, right?"

"Yeah, DS2." I nodded. "I'll be there just as soon as I get my fuel." I pointed at the counter ahead of me.

"Cool. See you there," she said and turned toward the door.

While I was gone, Providence had gotten a few more inches of snow. I trudged my way to the lecture hall, careful not to spill my precious coffee. The lecture hall hummed with muted conversations while we waited for Professor Vine to arrive. I pulled a chocolate chip muffin from my bag and peeled off the paper. Coffee and chocolate: the perfect combination for resuscitating a brain-dead coed on the first day of the semester.

Lecture commenced just the way I thought it would: a laundry list of projects to be completed before the Spring Showcase. By the time Professor Vine started to pass out her syllabus, I was doing my best to keep my head above water.

While Professor Vine continued her speech, my cell phone vibrated quietly in my pocket. *Meet 4 lunch @ dining hall?* Sarah texted.

I typed her a quick response. *Can't. Labs until 2. Dinner?*

Baja's? she suggested. I'd never been there, but I'd heard the food was great.

Sure! When do you finish class? I asked.

3:30.

Meet u @ the dorm, I said.

Professor Vine finished up the lecture portion of class by going through the exhaustive list of items we needed to bring to our afternoon lab. Her voice carried easily through the auditorium-style lecture hall. "I'll see you all shortly," she said, excusing us for a short break.

I stood up and stretched before I gathered my belongings. The classroom stirred to life and everyone else stood to leave, too. I tossed the syllabus into my bag and hurried to the door. I had exactly forty minutes to get back to Victor, grab my lab materials, and hike back to campus.

* * *

An afternoon of being cooped up in the windowless lab was exhausting, but thankfully not as intimidating as it had seemed first semester. It helped my stress level that I had a vision and direction for my collection (and that I'd started working on it over break). Now all I needed to do was reach into my brain, pull out the images, and dress the model who would strut my work down the catwalk.

By two o'clock, I'd finally paused long enough to survey the mess I'd made of my work station; scraps of fabric lay everywhere. An animated Jillian resembling the Looney Tunes Tasmanian Devil flashed through my head and I laughed. I envisioned shredded and torn pieces of fabric flying from a Jillian-shaped tornado. *What can I say, when creativity strikes, it can't be contained.*

I plugged earbuds into my ears, cranked up the music, and set about the task of cleaning up my mess. I wasn't going to lie; the creative juices flowing through my system felt fantastic.

While I danced and straightened up, someone tapped me on the shoulder. I glanced over and pulled my earbuds free. Chandra stood behind me. "Having fun over here?" she asked, smiling at my disaster area.

"I did get a little carried away, didn't I?"

She shrugged and pointed to her work station. It rivaled mine. "What's the fun of making something if you can't make a mess, right?" she said.

I agreed. "Exactly."

"We could help each other clean up," she suggested. Chandra was a genuinely kind person. She wore her heart on her sleeve and it showed in her designs and her willingness to help her classmates.

"Thanks. That would be great." This time I took her up on the offer. It was getting easier to let people in.

Chandra folded and stacked the larger pieces of fabric, admiring my choices. "You're really talented, Jillian," she complimented.

I turned to her and smiled. "Thanks. That means a lot coming from you. You're the most talented designer here."

"I wouldn't go that far," she scoffed.

I dropped the French curve onto the table and stared at her. *Is she serious?* "Come on. Your designs are outstanding."

"You really think so?" she asked humbly.

"Hell yeah." I couldn't believe what I was hearing; self-doubt from Chandra? I thought I'd bought all the property in that market a long time ago.

"Thanks, Jillian. I didn't realize how much I needed to hear that." Her lips turned up at the corners.

"What do you mean?" I was blown away. *How can she not know how talented she is?*

"Sometimes it's just hard to turn off your inner critic. You know what I mean?"

Boy, did I. My inner critic was a demonic monster from hell that never shut the fuck up. "Yeah, I definitely know what you mean." I looked around the table, picking up the French curve and shoving it into my bag. "Let's go get your mess cleaned up."

* * *

That night, Sarah and I waited in a long line at Baja's. Sarah said they had the best Mexican food in town and she wasn't lying. My chipotle chicken chimichanga was delicious.

"So, what do you think?" she asked, biting into her burrito.

I wiped the dripping cheese from my chin and said, "It's wonderful."

She grinned and took another bite, chewing before she spoke. "Good. How's Griffin?"

I picked up my Diet Coke and took a sip. "He's good. They just booked a tour over Spring Break," I bragged.

"He's going on tour? That's awesome! Where's he going?" she asked, grinning.

"Mexico and some other places in the U.S."

"I still can't believe your boyfriend is a rock star. That's so...cool." She scrunched her face up, shaking her head.

It *was* really cool, but I didn't see Griffin as a "rock star." Music was just a small part of what made him wonderful.

Sarah set her fork down and said, "Oh, I almost forgot. Your birthday is in two weeks. Do you have anything special you want to do?"

"I don't know," I exhaled. "Nothing extravagant, please."

"Gotcha," she agreed. But by the look in her eyes, I knew my request fell on deaf ears.

"I mean it, Sara. No fussing."

She put her hands up defensively and picked up her soda. "No fussing."

Sarah was a terrible liar. Her smile would give her away every time.

Chapter Twenty-Three

If the first two weeks were any indication of how the rest of the semester would pass, I'd be home in no time. As I'd predicted, labs sucked up my time like a black hole sucks up light. Going out for my birthday tonight had actually given me something to look forward to. It would be nice to see the world beyond the eye of a needle for once.

I unlocked my dorm room door, dropped my bag, and fell face-first onto my bed. I flirted with the idea of a nap but quickly shot it down, fearing Sarah's wrath if she found me asleep instead of getting ready for my party. Sarah hadn't divulged any information about what she'd planned for my birthday except that I needed to be ready to party.

A party sounded good. If I couldn't spend my birthday with Griffin, at least a party would keep my mind off of it.

"Jillian Lawson! Get your ass out of bed! Now!" Sarah yelled, throwing the door open.

Startled, I rolled off the bed and hit the floor with a *thunk*.

"Geez, Sarah!" I shouted. "You scared the shit out of me." I sat up, glaring at her.

"Why aren't you getting ready?"

"I just got back from class." I stood up and went to my closet, looking for something to wear.

"Likely story," she said brusquely. "But since you're the birthday girl, I can't give you too much shit."

I looked over my shoulder and saw her grinning widely. "Exactly." I nodded.

"You know what you're wearing tonight?" Sarah asked, clicking through the hangers in her closet.

"Not a clue. It would be a lot easier to find something to wear if you'd give me a hint as to where we are going?" I asked sweetly, hoping she'd eat it up.

"Nope. Not gonna happen. Besides, you're the designer; you're supposed to be dressing me."

"If I don't know where we're going, it's really hard to choose appropriate attire." My shoulders sagged. Arguing with her was hopeless; she never relented.

"Wear something fun…and sexy." She glanced over her shoulder.

"Um, Sarah? Why would I need to wear something 'sexy'?" I asked, wondering what she had up her sleeve.

She shrugged and looked back to her closet. "Or not. It's your party. Wear whatever you want."

Oh, dear Lord. What did she plan? I was legitimately worried now.

After several minutes of poring over her closet and my own, I pieced together two outfits that she deemed worthy, and went to get cleaned up.

Two hours later, we were ready to leave for my unknown birthday destination. I had rainbow-colored hair and wore a hot pink dress that hugged my curves nicely. It wasn't the sexiest dress I owned, but I loved the color. I pulled on my matching heels and looked at Sarah, "You ready?"

She put in her last earring and contemplated her reflection in the mirror. "Are you sure these pants look all right?"

"You look hot, Sarah." She'd borrowed my metallic royal blue leggings and paired them with her black, shimmery off-the-shoulder tunic. I warned her that Brandon wouldn't be able to keep his hands off of her.

"It's a little flashier than I'm used to," she confessed.

"You look great. I promise."

She turned away from the mirror and breathed. "All right, I'll put my trust in the fashion guru. You ready?"

"Yep." I nodded, handing Sarah my car keys.

She took them and smiled. "Let's get this birthday started then!"

* * *

Within minutes she parked down the street from Brandon's apartment. "Brandon's?" I asked.

"I had a little help," she said, shutting the car door.

Our heels clicked on the sidewalk as we approached the old brownstone that would soon be Sarah and Brandon's home. The front porch was littered with coeds in various stages of drunkenness. I pushed my way through the sea of unknown faces and wondered how Brandon had billed this party. I could hear the conversation in my head: *"Dude, I'm throwing a birthday party for my girlfriend's roommate."*

"Whose birthday?"

"Jillian Lawson."

"Who?"

"Never mind. Just come over Friday night. I'll have beer."

"Cool. I'll be there."

I figured Brandon's friends didn't really care who the party was for as long as the alcohol was free and readily available.

Weaving our way through the crowded house, Sarah held my hand, pulling me along behind her. We snaked our way through the living room on our way out to the back patio.

"Hey, baby," Sarah cooed when she spotted Brandon standing near one of the kegs. She let go of my hand in exchange for Brandon's waist and wrapped her slender arms around his middle. Brandon pulled her closer. Sarah stretched up on her tiptoes and met Brandon halfway as he lowered his head to hers. Their lips touched and I looked away. I couldn't watch their intimate embrace without missing Griffin even more than I already did. On the way over here, I'd tried texting him, but he hadn't responded. He'd said earlier that he'd be busy most of the night.

I stood next to Sarah taking in the throng of people who'd come out to celebrate my birthday…or better yet, the free beer.

"Let me get the birthday girl a drink," Brandon said, unwinding himself from Sarah. Brandon held a plastic cup under the tapper and passed it to me when it was full.

I held it up and said, "Thanks." Brandon turned back to the kegs and filled another glass, presumably for Sarah.

"Do you know any of these people?" Sarah asked.

"I know a total of…" I paused, making a show of counting the actual people I knew. "Two people: you and Brandon."

Brandon joined us, handing Sarah a plastic yellow cup. "Here, babe."

Sarah took it and drank liberally. "Thanks."

"Thanks for all of this, you two." I tapped my cup to Sarah's and said, "It's my birthday, damn it! Let's party!" I threw back the contents of my cup, chugging until I reached the dregs. It wasn't the smartest idea, but I had every intention of getting wasted tonight. Maybe it would dull the sting of missing Griffin.

"Woo!" Sarah cheered. Sarah downed her beer, too. "Thatta girl!"

"Want another?" Brandon laughed.

I nodded and went to refill my cup.

"It's cold out here, guys. Let's go in." Sarah said, her teeth chattering.

Brandon led the way, and Sarah and I followed. Inside, Brandon had transformed his basement into a dance hall; he'd even hired a pretty decent DJ. I couldn't believe he'd gone through all the trouble of planning a party of this magnitude just for my birthday. But there didn't seem to be any other occasion piggybacking on my day, so the sentiment wasn't lost on me.

"Let's dance!" I shouted over the pounding music. Sarah nodded her head and set her beer down on a small table. I did the same, and we made our way to the front of the grinding crowd. It felt amazing to throw my hands up and let go.

My hips dipped low, side to side. My personal bubble of space was popped by other people grinding their bodies on the makeshift dance floor.

"Jillian!" Sarah shouted over the music.

"What?" I didn't want to stop dancing. If I stopped, I would feel Griffin's void. The alcohol hadn't made me numb enough yet.

I needed more to drink.

Sarah smiled and pointed to Brandon, making his way through the crowd. "Look what I found for the Birthday Girl," he sang, holding up the answer to my problem. Tequila.

Hallelujah.

Brandon handed Sarah and I shot glasses and filled them up. "Now this is what I'm talking about." I tossed back the unassuming clear liquid, ready for the burn. The second it touched my throat, I cringed and shook my head forcefully, swallowing fire. "God, that's good!" I shouted.

Brandon held up the bottle and smirked. "Want another?"

"Hell yeah." I grabbed the tequila from Brandon's hand and poured myself another. "Thanks."

"No problem." He nodded and put up his hands. Smart man, he knew better than to get in the way of a woman and her tequila.

"I need another." Sarah held her glass out, waiting for me to fill it up. "Thanks. I'll be right back."

Brandon looked at her and asked, "Where are you going?"

Without answering him, she turned with her drink in hand, and walked toward the DJ. She tapped his mic a couple of times, checking to see if it was live. Brandon gave me a quizzical look, but I was too interested in pouring myself another shot of tequila to wonder what Sarah was about to do.

I tossed back my third shot and held my breath as the liquid burned a trail down my throat. I welcomed the fire warming my insides as a tingling sensation began to numb my lips and cheeks.

"Everyone!" Sarah shouted. "Hello? Shhh!" Her eyes roamed over the crowd, and a peeved expression fell on her face. People danced, drank, and completely ignored her request for attention. "EVERYONE! SHUT THE FUCK UP!" she yelled.

Everyone froze.

Including me.

"Thank you," Sarah smiled sweetly. "Today's a special day," she continued. "We're all here to celebrate my best friend's birthday." Sarah raised her glass. The rest of the crowd followed her lead, and the mass of people in Brandon's basement all held their drinks up in honor of my birth.

"Happy 19th, Jillian!" Sarah shouted into the mic. The crowd repeated her words and tossed back their drinks. I poured myself another shot and tossed it back as well. The DJ played a non-traditional birthday song that would have made my grandmother turn twenty shades of red.

Sarah relinquished the DJ's mic and skipped back over to where Brandon and I stood. "Are you ready for your present?" she crooned.

"Present? I think you've done enough." I gestured to the gathering of people I didn't know.

"Shut it! You only turn nineteen once." She leaned in really close, "If you had one wish for your birthday, what would it be?" she whispered in my ear.

I didn't even have to think; I knew exactly what I'd wish for.

Sarah backed away from me with a gigantic grin on her face and before I could question her actions there was a voice whispering in my other ear. "Happy birthday, Jillibean."

My reflexes were mired in alcohol, so my reactions were stuck on slow-motion. I turned around *Matrix*-style to see Griffin standing inches from my face. His dark eyes gleamed wickedly, lashing through the shroud of tequila covering my brain. I was suddenly hyperaware. My body zinged with electricity. He blinked and the corners of his mouth pulled up in a sinful smirk. I yearned to touch his gloriously masculine face, to run my fingers over the contours of his sharp cheek bones, over the scruff lining his jaw. His sex appeal was like gravity pulling me into him. Unable to resist his force, I stepped into his arms and gave myself a birthday present; I pulled his face onto mine and kissed him like he was my oxygen.

Now it was a happy birthday.

Chapter Twenty-Four

I couldn't believe he was actually standing in front of me, even though I was wrapped securely in his arms. "How did I not know about this?" We rested our foreheads together, looking into each other's eyes while we swayed to the song flowing from the sound system.

"Sarah swore me to secrecy," he said.

"So she's the mastermind?" I smiled and pulled my head away from his; I wanted to take in all of my birthday present. "How did you get away?"

"I told the guys I couldn't miss your birthday. Thor said he'd keep things going for the weekend."

I wrapped my arms back around his neck and brought him close. "Remind me to thank Thor."

Griffin smiled and bent down to kiss me.

We continued to get reacquainted with one another. I rotated my body so that my back was pressed firmly against his sculpted abdomen. Our bodies melted together, swaying and dipping as the music pounded around us.

Heat radiated through me. It could have been the dancing, the copious amounts of alcohol I'd consumed, or the fact that Griffin currently trailed sultry kisses down my neck. I was pretty sure Griffin's lips on my skin raised my internal temperature to combustible levels. When his hands moved over the curve of my hips and brushed lightly across my ass, I feared an explosion was entirely possible. Every nerve ending in my body was seared by the all-consuming heat we generated together.

"Griffin," I sighed, turning around in his arms.

His hands never left me and now he had even better access to my backside. He took advantage of the new position and cupped each of my cheeks in the palms of his hands and lifted up ever so slightly, pushing me up, closer to his mouth.

My body responded to his every touch. The second his lips touched mine, everyone else ceased to exist. It was only us.

Griffin pressed his strong lips to mine, giving me a couple of soft, tiny kisses before he latched on with the third kiss. Our lips fully connected and his tongue pushed into my mouth, begging to be met by mine. The deeper his tongue slid, the more he pushed me up with his hands. I was tempted to wrap my legs around his waist and make him hold me just so we could be closer.

I gripped his shoulders and ran my hands up his neck and into his hair, anchoring him to my face. I pushed my tongue against his, nipping at his lower lip. Our moans blended together as air escaped our lungs in short bursts of ecstasy.

I slid my lips to the corner of his mouth…his stubbled jaw…his neck. My tongue played at his lips, tasting him as I moved my way over his face and neck. His hands kneaded the cheeks of my ass, pulling me into him; I could *feel* how much he wanted me.

"Jillibean," he breathed in my ear. I worked my lips back to his. I wanted to taste my name on his lips. "Jillian," he said, pulling up my chin with his fingertips.

I stopped kissing him and stared into his eyes; desire poured from them and I couldn't comprehend why he'd stopped kissing me. "Hmm," I responded.

"Do you want to go?" he asked. His voice was raspy and deep.

I nodded.

He wrapped his arms around my waist and we made our way through the crowded dance floor. I hadn't realized how many people were still down here. Alcohol had bolstered my confidence to the point that I didn't really care who'd just seen me attack my boyfriend. Now all I wanted to do was get him alone.

Griffin and I made our way up the stairs. I saw Sarah and Brandon standing in the corner of the living room with cups in their hands, talking. "Sarah!" I called over the loud music. She didn't hear me so I called again. "Sarah!"

I looked over my shoulder and smiled at Griffin as we weaved through the living room toward my friends. Griffin smiled back and gave my hand a gentle squeeze. He seemed ready to leave, too.

"Hey, guys," I said, pushing through the throng.

"Hey, you two," Sarah sang, winking at me very conspicuously. "Did you enjoy your birthday present?"

Oh, I plan to. But I needed to get out of here first. "I still can't believe you two didn't tell me." I playfully punched Sarah in the arm and smirked at Griffin. He pulled me to his side and kissed the top of my head.

"It wouldn't have been much of a surprise if you'd known I

was visiting." Griffin pinched my side, and I squirmed beneath his hand.

I took a few steps closer to Sarah, just to make sure she heard me over the music. "We're going to bail," I said.

"Okay." She winked. "Happy birthday, Jillian." She tossed her arms around me and nearly knocked me over. With our arms locked around each other, we giggled like little girls as we wobbled on our heels. I felt Griffin's hand at the small of my back, steadying me as we righted ourselves. "I'm spending the night here," Sarah whispered in my ear. "So the room is all yours." She held my shoulders and pulled back, giving me a conspiratorial smile and a wink.

"Thank you, Sarah. For all of this." I swept my hand around, implying the entire party.

"No problem. I wanted you to have a good birthday." She hugged me again, but sweetly this time.

"I did. Thank you."

I turned to Brandon, ready to thank him, too. "Brandon, thank you for everything."

"Sure thing, Jillian." He patted my back a little too enthusiastically, and again I teetered on my heels. "Whoa, there." Brandon clamped a hand on my shoulder and steadied me. "Hey, man," Brandon said, looking at Griffin. "You'd better get her home. It looks like she's enjoyed her birthday a little too much."

"I did enjoy my party, but I am fine." I giggled. "I am not drunk." I was determined to make them believe me, but it was difficult when the giggles kept bubbling out of me.

Griffin reached around me and extended his hand toward Brandon. "That's my plan," Griffin replied with a smile. Brandon shook his hand and Griffin thanked him. "Thanks for having Jillian's party, man."

"It's cool," Brandon said, patting Griffin's shoulder.

I gave both guys a dirty look for implying that I was drunk when I clearly wasn't. I thought I'd like to see them try and stand in four-inch heels.

There was one more round of hugs and handshakes before Griffin and I finally made it out of the apartment. Griffin wrapped his arm around my waist and we walked toward my car as I dug in my purse for the keys. "Damn it!"

"What's wrong?" he asked.

"Sarah has my keys," I said, turning around to go back to Brandon's.

"Whoa, wait up a minute." Griffin grabbed my hand and pulled me back to him. "Sarah will bring your car back to the dorm in the morning. I have Ren's car."

"Ren's?" Her name came out of my mouth along with a hiccup.

"A thousand miles, and January air doesn't make for a very pleasant trip on a bike. Ren let me borrow her car."

"Oh. Okay," I shrugged.

"I'm parked over here." Griffin led me down a couple of sidewalks before he punched the locks and the car chirped to life. "I had to make sure I parked far enough away so you wouldn't recognize her car," he said, opening my door.

When Griffin shut my door, I leaned my head on the headrest and closed my eyes. The cold New England air wrapped my alcohol-numbed body in a welcome embrace. It had been really hot in Brandon's apartment. I inhaled large gulps of frozen air and ignored the rumbling in my stomach; there was no way in hell that I was going to let myself get sick. I exhaled slowly, hoping the growing nausea would pass.

"Bean, you all right?" Griffin asked.

"Mm-hmm," I nodded, making sure to keep my eyes closed.

Griffin laid his hand on my leg and squeezed. "We'll be back to the dorm in just a minute," he whispered.

True to his word, we were. I felt the car come to a stop and opened my eyes. Without a word, Griffin got out of the car and walked around to my side. The door opened and a *whoosh* of cold air swirled my hair onto my face. I didn't have the strength to lift my hand to push it off. I didn't even think I had the strength to lift my head from the head rest. I didn't feel very good.

"Come on, Jillibean," Griffin said softly, extending his hand for me to grab onto.

"I…can't…move," I mumbled.

"Take my hand, Bean." I felt him slip his hand into mine, but I was afraid to move.

My head swarmed with a thousand hornets. Their buzzing vibrated my entire body until I couldn't take it anymore. I thrust my body forward and leaned for what I hoped was the open car door. Before I could stop myself, every tequila shot I'd consumed spewed from my lips.

"Ugh," I moaned and fell back against the seat.

The buzzing in my head was replaced by a dull and constant ringing—reminiscent of the sound of a finger running along the rim of a half-filled champagne glass. While the champagne glass chorus rang in my ears, my body suddenly felt like it was floating. I wrapped my arms around a strong, sturdy column and rested my head while I floated away.

* * *

I prayed for unconsciousness to reclaim its hold on me, but it wouldn't. The jackhammer inside my skull hadn't shut off for the last twenty minutes, and I doubted it had an off button. I rolled onto my side and crashed into someone lying beside me. I pulled open one eye and saw Griffin's shaggy black hair spread across my pillow.

Griffin? When did he get here?

Despite the incessant hammering inside my skull, I recounted the events of my party last night. What was the last thing I remembered? Dancing…and…tequila? Dear God, the tequila. *Ugh! I will never drink tequila again.* I held my head and tried not to retch while I remembered powering down shot after shot of the vile liquid.

Breathe, Jillian. In…out…in…out….

Once I regained control over my spastic stomach, I tried remembering when Griffin had shown up and how the hell we'd gotten back to my room. It was useless; the tequila had sufficiently erased any memory of what happened after I'd started drinking.

I stared at Griffin sleeping soundly beside me. He was wrapped up like a burrito in the small travel blanket I kept in my closet. The wings of the griffin adorning his shoulders peeked out from underneath the blanket; I fought the urge to brush my fingers across the feathery artwork. I didn't want to wake him; he looked so peaceful.

What had I done to deserve his unconditional love? Even on my birthday, when no one in my family had bothered to call or even send a text, Griffin dropped everything and traveled eighteen hours to be with me. A wave of shame washed over me as the realization set in—Griffin had traveled all this way to celebrate my birthday with me, and I got wasted and couldn't remember any of it. What kind of girlfriend was I?

Tears stung my eyes, but I refused to cry. I was done with crying all the time. There was nothing I could do to fix what I'd done, so there was no reason to cry. I bit my lip and stifled the tears. Griffin stirred. His eyes were dark and shadowed with sleep. The second he focused his gaze on me, a sexy-sleepy smile brought color to his cheeks.

"Morning, Bean," his voice rasped.

"Morning," I whispered. My head pounded with the slightest noise.

"How are you feeling?"

I winced and shook my head. "I've been better."

"Sorry," he whispered. "I bet you're hurting." He sat up very slowly. I knew he was trying to be careful, not wanting to rock the bed on my account.

I rolled onto my back and stared up at him. The blanket fell away, revealing the broken guitar tattoo. Despite the fact that I felt like gum, on the bottom of a shoe, that had walked on hot asphalt all day, I still had the strength to appreciate the beautiful man lying in my bed.

"Griff, I'm so sorry." I wanted to apologize for behaving like an ass.

"Sorry? Why are you sorry?" Griffin sidled up next to me, lying on his side. His bicep flexed as he rested his head on his fisted hand.

"Not exactly my finest moment." I drew a hand over my hungover visage like a magic wand.

"Really? It's not the first time I've seen you drunk." His eyebrows pulled up, making his forehead crinkle when he smiled.

"I know. But you drove all the way out here, and I had to go and get fucked up. I was pissed that I had to spend my birthday without you, so I planned on drowning my sorrows in a bottle of tequila. Our time together is too short for me to be passed out during any part of it."

"Tequila. That explains it." He moved his hand over my forehead, brushing some of the shorter layers from my face.

"Explains what?" I asked.

"The puking."

I cringed. "Oh, dear Lord. I didn't. Please tell me I didn't."

Griffin's nose and eyes wrinkled up, and I knew he wasn't joking. "I don't remember shit about last night." I threw my arm over my eyes. I was so embarrassed.

The bed rocked and suddenly my head rested on top of Griffin's bicep. His other hand draped around my waist while his thumb drew lazy lines up and down the small patch of skin my cami failed to cover. "You don't remember anything from last night?" he asked. His eyebrow pulled up conspiratorially.

I shook my head.

"Nothing?" He grinned, like he had a secret.

Why did he keep asking? Did we do something that I should remember? Panic rose in my chest. What had we done?

Oh, God!

"Griffin…" I was on the brink of tears. I silently prayed we hadn't had sex. If I didn't remember our first time…*my* first time, I would be devastated. "Please tell me we didn't."

He shook his head and *shh*'d me. "No, no, no. We didn't. But…"

He fanned my faded-rainbow hair over his arm, drawing each colored strand slowly through his fingers.

"But?" I was about to eat anxiety for breakfast if he didn't start filling in the missing pieces of my memory. Alcohol and antidepressants weren't a good combo.

"You don't remember attacking me on the dance floor?" He smirked.

"I attacked you?" I hated not being able to remember anything.

He shrugged. "It's okay. I sort of attacked you back, so it wasn't all one-sided."

Mortification was seeping into my consciousness and I wanted to crawl under the blankets and hide. "Were we alone?" I asked the question even though I already knew the answer.

Griffin shook his head, never once losing his rock star grin.

"Ugh!" I rolled over and buried my face in his chest. "How bad was it?"

"Well, there was lots of tongue, some moaning, ass grabbing—"

I shook my head. "Stop. Just stop. I get the picture."

"Do you remember now?" he asked.

"No," I said, shaking my buried head.

"That's too bad. It was so fucking hot," he groaned, lying his head on top of mine. His shoulders shook and a rumble of laughter clamored from his chest.

"Why did you let me attack you? You were sober!" I said, lifting my head up, giving him and indignant glare.

"I really missed you. When you stick your tongue in my mouth, my self-control goes out the window. Sorry, Bean." He chuckled. "However, I am sorry that you don't remember it. It was by far the best kiss I've ever had. I guess we'll just have to do it again."

I was all for sticking my tongue in his mouth, but at the moment I was mortified by my drunken behavior. "This fucking sucks. Apparently we kissed the hell out of each other last night, and I can't remember even the smallest peck. That will never happen again." I pointed a finger at him.

"What?" Griffin screeched, sitting up. My head hit the pillow as I noticed the horrified look on his face.

"I didn't mean the kissing, you idiot." I pulled the pillow from behind my head and hit him with it.

He grabbed the pillow out of my hands and tossed it on the floor. "*Phew*, you had me worried. I've waited a long time to do that, and I am not about to stop."

I looked up into his eyes, wanting him to know how serious I was. "I meant that I am never getting trashed to the point that I can't remember kissing you. I will remember every single one of our kisses from here on out, and that's a promise."

"Well, enough talking. Let's start making some memories you'll remember." Griffin leaned down, but I squirmed my way onto the floor.

I pressed my finger to his puckered lips. "Hold that thought. From what you said I did last night, I need a few moments in the bathroom. I'll be right back."

I shot up from the floor, praying all the tequila was out of my system. My head felt slightly better than it had when I woke up, but the tequila didn't want to refund my birthday hangover. I shuffled to the closet, grabbed my toiletries, and rushed out the door.

"Hurry up. I have a birthday kiss to give you. I promise you'll remember this one!" Griffin shouted as the door closed behind me.

I ran to the bathroom…my hangover cured.

Chapter Twenty-Five

Y ou're hungry," Griffin said against my lips. "Your stomach sounds pretty pissed."

"I'll order a pizza. I don't want to leave."

Griffin grabbed my phone off the desk and handed it to me. Within minutes lunch was ordered and I resumed kissing my boyfriend.

"This has been the best birthday ever," I said happily. Griffin and I lay side by side on my tiny twin mattress. My hands were folded and pressed on the pillow between us. Griffin took the opportunity to put his hands over mine, running his thumb up and down my wrist.

"I haven't had a chance to give you your gift," he said thoughtfully.

"Are you kidding? You're here. That's beyond enough."

Griffin smoothed my hair back and smiled. "Of course I got you a birthday present." He leaned closer and kissed the tip of my nose. "But, before I give it to you, I want you to keep an open mind."

Uh-oh. Any gift that needed a buffer couldn't be good. "What did you do, Griffin?" I pushed myself up and sat cross-legged on the bed. Griffin did the same. He took my hands in his and squeezed them tightly.

Griffin's eyes blazed with an intense gaze. "It's nothing big or extravagant, but when I saw them, I thought of you…and us."

My eyebrows scrunched together. "What does that mean?" I was confused.

He got up off the bed and walked toward the closet. Reaching up, he moved a few of my things around before his eyes alighted on something shoved toward the back.

"What are you looking for?" I craned my neck to see.

Just then, my phone rang. I turned my attention to the ringing coming from my blankets and sifted through the tousled mess. "It's probably the pizza guy," I said, answering the unknown number.

When I answered the phone, Griffin guiltily whipped around like he'd been bitten by some monster hiding in my closet. He was acting so weird.

"I'll be right down. Thanks." I hung up the phone and sprang up from the bed, grabbing my purse from the floor beside my desk. "I was right; it's the pizza."

"Perfect timing," he mumbled. His demeanor visibly deflated and his shoulders slumped. He looked like he was pouting.

"I'll be right back." I walked to the door but before I opened it, I quickly wrapped my arms around Griffin's waist and pulled him to me. "You're acting very strange," I said, pressing my nose to his. "You don't need to worry. Whatever you got me, I know I'll love it. I've never disliked a present you've gotten me." Before he could answer, I put my mouth on his and kissed him with every ounce of confidence in my body. Whatever had him flustered, I hoped that I could transfer some of my confidence to him through my kiss.

I opened the door and skipped down the hall to get our pizza, leaving him speechless and standing in front of my closet.

After my short jaunt down to the common area, I paid the delivery guy and hustled back to my room. I'd deliberately deprived myself of food for most of the day, fearing my stomach would reject anything I put in it, but as the scents of cheese, pepperoni, and pineapple flirted with my nose my mouth watered and my stomach roared. If I didn't eat soon, my stomach threatened to jump out of my body and devour the pizza without me.

"Dinner is served," I announced, kicking open the door.

Griffin lay on the bed with his arm hiding his face. "You okay?" I asked, setting the pizza down on the desk.

"Yeah, I'm good." He sat up and smiled sweetly.

I pulled open a drawer and dug out paper plates and napkins. "So, are you going to give me my present?" I asked, opening the pizza box.

"Let's eat first. I'll give it to you later." He pushed off the bed and picked up a plate as he looked into the pizza box. "Pineapple? Seriously?"

"I only ordered it on my half, not yours." My eyes widened and I cocked my head to the side, giving him a sassy glare.

He wrinkled his nose. "Your taste in pizza is hideous."

The pizza was heavenly. I devoured my half in record time. "Ahh, that was fantastic," I sighed.

"Mine was fantastic…not so sure about yours," Griffin mocked.

I snatched a piece of pineapple from the empty box and popped it into my mouth. "You don't know what you're missing."

"I've watched you eat pepperoni and pineapple pizzas for what...thirteen years now? If I haven't indulged in your exotic taste in pizza yet, I think it's pretty safe to say that I don't believe I'm missing much."

"Your loss," I said, standing up. I tossed my plate and napkins into the pizza box and added Griffin's trash to the pile. Walking to the garbage can by the door, I tossed the box inside and glanced up into my closet, trying to get a glimpse of the present Griffin had hidden in there. Whatever it was, he'd hidden it well.

Griffin yawned and flopped on the bed. "I think I'll survive...somehow."

Turning back around, I brushed my hands together, dusting off the pizza crumbs. "So, when do I get my present?" I asked, wringing my hands together greedily.

"Your present, huh?" He sat up with a grunt and took two large strides to stand next to me, in front of the closet. His arms were around me instantly. "I will give you your birthday present on one condition." He rocked me back and forth as he awaited my compliance to his condition.

"What?" I looked up at him, suspicious of his motives.

"You can't hide them." His lips spread into a tender smile.

I was thrown off by his request. "Okay? But that's a silly condition. Why would I want to hide something you got me?"

"I'll explain once you open them." He tickled my sides and tapped my nose with his finger.

I giggled and slapped his hands away from my sides. "Got it. Now give me my present damn it!"

Griffin kissed the top of my head and stepped to the closet. Behind several of the small boxes I had on the top shelf, he pulled forward a brightly wrapped, large, square package. He held it in both hands, presenting it to me with a warm smile. I took the sparkly gift and looked up at him.

He wrapped his arm around my waist and guided me over to the bed. "Do you remember the day you moved in with Jennifer?" he asked as we sat down.

The memory flickered to life like an old movie inside my head. So much had happened that day, I wondered what memory he was thinking of. "Yes," I groaned. "She wasn't very happy to have me there and she made sure I knew it."

Griffin scooted back on the bed and held his arm up, waiting for me to snuggle in close. "But I was there to help you," he said.

I leaned my head on his shoulder, holding the package in my lap. "I remember. She loved that, too."

"It was fun to get her riled up." He smirked, before he went on with his story. "I remember unpacking a box with pictures, and you just lost it. It scared the fuck out of me. I didn't know what to do. I tossed the pictures into a random drawer and went to you."

Those same pictures were hidden away again. I looked down at the gift and ran my fingers over the smooth paper. *Where is he going with this?* "I didn't want those unpacked and when I saw them…"

"I know." His fingers brushed against my cheek.

"You wouldn't let me go until I stopped crying."

"You cried so much back then." He exhaled. "I wanted to help, but I was…"

"Only sixteen years old," I countered. "You were just a kid too. I don't know many sixteen-year-old boys who would have put up with a broken teenage girl."

His dark eyes surveyed my face, then he shifted his arms and pulled me onto his lap. "You weren't just some broken teenage girl. You were my girl. The girl I promised to make happy when she was sad." His strong arms held me close. "I tried to make you happy, but I failed miserably."

"Griffin, why are we talking about this?" I asked. "Can't I just open the gift?"

He shook his head. "Hear me out, please. I've got a point, I promise."

Still wrapped safely in his arms, I rested my head against his chest. I could hear his heartbeat, a swift constant rhythm.

"Before your parents died, you loved to take pictures. Especially with your mom and dad. But once they were gone, that little girl wouldn't smile for the camera anymore. Anger and sadness had wiped away the happiness of the little girl I used to play with when she'd visit her grandparents." Griffin took my shoulders and held me, looking into my eyes. "I want to see that happiness on your face again." His eyes searched mine, pleading. "Open it," he said.

I looked at the gift in my lap, sliding my fingers to the edges. Peeling back the paper, I unwrapped two wooden picture frames. The frame on top was a blonde oak color, engraved with one word across the top: *Promise*. Inside this frame was a picture of Griffin and me—one that his dad had snapped at my going away party, the night before I left for school. Griffin towered over me. Our bodies were pressed together in a tight hug, and we both wore huge smiles on our faces. It was beautiful. I loved it.

I glanced up at him, running my fingertips over the engraved lettering. "This is perfect," I said.

"Look at the other one." He nodded.

I removed the top picture and stared at the frame underneath. It was identical to the other, except for the engraved word. This one said: *Forever*. Promise and forever...those were our words. "This one's empty?" I held it up, puzzled.

"That one is for your parents." He ran his hand over my head. "About a week ago, I went over to Jennifer's house."

"Wha—"

He put his hands up, cutting me off. "I knew those pictures I'd thrown in the drawer five years ago would probably still be there. I went to Jennifer's and asked if I could look for them. Surprisingly, she let me. When I pulled the drawer open, it was empty." His eyes flashed. "You had packed them up and brought them with you." He grinned. "You kind of foiled my plan, but I was so happy that you were brave enough to bring them with you."

I harrumphed. "Not that brave." I pointed to the closet. "They're still packed in there."

He took both of the frames and laid them on the bed in front of us. Pointing to the one that said *Promise*, he said, "This is you and me. We have the promise of a happy future ahead of us." Then he pointed to the empty frame that said *Forever*. "This one needs a picture of you and your parents. They're a part of you, and are with you forever."

I had a lump in my throat. I tried to swallow it down but it wouldn't move. Without a word, I pushed myself off of Griffin's lap and stood. "Where are you going?" he asked.

I turned and walked to the closet, bending down to drag the box from the back. Griffin got up off the bed to help me, but I put my hand up to stop him. "I got it," I croaked. He sat back down and watched me pull the box over to the bed. I plopped down beside him and we both stared at the box. "They're in there." My voice was hoarse.

"Are you going to open it?" he asked.

I nodded.

Griffin leaned behind me and pulled a pen off my desk. He handed me the pen. I took it and poked through the tape stretched across the flaps. Running the pen down the seam, I split the tape in half and the flaps of the box popped up. Griffin put his hand on my leg, letting me know I wasn't alone.

I pulled the cardboard back, and inside were the pictures that I'd always wanted to keep hidden. But now that I'd said good-bye, looking at them didn't hurt so much. I reached inside and pulled out the tiny black frame from the top of the stack.

My little five-year-old face smiled toothlessly at the camera. I was sandwiched between Mom and Dad. The tassel of my kindergarten graduation cap hung nearly in Dad's face, but he didn't seem to care. All three of us smiled so big. I smiled, vaguely remembering when the photo had been taken.

Griffin put his arm around me, holding the new frame in his hand. I looked up at him and said, "Thank you."

Chapter Twenty-Six

Griffin helped me exchange the old frame for the new one. I got up from the bed and set them both side by side on my dresser.

Griffin patted the bed, asking me to come back. He scooted closer to the wall and opened his arms wide for me. I lay down next to him and he wrapped me in his arms. "You're amazing," he whispered at my ear. He pressed feather-light kisses all along my jaw and down my neck. Every kiss was kindling, feeding the growing fire burning beneath my skin. I shifted slightly and he took advantage of my closeness, climbing on top of me. He pressed his body into mine, never removing his lips from my skin. My hands traveled over the flexing muscles of his arms.

I opened my eyes and watched him move his lips toward the cleavage that teased over the top of my cami. I placed my hand under his chin and drew his attention to my face. "Griffin," I said breathlessly.

Although no words left his mouth, the look he gave me spoke paragraphs. I focused on his breathing, trying to match mine to his. With each hurried exhalation our breath twisted together in the infinitesimal space between our lips, until there was no space left.

Hungrily, I tasted him. I wanted him. Until Griffin, I'd never understood what that expression meant. I'd never *wanted* anyone. I'd especially never wanted anyone to touch me…to see me. I'd never wanted to explain my past to someone, the past documented on my skin. With Griffin…I didn't have to.

Griffin's hands slid over my waist, grabbing the stretchy material and bunching it up so his hands would have access to my skin. During the very few times I'd ever made out with a boy, if his hands ever made it this far, I would completely shut down. The thought of explaining what was underneath my clothes scared the hell out of me. But Griffin was different—he knew my past. He'd never seen the whole story written beneath my clothes, but I still knew I was safe with him. Every breath…every kiss…every touch…felt right.

I wanted him…to read my story.

I stilled his hands between mine. Our hands folded together on my stomach, Griffin's passionate stare sent shivers across my skin. Goose bumps prickled their way down the length of my arm. "Griffin…"

"What?" he breathed.

"Make love to me," I whispered.

I slowly loosened my grip on his fingers and moved my hands up the length of my torso. The cami bunched in my fingers as I pulled it over the swell of my breasts, up my neck, and over my head. My chest rose and fell rapidly with each of my staccato breaths. The royal blue lace bra I'd slipped on this morning stood out against my pale skin. My scars were willingly on display before the man I loved.

"Jillian…" he whispered. Griffin's eyes never left mine, almost as if he were scared to take in my almost naked form.

I supported my weight on my elbows, bringing my face millimeters from his. "I want this. I want you."

He transferred his hands from my middle and slowly ran them down my flexed arms. He pushed lightly, and I fell back onto my pillow. Griffin's eyes traversed the plains of my marred skin like a roadmap. Each whitish slash across my chest represented a ruin—something that once had been beautiful, but crumbled to pieces in the wake of disaster. Though ruins, they still retained their majesty—a whisper of their foregone beauty still lingered within. My ruin of a body spoke of a time wrought with sadness, helplessness, and destruction, but I prayed Griffin would find some remnant of beauty.

Despite being an expert in reading his facial expressions, I'd barely pass as a novice at this moment. "Griffin," I whispered.

His eyes left my skin and he looked me. "Bean," he choked. His hands slid from one puckered slash to the next, almost as if his hands were performing some sort of silent prayer over the sight of a tragic accident. "I'm so sorry," he said, barely above a whisper.

His words landed on my ears like a butterfly—barely there. I wasn't sure if I'd heard him correctly. "Sorry? Why are you sorry?" I didn't understand. He had no reason to be sorry. Then it hit me. Maybe he was sorry because he couldn't….not with a scarred, ugly, mess. Why did I ever think he'd want me…or touch me…or be with me? My heart beat into my throat, blocking my airway.

Unexpectedly, Griffin whipped his shirt up and over his head, and tossed it across the room. I jumped, surprised by his abruptness. Griffin gripped his right bicep with his left hand. He pressed so tightly that the knuckles of his left hand turned white. Five fingertips tried their hardest to depress the skin around his arm, but the flexed muscle beneath made it impossible.

"Griffin?" Tears sprang to my eyes, and I scrambled to sit up. My desire to be naked vanished with the disgusted scowl on his face.

I pushed against him, wriggling my way out from underneath his weight. "Let me up," I demanded. I had nowhere to hide. "Damn it, Griffin! Let me up," I said through clenched teeth.

"Jillian, what's wrong?" Griffin asked, suddenly returning his attention to me.

I pushed on his chest, desperate to cover myself. "Nothing. Just let me up." He rolled off of me and fell back against the wall.

Finally. Freedom.

I scrambled for my shirt and threw it on quicker than I'd pulled it off. Rejection was a bitch. I walked over to Sarah's bed and fell onto the mattress.

"Jillian?" Griffin asked quietly.

Sarah's bed dipped as he pushed my body toward the wall, making room for him to curl around me. His hand smoothed the hair away from my face while a few strands pulled, adhered to my cheeks by sticky tears. "Bean?" he whispered in my ear. "I'm sorry."

"I get it, Griffin, you don't have to explain. How I ever expected another person to want me...I'll never know," I choked.

"You think that's what I'm sorry about?" He gripped my shoulder and forced me to roll over. "Jillian Helene Lawson," he scolded. "Come on, you know me better than that." His eyes searched my face, the hint of a smile pulling at the corners of his lips. "Do you remember when I got this?" He pointed to the biblical words branded around his arm.

"Yes." My voice cracked. "Junior year."

He nodded his head. "I got this right after I found out what you were doing to yourself. I hated the fact that I couldn't take your pain away," he said, brushing my cheek with the back of his hand. "I felt powerless. There was *nothing* I could do to help you, and I *hated* that. My own powerlessness made me sick. I was your best friend, and I couldn't save you."

"Nobody could, Griffin. The voices in my head were so much easier to believe—their lies so much more convincing than the truth."

"When I got this tattoo, I made a promise to myself and to you. I would *always protect* you, *always trust* you, *always hope* for you, and *always persevere* for you." Each time he spoke, his fingers touched the words written on his skin. "This is what love means to me. That's why I got this, a physical reminder that I would never give up on you…or us."

"What about this?" I touched the sentence *Never Fails.*—the one he hadn't mentioned.

"To remind me that failure wasn't an option. I wouldn't ever stop trying." His eyes focused on mine, taking on a serious quality. "Jillian, I had no idea. I didn't know how much you were hurting. Each one of those scars represents a time that I didn't protect you." He pointed to the words on his arm. "I feel like I failed you. Something love isn't supposed to do."

"Griffin," I gently kissed his lips, trying to remove the sadness I had put in his heart. "You couldn't have saved me. I had to do that myself. But if you hadn't been by my side through all of that, I wouldn't have survived. You didn't fail me. You found me dying on the bathroom floor. You forced me to get help even when I didn't want to. You took whatever wrath I unleashed on you and willingly stood by my side. I'm here, wrapped in your arms…*because* of your love for me. I don't deserve it, but for some reason you think I do." I blinked and a single tear fell down my cheek.

Griffin's fingers lingered at my waist before they pinched the fabric of my shirt and pulled it over my head. He pushed my shoulders back and positioned himself astride me. Now he stared at my nearly naked form with admiration. He reverently touched each reminder of my sadness. His touch warmed my skin, sending tingles of electricity through each pore.

"Jillian," he said, bending down to kiss my lips. "I promise I will always protect you." His lips moved to the scar just above my left breast. "I promise I will always love you." He kissed the scar that disappeared beneath my bra. Griffin continued to kiss each of my scars; each one punctuated with the promise of his unfailing love.

His lips on my skin drove me crazy. I arched my back as he worked his way across my chest. "Make love to me…please," I begged.

Finally resting his weight on top of me, he whispered in my ear. "I want nothing more than to make love *with* you, Jillian. But when I do make love *with* you, I plan to hold you hostage in bed for several days. I don't want to wake up tomorrow and have to leave your side. Our first time will be perfect." His lips rested on mine. "I promise."

My body despised his answer, but my heart leapt for joy. I wanted him more than anything, but he was right; if we made love, it would be a zillion times more difficult to say good-bye in the morning.

For the rest of the night, we settled for exploring each other's bodies with our lips and hands, rejoicing in the growing anticipation that would make our first time together perfect.

Chapter Twenty-Seven

After a long good-bye, Griffin drove away in Ren's Miata. The next time we'd see each other wouldn't be until May, when I finished for the semester. Our schedules over the next few months were insane. Mine Shaft had their Mexico/U.S. tour, and I had plenty of sewing to keep me busy until the Spring Showcase. I was thankful for the distraction of my looming debut. At least I'd have plenty to keep my days filled, so I wouldn't think about the 102 days separating me and Griffin.

Today promised to be a long day of lecture and studio, and I was prepared to buckle down and get my shit done. That's why I was here in the first place. I grabbed my bags and locked up the room, ready to put pen to paper and scissors to fabric.

I walked into the empty lecture hall and sat down with my coffee—the only plus side to Griffin departing before the sun rose; I had time to get coffee. Which I desperately needed.

I yawned and took a sip of my coffee before I pulled my iPad from my bag. I checked the time on my phone and noticed a missed text message from Sarah, *How was your weekend, birthday girl? I WANT ALL THE DEETS!*

Perfect! Lunch @ dining hall? 11:30? I typed back.

Can't. Class until late. See you tonight?

Damn, I really wanted to see her. *See you later, then.*

"Hey, Jillian. Did you have a good weekend?"

I jumped when I heard my name. My coffee cup teetered near the edge of the small desktop and my hand shot to save the precious liquid from a fatal tumble to the floor. After I'd balanced my coffee cup, I looked up and saw Chandra smiling, plunking herself down in the seat next to mine.

"Sorry, I didn't mean to scare you," she said, pulling her laptop from its case.

"No, it's okay." I smiled. "My weekend was great. How was yours?" I asked.

"Quiet," she said. I noticed a look of relief on her face. "It's nice to have those every once in a while." She flashed me a smile and then went back to logging on to her computer.

"It is," I agreed.

Both of us sat quietly, waiting for Professor Vine to begin class. I drank my coffee and checked my Twitter feed. Listening to Chandra clicking away at her keyboard, I realized I knew nothing about this girl, besides her propensity toward kindness and the enormous amount of talent she possessed. I turned in her direction and asked, "Would you want to get lunch after class?" Since Sarah couldn't make it, I could use the opportunity to get to know Chandra a little better.

She looked up from her screen, and the hint of a smile lit up her face. "Sure."

"Good morning," Professor Vine announced, walking into the room. "Today's lecture will focus on pattern basics. Since all of you are beginning to put together the bulk of your designs for the Showcase, I want to review basic patterning techniques."

"Awesome," I said in a hushed tone. I smiled and settled into my chair, ready to listen, while Professor Vine loaded her presentation.

* * *

For two and a half hours, I dutifully took notes. This was a helpful lesson, since pattern making wasn't a strength of mine. "That's all for the lecture today. I'll see you in an hour for the first of our labs today." Professor Vine chugged the dregs of her water bottle and gathered her lecture notes.

I saved my notes and clicked off my iPad. Chandra was in the process of shutting down her computer. "Ready for lunch?" she asked, turning in my direction. "I'm starving."

"Yep." I stowed my iPad and stood up.

On our way to the dining hall, Chandra and I made small talk. When we got to the dining hall, it was jam-packed. "This place is insane," I said, stretching on my tiptoes, scanning the room for an open table.

Chandra did the same, looking all over for somewhere to sit. "No kidding. Did they hire a professional chef over break? I don't recall the food being that good here."

"Let's get in line, maybe something will open up," I offered.

We grabbed our trays and bypassed the hot food line, opting for the salad bar. After we loaded our plates with colorful fruits and veggies, we went in search of a place to sit. As luck would have it, a couple vacated a seat for two just as Chandra and I left the salad bar. We booked it to the table before someone else could snatch it up.

We sat down and dug in. "So, tell me about Paris," I said, taking a bite of my salad.

"Oh…" She covered her mouth, chewing her food before she continued. "It was so amazing," she gushed. "Even though it was a small house, I was able to get some real life experience."

"What a fabulous opportunity," I said. "What made you want to be a designer?" I asked, wanting to know her better.

"I grew up in Michigan. Just my mom and me. My dad skipped town when I was little. My mom's a waitress. She doesn't make much money. Growing up, my mom couldn't afford much, so we'd spend our evenings making clothes. I eventually got to the point where I didn't need a pattern, and I was making up my own designs. My mom encouraged me to continue designing. At the end of the day, I got a scholarship into the design program, and here I am now." She shrugged. "I hope that one day I can make enough money to buy my mom a new house."

I admired and understood her drive to succeed so much better now. "I have no doubt you're going to make it big. Hell, you've already been to Paris. That's amazing." I reached across the table and squeezed her hand.

"Thanks, Jillian." She swiped at the tears glistening on her eyelashes and smiled. "So, tell me about you," she asked, taking a deep breath. "What's your story?"

We certainly didn't have time for me to lay my story out there, and I didn't really want to rehash my past again. I was finally moving in the right direction, and wanted to keep it that way. "My mom encouraged me, too," I said, remembering how often I gave my mom childish drawings, and the way she would praise my efforts. And Griffin came to mind, too—his endless support and love. "But my boyfriend was the one that made sure I followed through on my dream."

"What's his name?" she asked, poking a cherry tomato with her fork.

I smiled. "Griffin Daniels."

Chandra swallowed and took a quick drink. "The lead singer of Mine Shaft?"

My eyebrows pulled together. I wasn't used to people recognizing Griffin's name. "Uh, yeah? How do you know about Mine Shaft?"

She sat her Styrofoam cup on the table and grinned. "I love indie rock. I've downloaded the few songs they have on iTunes. Your boyfriend is Griffin Daniels?"

It was hard to comprehend that the guy I'd known since I was six years old was becoming a public figure—a name and a face people would instantly recognize. *So weird.* "Yeah," I answered. "We've been friends since we were kids. It's a long story, but over Christmas, things changed."

"Wow. That's so cool." She smiled. "It really is a small world." Chandra shook her head, looking a little starstruck.

"I'll have to tell Griffin he's got a fan from Michigan. He'll love it." I ate the last cucumber and pushed my plate away. "Are you ready to get to the lab?" I asked.

She looked at her watch and finished the last of her soda. "Yep, we need to go."

We discarded our trash and walked briskly through the quad on our way back to the studio building.

Once Professor Vine got the lab started, Chandra and I were so busy we didn't have time to talk. The pattern for our third ensemble was due today, and I had yet to finish mine.

* * *

By the time I glanced at the clock, I had less than twenty minutes to wrap up my spandex pencil skirt template and hand it in to Professor Vine. I'd make it; pencil skirts weren't that difficult to make, which meant their patterns weren't that hard to draw.

I'd chosen a model from Professor Vine's list of TAs. My patterns were drawn to Tina Nelson's specific requirements as listed on Professor Vine's syllabus. I prayed that Tina's measurements hadn't changed, I'd tried contacting her, but she was impossible to reach.

"Five more minutes," Professor Vine called out. The room got louder as everyone hurried to finish and put things away. It had been a long day, and I was ready for it to end. Thankfully, after this class, I had the rest of the day off.

"Need any help, Jillian?" Chandra asked as she cleaned up her work station.

I ignored Chandra for one second while I finished up. "Just one…more facing…dart…and I'm….done." I snipped through the top of my pattern, cutting away the paper that would be used to make the facing of my skirt. I turned to Chandra and smiled. "Nope, I'm finished." I held up my pattern and smiled at my handiwork. "Thanks, though."

"No problem." She placed all of her utensils in a carrying case and zipped it shut.

"Well, three down, two to go," I sighed, gathering my scraps together.

"I think I'm going to be living here from now until the end of the semester," Chandra added.

I tossed the scraps into the recycle bin and agreed. "I think you're right."

"Do you have any of your pieces finished? Besides the one you completed last semester," she asked.

"Yeah. Over break I made another dress." I hoped it would fit Tina. "Do you?" I asked, putting my things away.

Chandra shook her head. "Just the two pieces from last semester, I haven't worked on anything else since break. That was the downside to going to Paris."

"Jillian, do you have your pattern?" Professor Vine asked, walking over to my station.

My eyes scanned the table. "Oh, yes, right here. I'm sorry. I meant to bring it up." I plucked it from the table and handed it to her.

"Thank you." Professor Vine took my pattern. "I'm on my way out, ladies. Since you're the last two here, please lock up on your way out."

"We will, Professor," Chandra answered.

After I finished cleaning up my work station, Chandra and I locked up the studio and headed back to our dorms. Chandra's dorm was closer to campus than mine. She dug her access card from her purse and said, "Thanks for lunch, Jillian. It was nice talking to you."

"Yeah," I agreed. "I'm sure we'll have plenty more opportunities as the Showcase gets closer."

"I'm sure you're right." She started walking up the sidewalk and waved. "'Bye, Jillian."

I trekked across campus, toward Victor. Sarah wouldn't be back until later, so that left me with some quality time with my sketches. I planned to work on my remaining three patterns. Once I got those out of the way, the real fun started…bringing the images inside my head to life.

Chapter Twenty-Eight

Griffin!" I yelled. Since he'd been touring Mexico for the last three weeks, it felt like ages since I'd heard from him.

Even with the grainy FaceTime picture, I could still see a wide grin across his face. "Hi, Bean." His voice came over the iPad, garbled and hard to understand. We had a terrible connection.

I stood up from my bed and moved closer to the door, hoping my proximity to the router would strengthen the signal. "Where are you guys now?" I asked. He'd been to so many different cities, I couldn't keep them straight in my head.

"We're in Cancún," he shouted. It was really noisy there.

"Awesome. It looks like you're getting some sun," I said. His usual olive complexion was much richer.

"Yeah, most of our shows have been open-air venues," he commented. "We're headed back to the States in a couple days," he added. "We've got shows booked in Texas, Oklahoma, and Missouri before we get to come home."

"You're a busy man." I nodded.

I could tell Griffin was walking. The picture on the screen kept bouncing. "What are you doing?" I asked.

"We've got a show in twenty minutes. I'm just getting things together." He picked up his bass, holding it up to the screen.

I smiled. "That one's cool, but I much prefer its likeness on *you*," I said, wagging my eyebrows for effect.

Griffin got really close to the screen and whispered, "And I like when you *play* that one." His voice was low and insistent.

Heat spread over my cheeks and a slow, burning want spread through my core. It had been two months since I'd kissed him...two months too long. "I miss you," I breathed.

"It's been too fucking long." He nodded in agreement.

Walking up behind Griffin was Pauly, Mine Shaft's keyboardist and guitarist. He rested his chin on Griffin's shoulder and waved. "Hi, Jillian. You better be sweet talking this dude." Pauly turned to look at Griffin. "He's feeling left out."

Griffin scowled. "Shut the fuck up." He shrugged and put his hand in Pauly's face, clearing him off his shoulder. "Don't listen to a thing he says, Bean."

I was confused. "Why are you feeling left out?" I asked.

Pauly stuck his head back in the screen, "There's a lot of tail here, girl. But, no worries, your boy is behaving himself." Now I understood. The others were all hooking up.

"Fuck, man. Back off!" Griffin yelled, knocking Pauly out of the way.

"'Bye, Jillian!" Pauly shouted as he stumbled to the side. I could still hear him laughing in the background.

Griffin righted the iPad and his face came back onto the screen. "I'm sorry," Griffin said, running his hand through his hair.

I smiled. "It's okay. He seems to be enjoying himself." I chuckled.

"Let's just say Adam and Pauly are taking full advantage of spring break." Griffin rolled his eyes.

"Adam? What happened to Trina?" I asked. The last I'd heard they were still going strong.

"She dumped his ass," Griffin smirked. "She said he was a hothead, and she was tired of his outbursts."

I nodded, raising my eyebrow in understanding. "He doesn't seem too broken up about it."

"Not in the slightest," Griffin crooned.

"And Thor?" I asked.

Griffin climbed a flight of stairs and the sun beat down onto the screen. He turned around, and I could see his face again. "Nope. He's still into Harper. Hey, Bean," Griffin said abruptly. "I've got to go; they're calling for me."

"Oh, okay." Disappointment shot through me. I wasn't ready to say good-bye. "Good luck," I said, trying to hide my sadness. "I love you."

"Promise?"

I smiled. "Forever."

"I fucking love that," he said, grinning from ear to ear. A curl fell onto his forehead and he shoved it back. "I love you, Bean. Talk to you soon."

"Soon." I kissed my fingers and pressed them to his lips on the screen. He smiled and the call ended.

* * *

For the last two months, Chandra and I had spent all of our free time in the studio. Our designs were taking shape along with our friendship. I saw Chandra more often than I did my own roommate. On occasion, Sarah would visit us or bring us food when we were too busy to leave the studio. But for the most part, it was just Chandra and me.

"Will you help me pin this fabric?" Chandra handed me a pin holder shaped like a cat. I took the cat and slipped a few pins between my lips, then pulled a few more out, pinching them between my fingertips. Chandra stretched the material across the dress form while I pinned.

"How's your mom doing?" I asked. Chandra's mom had lost her job and wasn't doing so well financially. "Any job prospects?"

"No. I'm still sending her the small paycheck I get from working at the Student Union. I keep hoping something will open up for her, though. She's so proud; she hates that I have to send her my spending money."

"I don't know how you do it. You work, go to class, and spend every other hour of the day here."

"Sleep is for the weak!" She laughed. "I need a pin right here." Chandra nodded with her head.

I slid the pin through the fabric where she indicated and said, "I'll remember that."

"Have you met with your model lately?" she asked. "What's her name again?"

"Tina." I growled her name as if it was a swear word. "Funny you should mention her. We're supposed to have another fitting in—" I checked the clock— "twenty minutes."

Chandra walked around to the other side of the dress form and started draping the back. "She can't be that bad."

I followed her, sliding pins into place. "She's not *that bad*...she's the devil. Stick around, you'll see."

"I think I'll pass. Besides, I have to work." I slipped the last pin into place and Chandra let go of the fabric. "Hey, I'm sorry to leave you with this mess, but I've really got to get to the Union." Chandra pinned her name to the partially draped form and wheeled it into line with the rest of the headless torsos.

I waved her on. "Go, I've got this."

"Good luck with your fitting." Chandra hugged me and slung her bags over her shoulder. "Talk to you later."

"See you," I said as she ran out of the classroom.

I had ten minutes before Tina's fitting. I gathered my equipment, sure to have everything ready. I didn't want to deal with her any longer than necessary. I glanced at the clock: 7:00 p.m.

Twenty minutes later, Tina waltzed in like I should be bowing at her feet.

"Can we get this over with? I have a date," she snapped.

I was tempted to tell Professor Vine how unreasonable Tina was to work with. For someone being paid for her responsibilities as a TA, she certainly wasn't very approachable. "Why did you schedule a date when you knew you had a fitting tonight?" I asked.

She glowered at me. "What am I trying on today?"

I held up the dress I'd made at Christmas. Even though I had made it according to my measurements, Tina would have to wear it in the show.

"Here." I tossed her the dress. She stalked to the corner and slipped behind the decorative accordion room divider—the studio's makeshift dressing room.

As Tina removed her clothes, she flipped them over the top of the divider. "Did you even *look* at the measurements in the syllabus," she grumbled.

"Yes," I sighed.

"Then you might want to brush up on your measurement skills because this dress does *not* fit."

She stepped out from behind the divider and it took all my strength not to erupt into a fit of laughter. I literally bit my tongue. Tina was taller than me (most people were), but where the dress fell just above mid-thigh on me, it fell about mid-buttocks on Tina. It looked ridiculous.

"I am *not* wearing this dress," she said.

While possible solutions to the problem ran through my head, I also pondered why Tina felt the need to overemphasize at least one word in every sentence she spoke.

"Relax. I'll fix the dress." I picked up my measuring tape from the table and measured from the hem of the dress to Jillian's mid-thigh. The dress was a good five inches short. Damn. I would have to alter my design to fix this problem, and I didn't have time for this kind of setback. "You can take it off," I said, folding my measuring tape.

She eyed me balefully. "Are we finished?"

"Yes." I nodded.

"Thank *God*," Tina said.

Tina ran back behind the divider and changed back into her own clothes faster than she'd got into my dress. She tossed the dress in my direction. "Good luck with this piece of crap," she said, grabbing her purse and walking toward the door.

"Thanks for all your valuable help. I really appreciate it." Little did Tina know, I used to live with someone who spewed vitriol. A younger, more impressionable me would have cowered under a table the second Tina opened her mouth, but I wasn't that scared little girl anymore. Griffin was proud of me. So were Sarah and Chandra. I had an Army of Proud behind me, but most important of all...*I* was proud of me.

***

I locked up the studio and stepped outside. A warm breeze tossed my red-streaked hair into my face. I brushed it out of my eyes and walked briskly to Victor, listening to Griffin's voice streaming through my earbuds.

Mine Shaft's first LP, *Buried*, had skyrocketed to the top of the indie charts within a week. Like any fangirl, I'd downloaded the album the day it was released, and I hadn't stopped listening to it since. Even though we couldn't be together, I still had the benefit of hearing his voice whenever I wanted. Or needed.

"About Time", my song, filtered through the tiny speakers as I walked through the deserted quad on my way back to the dorm.

I unlocked my door and pushed it open. "Hey, Sarah," I said, dropping my bags in front of my closet.

"Hey. How was Modelzilla?" she asked, looking up from the stack of photos on her bed.

I dropped on my bed and groaned. "Oh, so pleasant...as she stomps through my city of dreams leaving nothing but destruction in her wake," I said sarcastically.

"Nice," she crooned.

I looked over at her and asked, "How's your project coming?"

"I'm getting there. I've decided that my feature will be the Spring Showcase. I'm going to chronicle several designers as they work their way to the big day. So, I was thinking." She pushed the snapshots to the side and stood up, batting her long eyelashes at me. "Would you and Chandra mind if I hung around while you worked? I need tons of photos."

I sat up and smiled. "I think that's a great idea. We don't get to see each other enough as it is. I'd love to have you around, and I'm sure Chandra wouldn't mind."

"Really?" she smiled hesitantly.

"Of course," I reassured her.

"You know," she shrugged, "some designers like their stuff to remain a secret until the big reveal on the catwalk. I didn't want to pry or anything."

"Nonsense. You're welcome in the studio any time. My designs are by no means 'top secret.'"

"Awesome." She smiled and bounced back over to her bed. "What are your plans tonight? Want to get some dinner?"

"I'd love to, but unfortunately Modelzilla happens to be very tall and my dress looks like a shirt on her. I have some serious alterations to work on." I cringed.

I collapsed back onto my bed, trying to locate some untapped reservoir of energy. I needed it; those aforementioned alterations were as daunting as hell. Right as my eyes closed, a muffled Mine Shaft song began to play. I was across the room in an instant, pulling my phone out of my purse.

"I'm going over to Brandon's. I'll be back in a little bit." Sarah said, slipping on her shoes. She picked up her keys and purse. "Tell

Griffin I said hi." She winked at me and was out the door as I accepted the call.

"Hey, Griff!" I said breathlessly. It'd been a damn long week since we'd last talked.

"Hey, Bean!" he shouted. I could hear a punk band playing in the background. "Ahh, it's good to hear your voice. God, I needed that."

My heart skipped a couple of beats. "Sorry, I don't know what that's like," I teased. "I get to hear your voice whenever I want."

He let out a short chuckle. "You keep talking like that, and I'm going make you record me an album."

I laughed. "Ha! I don't think so!"

"It's nice to hear you laugh."

"I miss you, Griff," I said, getting serious. "Would you send me a picture of the show?" I felt like I was missing so much.

"Sorry, Bean…I…didn't…What did…say?"

The line was breaking up. All I could hear was static. "Send me a picture!" I shouted.

"A picture?" he yelled.

"Yes!"

"I'll have one of the roadies take one while I'm on stage. I'll send it after the show."

I smiled, glad that he'd heard me. "Thanks. I'm so proud of you, Griffin."

"I'm proud of you too, Bean. Look, the opening act is finishing up. I gotta go. I love you, Jillian."

"Griff," I said loudly. I didn't want him to hang up yet. "Be careful flying back tonight." It made me sick that he was taking a flight to his next tour stop in Texas.

"I'll call you before I board, and the second I land." He promised. "I love you, Jillibean. I gotta go."

"I love you, too, Griffin."

He clicked his line off just as the announcer shouted "Mine Shaft!" over the PA system. I heard the crowd roar and then nothing. Silence. He was gone.

Chapter Twenty-Nine

The second Chandra opened her door, I unleashed all of my pent-up fury. I threw my messenger bag on her bed and screamed, pulling fistfuls of my purple hair. "Ugh! I fucking HATE her! She's horrible!"

Chandra stood back, not accustomed to seeing me in freak-out mode. "Whoa, calm down. What happened?"

"Tina happened…again." I paced.

"What happened now?" she asked, sitting on her bed.

"She had a fitting two weeks ago. I took her measurements and altered the shit out of my designs. They don't even look like my original sketches anymore. Today, we had another fitting and none of the clothes fit right."

"Have you talked to Vine?" Chandra asked.

"It's too late now. The show's only a month away." I griped. "It's my own damn fault. I should have talked to Vine and gotten a different model." I finally tired of pacing and sat beside Chandra on her bed.

"I'm sure the show will be fine." Chandra patted my back reassuringly. "Tina won't do anything to put her reputation on the line in front of Vine. She'll play nice when she's being watched. I'm sure of it."

I admired Chandra's confidence. I just wished I had some of my own. I turned and looked at her. "I hope you're right."

"Hey, guess what?" Chandra said, getting up.

"What?" I shifted my bag to the floor and stretched out, making myself comfortable. Over the last few weeks, I had spent more time at Chandra's than in my own room. Sarah worked on her project or was with Brandon most of the time. I barely saw her anymore. Chandra and I kept each other company during marathon work sessions. With the show only four weeks away, things were getting crazy…for everyone.

"My mom found a job!" Chandra announced.

I sprang to my feet and gave her a big hug. "Chandra, that's awesome!"

"Yeah, it is. She's working at a doctor's office as a receptionist. She has benefits for the first time in her life. But do you know what she's most excited about?" I could see tears welling up in her eyes.

I shook my head. "No, what?"

"She gets to sit."

"Sit?" That seemed like an odd thing to be excited about.

"My mom's been a waitress for twenty years. She's worked on her feet for twenty, long years. My mom gets to sit down at her new job." Chandra's love for her mother was evident in the way she spoke of her.

I got up from the bed and gave her a hug. "I'm so happy for her," I said.

Pulling away, Chandra smiled at me and said, "Thanks. She's going to be okay now." I could hear the relief in her voice. "Hey," she squealed. "I almost forgot. I've got a surprise for you."

"A surprise?" I asked, puzzled.

"Yeah. It's actually why I asked you to meet here instead of the studio." She pulled her computer out of its sleeve and set it on her desk.

"What is it?" I walked over to stand beside her.

She looked over her shoulder and smiled. "Griffin has a concert tonight, right?"

"Yeah," I nodded.

"They tweeted a link to a live feed of the concert."

I remembered reading that in one of the e-mails Griffin sent me. "I totally forgot they were doing that," I said.

"If I can find the link, we'll be able to watch the concert," she said, scrolling through her Twitter feed. "Here it is." She clicked on it, and a new tab opened in the web browser. Mine Shaft's YouTube channel opened. The feed took a minute or two to load, taxing the dorm's shitty Wi-Fi capabilities, but once enough of the feed buffered, a grainy image of Griffin, Thor, Adam, and Pauly filled the tiny box.

Chandra clicked on the full screen button and filtered the sound through an external speaker. The enlarged image was even grainier, making the four members of Mine Shaft completely indistinguishable from each other, but I didn't care. Griffin was on a stage in Kansas City, Missouri, giving a concert to hundreds of people, and now I was a part of that concert, too. His voice came through Chandra's speakers loud and clear.

"This is awesome," I said, watching the screen. "Thanks, Chandra." I looked at her and smiled.

"You're welcome. But we still have to work." She pointed a finger in my direction.

"Party pooper." I stuck out my bottom lip in protest.

"Yep." She smiled and threw a folded, half-sewn skirt in my face as she turned up the music.

* * *

After my draping class let out, I stopped by the coffee shop to load up on the three C's: coffee, chocolate, and carbs. Chandra and I had planned an all-nighter, and we were determined to finish our last pieces if it killed us.

I pulled open the door to the shop and my phone played Griffin's signature ring tone—"About Time". Griffin's tour had ended two weeks ago and he was enjoying some well-deserved time off. I pulled my phone from my pocket, sliding my finger across the screen. "Hey, Griff," I answered.

"Hey, Bean. What are you doing?" He was quiet. Something was on his mind…probably a new song.

"I'm heading into the coffee shop. Is everything okay?" I asked.

"Yeah. I'm working on a new song, and I got stuck." After being on the road for over a month, Griffin's usually smooth, deep voice was gruff and scratchy from overuse. No matter what his voice sounded like, it still sent chills down my spine and melted my insides.

"Does your new song have a title?" I asked.

"Uh-uh," he answered. "How many days until you're home?"

"Who says I'm counting?" I teased, walking over to a table so I would be out of the way.

"I know you're counting." Griffin paused for a moment before he spoke again. "I need to kiss you so fucking bad it hurts." I could hear the pain in his voice.

I would give anything to feel his lips on mine, too. "Twenty-one days," I sighed.

"Jesus," he cursed. Or was that the beginning of a silent prayer? I couldn't tell. "Be prepared, Bean," he rasped. "I fully intend on holding you hostage when you get home."

Desire pooled low in my abdomen. This was going to be the longest twenty-one days of my life. "How am I supposed to get any work done tonight? All I can think about is your hands on me."

"Just my hands?" he groaned.

His tired voice rumbled deep in his throat. It sounded so fucking hot. "Oh, no," I crooned. "I want every part of you." *Dear Lord, did I want him.*

"Anytime, Bean," he teased "I'm all yours."

"Promise?" I asked.

"For-fucking-ever," he growled.

* * *

After I hung up with Griffin, I had to take a minute to compose myself before I got up to order. I took a couple of deep breaths in, then out. I smoothed my hair back and stood up, shaking off the reaction Griffin's words had elicited from my body.

I walked to the counter and was greeted by a perky barista. "Good evening. May I take your order?" she sang.

I took another breath, still feeling Griffin's voice resonating in my ear. I exhaled and gave her my order. "I need five extra-large espressos—double shots in each, please. I will also take two brownies, two blueberry muffins, four chocolate chip cookies, and four sugar cookies. And these, too." I laid four packages of M&M's down on the counter. The barista stared at me like I'd just ordered a side of diabetes with my purchase. "It's going to be a late night," I added.

"Apparently so," she remarked, ringing in my order. I handed over my card and she ran it through. "I'll get your bakery items. Your drinks will be ready down there." She returned my card and busied herself, gathering my order.

"Thanks." I stepped aside, giving the next customer room.

The barista loaded my drinks into a tray and packaged my food items into a bag. Balancing the large order, I was glad the coffee shop wasn't that far from the studio.

"Are you going to make it?" she asked before I stepped out the door.

"I'm going to find out." I smiled wearily. "Thanks for your help." I pushed the door open with my hip, balancing everything precariously.

Chandra was waiting for me outside of the studio. She helped alleviate some of the load and took the coffees off my chest. Literally. "Thanks," I said, drawing in a huge gulp of air. I hadn't attempted to breathe the whole way over, fearing I'd upset something and spill it all over the ground, or me.

"You should have told me you were going. I would have met you there," she scolded.

"Ah, it's okay. I went on a whim. We're not leaving until we're done." I needed to close this year out and get home.

"You got the three C's?" She asked, peeking in the bag.

"And then some," I added, shrugging my jacket off. "Let's get to work."

I docked my phone onto my portable speaker, grabbed an espresso from the tray, and cranked the music.

Chandra rolled two dress forms over to our work stations, and I grabbed two sewing machines. We pulled out the last of our pieces and got to work. Mine Shaft had become our music of choice. I was glad Chandra was a fan and my obsession didn't bother her.

By the time I'd finished my second, extra-large cup of espresso, the sewing machine I used could be classified as a dangerous tool. I nicked my finger at least four different times swapping different gauge needles in and out of the needle bar. Each time my finger bled, I stared at the red bead. I waited for the rush of endorphins but for once, they never came.

"Hey workaholics, I brought dinner!" Sarah shouted from the doorway. In her hands she carried takeout from Baja's.

"Sarah! I could kiss you!" I shouted. I pushed away from the machine and stood up, stretching my back.

"Seriously," Chandra agreed. She stood up and stretched, too.

"Bring it on, girlies!" Sarah puckered her lips and made kissy noises.

"No offense, but I'm making out with this," I said, reaching into the bag and pulling out a burrito.

"You two crack me up." Chandra laughed and bit off a huge bite of her burrito.

"Ugh, this is so good," I moaned.

"Mmm. So good," Chandra agreed.

"Aren't you eating, Sarah?" I asked, wiping away the string of cheese that hung from my chin.

"Brandon and I ate at Baja's. I got you two carry-outs." Sarah walked around the studio, camera in hand. Occasionally she'd snap a shot of some material spread out on a table or a partially draped dress form. The way she carried herself, she resembled a cat stalking its prey. Sarah's claws were her camera, and her prey, the perfect shot.

"I don't know if I actually *ate* that burrito or if I just inhaled it." I wiped my mouth again and crumpled up the greasy burrito wrapper, tossing it in the garbage. "Thanks, Sarah. I needed that."

"Sure thing." Sarah looked over the top of her camera and smiled. "How much longer do you ladies plan on staying?"

"Until we're finished," Chandra and I answered in unison.

After we cleaned up our dinner mess, I cranked the music. Chandra went to her machine, I returned to mine, and Sarah documented our progress digitally. We were a rather reserved bunch, very different from a Friday night frat or house party.

As I fed the denim of my soon-to-be jeans through the sewing machine, I wondered if Griffin was making any progress on his new song.

"Oh, turn it up!" Chandra shouted.

I was just about to slide my chair over to the speaker but Sarah beat me. "This is my favorite Mine Shaft song!" Chandra said enthusiastically.

The heavy, upbeat tempo of Adam's drumbeat pulled at my feet, and I couldn't resist the urge to dance. "Buried" always had that effect on me. I stood up from the rolling chair and danced over to Chandra. I grabbed her hands and pulled her up, too. We met Sarah in the middle of the room and had our own impromptu party.

Each time Griffin strummed his bass, I'd throw my hip into Sarah or Chandra, flinging my hair around wildly. I was just about to toss my hip in the other direction, anticipating Griffin's next chord, but it never came. The music stopped.

We froze.

My generic ringtone sounded through the studio. This was a ringtone I didn't have assigned to anyone. "Who'd be calling at this hour?" I said. My eyes automatically went to the clock. It was 10:30 p.m.

I tiptoed toward the speaker where my phone was docked as if I expected it to bite. Every horror movie I'd ever seen began this way. Three college females, alone, having a good time…then bam: cue psycho killer.

I slowly reached for the phone, cringing as I pulled it from the dock. I pressed the answer button and held it to my ear. "Hello?" I whispered. Chandra and Sarah inched closer to each other, ready to run when I gave the signal.

"Oh," I exhaled, relieved that it was only Ren.

I listened to her frantic voice at the other end of the line…then I fell.

Sarah and Chandra were at my side in a second, but all I could hear was Ren's voice, "Did you hear me, Jillian?" she asked.

Her words hurt. I didn't want to listen to anymore. "Uh-huh," I croaked.

"Jillian, you have to get here," Ren commanded through heavy sobs.

"Okay," I answered robotically.

Then the line went dead.

Griffin's next bass chord picked up right where it had left off, followed by his booming voice. I stared at my phone, at the picture of Mine Shaft's album cover displayed on the screen. I couldn't stop the tears now…not with Griffin's voice…in my hand.

Sarah grabbed the phone and stopped the music. "Jillian! What's wrong?" she shouted, hovering over me.

"Jillian?" Chandra brushed my hair back.

Seconds ago, his voice had filled this whole studio. With one click of a button, he was silenced. I had to get to him. He needed me. "I have to go." I sucked up my tears and pushed off the ground with determined strength.

"Jillian. What's going on? Where do you have to go?" Chandra asked.

I turned around and looked at both of my friends. "Griffin was in an accident." I forced the words out. "The roads were wet and he lost control of his bike." The only thing that gave me any hope was the fact that he'd worn his helmet.

"He's going to be okay, though, right?" Sarah's voice shook, too.

"The paramedics were loading him into the ambulance while she was on the phone with me. That's all she knew." My heart was beating so hard, I feared it might stop.

"Oh, Jillian." Chandra came closer, ready to hug me. I took a step back. If they hugged me, I'd fall apart for good.

I shook my head. "I'm sorry. I have to go. I need to get there." I searched around frantically, not knowing what to take, or where to go. I felt lost.

"Go," Chandra demanded. "I'll clean up here. Sarah, you take her back to the dorm and help her pack."

"Got it. Come on, Jillian." Sarah grabbed my hand and pulled me toward the door.

Sarah and I ran back to Victor. The whole way, she formulated a plan to get me home to Griffin. "When we get back to the room, you pack whatever essentials you need. I'll book your flight."

Flight. I stopped dead in my tracks.

It hadn't even dawned on me that the quickest way to Griffin was by plane. I couldn't drive. That would take too long. I'd have to board an actual airplane.

Sarah turned around and saw that I wasn't moving. She backpedaled and grabbed both of my shoulders, forcing me to look at her. "Jillian, I know what you're thinking, but it's the only way."

I stared into her eyes. Since Ren's call, a high-pitched buzz had droned in my ears like a swarm of hornets. But Sarah's words muted the noise, and I could think clearly. Griffin needed me. "I know," I whispered. I'd get on that plane for him. "Let's go," I said, steeling my resolve.

***

Within twenty minutes Sarah had booked my flight, and I had my carry-on filled. "I'll drive. I texted Chandra; we'll pick her up outside the studio and get you to the airport." Sarah ticked off everything we needed to accomplish in order to get me home to the St. Louis area. "Ready?" she asked, pulling open the door.

I nodded, pulling my suitcase behind me. Quietly, Sarah and I took the staircase on our way down to the parking lot. Reaching the bottom, I pushed the crash bar on the heavy steel door and froze. "Wait!"

"What?" Sarah replied, startled.

"I forgot something." I dropped my hands and the heavy door

slammed shut. Frantically, I searched my pockets and turned to Sarah. "I don't have my keys!"

"Here, take mine." She pushed her dorm keys into my hand. "I'll put your suitcase in the car."

"Thanks." I sighed, taking off back up the stairs.

Racing down the hall, I skidded to a halt at my door, slid the key into the lock, and threw the door open. I ran to my desk and pulled the two picture frames off the shelf, hugging them to my chest. "I'm ready now."

Once I made it to the parking lot, Sarah had the car pulled up to the curb, ready for me to climb inside. "Thanks," I croaked. My hands shook as I pulled the door closed. I was so scared.

"Jillian, he's going to be okay." I knew she was trying to be reassuring, but it wasn't helping.

"But what if he's not?" I turned and looked at her profile.

She glanced at me. "He will. You have to keep thinking that."

I nodded, forcing myself not to think the worst. I held the picture frames tightly, the one of Griffin and me on top. My finger traced the word *Promise* over and over again.

Chapter Thirty

Sarah pushed the speed limit as we sailed down I-95 toward the airport. I stared out the window even though the blackened sky swallowed the landscape. Inside my head, the same question looped endlessly: *What if?*

"Jillian," Sarah said, looking over at me. "Chandra and I won't be able to go with you past security." She continued to walk me through the steps I'd need to complete in order to get on my flight. "We'll help you get your boarding pass when we get there. Your flight takes off at 6:00 p.m. You'll arrive in St. Louis at 10:43 p.m."

I stared at her, nodding my head. "That's so far away," I whispered.

"I know, but that's the earliest flight they had." She grabbed my hand and squeezed.

Chandra reached around from the backseat and rubbed my shoulder. They both tried to comfort me the best they could.

My phone rang again, and I quickly fished it out of my purse.

Ren's number lit up the display screen. "Hello?" My voice was frantic; I was craving information.

"Jillian." Ren breathed heavily.

"What's going on? How is he?" Questions tumbled from my mouth faster than she could answer.

"He's in surgery right now."

"Surgery? Why? What's wrong?" I shouted. Sarah's eyes darted from the road to my face as she tried to fill in the missing pieces of the conversation.

"I still don't know any more than I did the last time we spoke. I haven't talked to anyone. But—"

"Call me as soon as you know anything," I demanded, cutting her off before she finished her sentence.

"I will, Jillian. Are you on your way?" she asked.

"Mm-hm. The earliest flight I could get leaves in two hours, but I'm coming."

"He's going to make it. He's going to be all right," she chanted. I didn't know if Ren was trying to comfort herself or me. *Did it really matter?* At this point, any consolations were meant for the both of us.

"He is," I affirmed. "Ren?" My voice quivered. "If you see him before I get there, tell him I'm on my way, and that I love him."

Ren inhaled a sob. "I will. See you soon."

"Soon." I disconnected the call and dropped my hands to my lap.

"What did she say?" Sarah asked.

"He's in surgery, but she doesn't know why. The doctor hasn't been out to talk with her yet. That's all she knows."

"That's good, then. Surgery, I mean. He's hanging in there. He's still alive." Sarah rambled as she turned the car onto the exit for the airport.

Chandra patted my shoulder. "I agree with Sarah. He's fighting for you, Jillian."

I wanted to believe them, but the *what ifs* were louder than their words of comfort.

The airport was deserted. Sarah, Chandra, and I walked right up to the ticket counter and got my boarding pass. As we walked the short distance between the ticket counter and the security line, my stomach knotted as realization set in—I was about to board a plane. But knowing Griffin lay unconscious on an operating table spurred me onward.

I could do this. For him.

"This is as far as we can go," Chandra said, stopping at the security barriers. Chandra didn't hesitate to pull me into a warm hug. "He's going to be all right," she whispered in my ear. I wanted to believe her. "Call us when you know more."

I pulled away, looking into her dark eyes. "I will." I nodded.

She released me and Sarah immediately jumped in her place. Her arms were around me instantly. "What if…he…doesn't…?" I stuttered.

"Shhh," she whispered in my ear. Her hand ran over the back of my head, trying to soothe away my fear. "You get on that plane. Get to him. And when you see him…you tell him that *you* got on a plane for him. He'll wake up from shock alone."

A smile tried to break through my fear, but it didn't quite make it. "I love you, Sarah."

"I love you too, Jillian." She squeezed me tight before I moved toward the scary, empty security line…alone.

Security didn't prove to be as daunting as I'd expected, at least not this late at night. I slipped my flip-flops back onto my feet and grabbed my belongings from the conveyer belt.

I found the gate for my flight easily and plopped down in a seat near a window. A couple of planes were docked at nearby gates. I stared at them, feeling my pulse quicken with each passing second. Two hours separated me and my inaugural flight. Six hours separated me from Griffin.

The gate was quiet. Eerily quiet. The only sign of life I'd seen since I'd sat down was a maintenance person polishing the tile. For the next two hours my mind raced from one terrible scenario to the next. Stretching out across several seats, I closed my eyes and forced myself to picture Griffin's smile...the feel of his hand in mine...the sound of his voice whispering in my ear...any positive memories I could cling to.

"We are now boarding all passengers for Delta Air Lines Flight 1619 to St. Louis."

The voice on the PA system boomed, and I started at the sound. I hurriedly checked my boarding pass for my flight number. The numbers 0307 were printed at the top of the ticket. My flight was now boarding.

I dug my phone out and sent Ren a quick text: *I'm boarding the plane now. If you have any info, text me. I'll check my messages the second I land.*

Before I powered my phone down for the next four hours, I had one more text to send. I found Griffin's name and typed, *I love you. I'm coming home.*

* * *

The hospital doors parted, allowing me entrance. I lugged my suitcase behind me, searching the waiting room for Ren or Griffin's
parents. My eyes were so tired and sore from sleep deprivation and
crying they barely functioned.

"Jillian! Over here," Ren called from the very back of the room.

I summoned whatever energy I had left and ran to her. She
held her arms open wide and I fell into them. Ren's arms
wrapped around me, and we both held squeezed tightly, praying
the other had a reserve of strength to share. "You made it," she
exhaled.

I pulled back; I needed to see her face. She looked beaten, tired,
and lost. "How is he?" I asked.

"I don't know." She shook her head. She brought her hand up to
her mouth and chewed on her thumbnail. "He's still in surgery."

"Still?" I whined. "How long has he been in there?"

"It's going on seven hours now," she choked. "Let's sit down."
Ren pulled me over to an empty chair and I collapsed. "You look
tired. Why don't you try to get some rest?" She offered.

I stared into her brown eyes. "No, I can't sleep. Not until we
hear something." I shook my head defiantly. "Where are your mom
and dad?" I asked.

"They're coming. They were in Phoenix, remember?" She continued to bite at her thumb, a nervous habit.

Shit, I'd forgotten they'd left after Christmas. "When are they
supposed to get in?"

"I don't know. Mom said she'd call me the second they landed."

I sat back in the chair feeling completely useless. There was
nothing I could do now but wait. I looked at Ren again. "Do you
know what happened?" I asked.

"When I talked to the paramedics, they said another motorist called in the accident when they came upon it. No one knows for sure." Ren stopped, getting choked up. I put my arm around her. She wiped her eyes and steeled her will to finish the story. "The only thing the paramedics could deduce from the scene was that Griffin had lost control of his bike on the wet pavement. They found him lying five feet away from the motorcycle."

My hand covered my mouth. "But he was wearing his helmet, right?"

Ren nodded. She'd told me earlier that Griffin had worn the helmet, but I just needed to hear it again. I breathed a sigh of relief. I was so glad I hadn't backed down about that damn thing.

Ren and I sat next to each other for a while, but eventually fatigue took over, and I needed to lie down. Like I had at the airport, I stretched my body across several chairs.

Ren sat on the floor with her back against the wall. Her eyes were closed, but I knew she wasn't asleep. Every time the automatic doors opened, her eyelids shot up, anticipating the arrival of her parents, or word from the doctor.

"Ren," I whispered. "Why do you think it's taking so long?"

"I don't know," she answered, sounding defeated.

There was really nothing more to talk about. All we could do was "hurry up and wait." I popped in my earbuds, craving Griffin's voice. I scrolled through my songs, looking for one in particular—*my* song—"About Time". I set it on repeat and closed my heavy eyelids. Sleep finally pulled me under.

* * *

"Jillian. Wake up, Jillian," a quiet voice said.

"Hmm?" I shifted and lost my balance, falling off the seats. "Ouch!" I cried out, blinking my eyes open. "Damn, that hurt." I rubbed my shoulder and bit my tongue, staving off the other curse words that threatened to spill out.

"Jillian," Mrs. Daniels and Ren both exclaimed "Are you all right?" Mrs. Daniels was crouched down beside me with a shocked expression on her face. Ren stood beside her.

"Mrs. Daniels?" I asked, confused and disoriented.

Her arms went around my back, trying to help me off the floor. Ren tried to help us both up. "You took a nasty spill off those chairs. Are you all right?" Mrs. Daniels asked.

I stood up and looked at the chairs.

Hospital.

I was still at the hospital. Griffin.

My brain played connect-the-dots as it regained clarity. "Is he okay?" I prayed I hadn't missed any news.

Mrs. Daniels shook her head, pulling me into a hug. She rocked me in her arms as she spoke. "No word yet. Bill went to track down someone."

Bill. Griffin's dad. He'd find some answers. After being a high school football coach for twenty-five years, he'd mastered the art of intimidation.

"Are you sure you're okay, Jillian?" Ren asked.

I nodded my head and pulled out of Mrs. Daniels's embrace. "I'm fine."

Ren flashed a weak smile and said, "I'm going to go sit back down. You okay, Ma?" Ren sounded like Griffin when she called her mother by that name. Griffin always called her that.

"I'm good." She patted her daughter's hand.

Mrs. Daniels and I sat down while Ren went back to her spot on the floor. "When did you get here?" I asked.

"Just a few minutes ago," she sighed. "How long have you been here?"

"I don't know." My heart was racing again, and I couldn't slow it down. "I don't know what time it is. I don't know how long I've been here. I don't know anything." I was so overwhelmed.

"I know you're scared, sweetie. We all are." She wrapped her arm around my shoulder, comforting me like a mom. "But, if I know my son," she went on, "you're the only person that's keeping him alive right now."

"Me?" My voice cracked.

She offered me a reassuring smile. "Absolutely," she said confidently. "That boy loves you something fierce. Always has."

I lay my head on her shoulder and said, "I love him, too."

"I always knew you did." She hugged me tightly, and I felt safe in her arms. But the reality of the situation weighed on my heart. "What if—"

"Nonsense," she interrupted. "He's going to pull out of this. I know my son." Her answer was emphatic. "He's strong. He loves you. He loves us. He's going to make it."

Mrs. Daniels was right; Griffin's strength did come from his unconditional love. He had never given up on me. I wouldn't give up on him now. The images of Griffin's tattoos popped into my head—*Always hopes. Always perseveres.*

I'll hope. I'll persevere.

Chapter Thirty-One

Mr. Daniels came into the waiting room and shook his head. "All these smartass doctors and none of them know a goddamned thing," he growled.

I could tell he'd been reading someone the riot act; his red face and labored breathing were telltale signs of a Bill Daniels ass-chewing.

"Bill," Mrs. Daniels said, her voice thick with concern.

Mr. Daniels lumbered over to his wife and sat down. He put his arm around her and she collapsed against his shoulder. Her brave front had disappeared the second she saw her husband.

"Daddy," Ren cried. She stood up from the floor and ran to his side. He stretched his other arm around Ren and supported both of the women in his life. What was it like for him? He didn't know if his son was alive or dead, yet he still remained the pillar of strength for the Daniels family.

Mrs. Daniels slipped her arm around me and spoke softly, "He knows his family's here for him." I didn't know if she was speaking to us, or if she was trying to vocalize reassurances for her own sake, but regardless of her motivations, I felt stronger knowing I was considered a part of their family.

"Mr. Daniels?"

A white-haired man with a dark tan and a white coat walked into the waiting room. Instantly, the four of us were on our feet.

"Yes, that's me," Mr. Daniels said gruffly, swallowing back his fear.

"You're Griffin Daniels's parents?" the doctor said, looking to Mr. and Mrs. Daniels.

"Yes. Please, is he okay?" Mrs. Daniels stuttered.

"I'm Dr. Adler, Chief Neurosurgeon." He held his hand out for Mr. Daniels to shake. Griffin's dad took the doctor's hand in his firm grip. "Griffin just came out of surgery. He's in recovery now," Dr. Adler announced.

"So he's okay?" Ren asked, holding her breath.

Dr. Adler looked at Ren and said, "He's alive, but not out of the woods."

"What do you mean?" I interjected. "Is he going to be okay?" Impatience permeated my voice. Why couldn't doctors just spit out what they meant?

"Griffin suffered a severe head trauma when he was thrown from his motorcycle. Luckily, he was wearing a helmet; it saved his life."

When I heard those words, I gasped. My insistence had saved his life. Tears stung my eyes and I bit my lip to keep from crying. I tried to focus my attention on what Dr. Adler was saying.

"However, when his body hit the ground the impact was

extreme, and his brain was severely jostled. Blood vessels ruptured, causing swelling to the brain, and surgery was needed to alleviate the pressure. Right now, we have him in a medically induced coma until the swelling goes down. In a few days, we'll gradually reduce the amount of medication he's receiving. Once he's off of the IV, we wait to see if he regains consciousness. Even though the initial brain scans we've taken are promising, we won't know if there is any permanent damage until he wakes up."

I didn't understand most of what Dr. Adler had said. My brain kept sticking on the word "coma." The more Dr. Adler talked, the harder it was to focus my thoughts. All I wanted at this point was to see him. If he knew I was here, he'd be all right. "Can we see him?" I asked.

Dr. Adler looked at me and smiled. "Soon. I'll send a nurse to escort you to his room once he's out of recovery."

"Thanks, Doc," Mr. Daniels said, offering his hand again.

Dr. Adler's lips pulled into a tight smile and he shook Mr. Daniels's hand. "We're doing everything we can," Dr. Adler promised before he turned to leave us to wait again.

"He's going to be fine, girls. He's going to be fine." Mr. Daniels held his hands open wide. Ren and Mrs. Daniels stepped into his mammoth arms, and each woman cried on a shoulder. "Get over here, Jillian. I need all of my girls if I'm going to get through this." Mr. Daniels waved me over.

Tears streamed down my face as I took two big steps and pressed myself against Griffin's dad. I laid my head on his heart and he closed his arms around "his girls." I was sandwiched between Ren and Mrs. Daniels, barely able to breathe, but I didn't care. Griffin was a part of each one of them. Being caught in the middle of his family was like being caught in one of his all-consuming hugs. All of them gave me strength.

* * *

It seemed like Griffin was in recovery forever. A nurse would periodically update us on Griffin's status, but it was always the same: "His vitals are strong." After five hourly visits, a nurse returned with what we all expected to be the usual statement.

"Still no changes?" I asked, having no energy to get up off the floor.

"No, not yet. But..."

The moment she said "but" I lifted my head. "But" was good. "But" was new. "But" was an improvement.

"He's been moved to his room in ICU," she continued. "I'm here to take you up."

That was all I needed to hear. I was off the floor in a hurry. "Yes, let's go," I said urgently.

Griffin's family and I followed the nurse down several corridors and into the ICU. A couple of nurses looked up from their computer screens and gave us tight-lipped smiles as we passed by. When we came to Griffin's door, the nurse stopped and rested her hand on the handle. She turned around with a grim look on her face.

"Before we go in, I have to warn you. He's suffered a lot of injuries. He's got quite a few lacerations and contusions on his face. There's also a significant amount of swelling. The right side of his head has been shaved and bandaged. Try to keep a positive outlook. Talk to him. Touch him. Let him know you're here. That's the best thing you can do for him now." She smiled somberly and pushed the handle down.

Griffin's room was dimly lit. An occasional beep echoed through the silence from the machines monitoring his vitals. I was anxious to see him but scared as hell. Griffin was the strong one; he'd been the one protecting me from all the bad shit. I didn't have a fraction of his strength, and I worried I wouldn't be strong enough.

Silent tears rolled down my cheeks when my eyes finally adjusted to the quiet light. My strong Griffin lay motionless on the bed. His chest rose and fell as the machine attached to him commanded. Despite the nurse's warning, I wasn't prepared to see him like this.

A heavy gauze bandage covered his right cheek, which led right into the thick bandage wrapped around his head. His right eye was black and swollen. Large, overlapping scratches crossed the length of his chin. Most of the damage was to the right side of his body—if I had to guess, it looked like when he'd been thrown from his bike he'd slid across the pavement. Even his right arm was wrapped up tightly.

Mrs. Daniels flew to his left side. She kissed his cheek and nuzzled his face with hers. "Oh, baby," she cried. Her tears left shiny streaks of wetness on his face; I expected him to wipe them away and groan over his mother's fussing.

He didn't.

Her tears remained on his cheeks.

Ren stood behind her mom and Mr. Daniels pulled up a chair to his son's right side. I suddenly didn't feel like I belonged. Where did I fit in to this picture? There was no room for me. I shuffled back toward the wall; its strength held me up.

"Jillian, get over here," Mr. Daniels commanded, holding his hand out to me. He patted the bed, calling me over.

I shuffled from the shadowed wall toward Griffin.

"That's it," Mr. Daniels coaxed. "Let him know you're here. He needs his Jillibean right now."

Once I was within Mr. Daniels's grasp, he planted me on the edge of Griffin's bed. "If anybody can pull him through this, it's you."

I turned my head and stared at Griffin. The tips of his fingers weren't covered by gauze, and begged to be held. The second my fingers came into contact with his, a jolt of electricity surged between us. I felt it so acutely I knew he had to have, too. I grabbed his hand, and there was no way in hell I was letting go. His hand wasn't enough. I needed to hold him. Transfer my strength to him somehow.

I didn't care that his family was in the room. I turned on my side and slipped my body right next to his, stretching out on the bed next to him. Mrs. Daniels was still bent over Griffin's left side in a silent vigil. Bill rested his hand on my shoulder, keeping me from rolling off the bed, and Ren pulled up a chair at the foot of Griffin's bed. None of us spoke.

I prayed. Over and over and over again, I prayed, "Dear Lord, please…"

I closed my eyes and breathed him in. He smelled sterile, like the hospital, but somewhere beneath the antiseptic tang was him…my Griffin…like wind and leather. Yep, beneath all the hospital garb, my Griffin was still there.

Moments later a nurse came to the door. "I'm sorry, but it's time to leave. Mr. Daniels needs his rest," she said quietly, waiting for us to follow her directive.

My eyes opened at her command. I had no intention of removing myself from his side. "I'm not leaving," I said.

"Candace, Ren, let's give Jillian and Griffin a minute," Bill said quietly.

Mrs. Daniels looked from Griffin to me, our gazes connecting. She smiled and kissed his cheek again. "Rest now, sweet boy. Hang in there." Mrs. Daniels stood and ran her hand down his cheek. She turned her eyes to me again. "It's been a long time in the making; it's good to see you two like this. He's waited a long time for you, Jillian. He'll come back."

Mrs. Daniels stepped away, and Ren moved over and kissed her brother's cheek. "Take care of him, Jillian," Ren whispered.

I nodded. "I will."

"Miss, visiting hours are over," the nurse insisted. Even though I couldn't see her, I knew she was talking to me.

"Ma'am," I heard Mr. Daniels say. "I'd really like her to stay with my son. Trust me; she's better than any medicine you can give him."

"Sir, I really can't allow that," she said, annoyed.

"I don't want him alone. She stays." Mr. Daniels's voice instantly transitioned to football coach mode.

"Yes, sir," she acquiesced. She stepped around the bed and glared at me, hating that I'd won the battle. "Miss, I am going to need you to stand up for a moment. I need to check his dressings."

Before I lowered my feet to the ground, I glanced at her name tag: Sheila. Sheila needed to work on her bedside manner. As slowly as I could, I slid from the bed. Sheila gave me a stiff smile and smoothed the wrinkles my body had left on the sheets. I sat down in the chair Mr. Daniels had vacated and waited for Sheila to finish.

"We'll be in the waiting room, Jillian," Mr. Daniels said, squeezing my shoulder.

"I'll come get you if anything changes." I put my hand on top of his and looked over my shoulder.

Mrs. Daniels, Ren, and Mr. Daniels left the room. Now it was just me, Griffin, and the ever-pleasant Nurse Sheila. She flitted around the room checking monitors, copying numbers onto Griffin's chart, and double- and triple-checking his dressings. When she felt she'd poked and prodded him sufficiently, she left.

Now we were finally alone.

I reclaimed my perch on the bed, gently lifting his arm so I could snuggle up next to him. I rested my head on his chest, listening to the strong, steady beat of his heart. Tears slid down my cheeks and seeped into Griffin's hospital gown.

I tilted my head up so I could look at him. "Hey, Griff," I said, brushing my fingers over the few strands of hair that weren't bandaged. "You won't believe how I got here." I let my fingers trail down his cheek, over the bruises and scratches. "I flew. I got on a plane, and I made it here…to you." A despondent laugh escaped my mouth. I watched his face intently, hoping that the monumental fear I'd overcome would be enough to wake him up. But it wasn't.

I cupped his bristly chin in my hand and prayed. "Dear God, please let him be okay. *Please*!" I begged. Sobs wracked my body. I tried to hold them inside, but I didn't have the strength. "Griffin

Daniels, you can't do this to me!" I clung to him, burying my face in the hollow of his neck, breathing him in. The sterile odor of the operating room lingered his skin, making my stomach roll. I pulled back, expecting him to thwart my efforts and hold me to his chest. He didn't do that this time. This time I was on my own to find comfort.

"I need you, Griffin." I lay my head back down on his chest, needing the comfort of his heartbeat. "What about your promise? What about our happy future together?" I shifted, getting a better look at his face. "You've never broken your promises to me, Griffin. Don't you dare start now."

Chapter Thirty-Two

*G*riffin?" Even though my eyes were open I still couldn't figure out where I was. "Griffin?" I called again, a little louder this time. My throat hurt.

"Shhh, Bean. I'm here." I felt a warm hand brush over mine.

Griffin's head pulled away from the shadows and he leaned forward, hovering close to my face. A moment ago I hadn't been able to feel anything, but now I did. His strong fingers latched onto my hand and refused to let go.

"Where am I?" I asked groggily. I felt so weak.

"The hospital," he answered softly.

I tried to sit up, but I couldn't. "Why?"

With his free hand, he brushed my forehead and down the side of my face. "You don't remember?"

I barely shook my head. It was so heavy.

Even in the dimly lit room, Griffin's dark eyes pulled me in, commanded my attention. But for some reason, they glistened with sad-

ness. Their usually dark chocolate warmth was gone, completely devoured by sorrow and worry.

"Jillibean." He whispered my nickname reverently, like a prayer. "I almost lost you."

"Huh?" My voice caught in my throat.

Griffin let go of my hand, moving his fingers up my arm. I felt safe and secure with his fingers connected to me, but then all of a sudden they vanished. I couldn't feel him anymore. I looked down to see why he'd stopped touching me, and that's when I saw that he hadn't. His hand was still anchored to me. But the thick bandages wrapped around my arm, from my shoulder to my elbow, hindered my brain from registering his grounding touch.

I lifted my arm, trying to understand what had happened. Alarm happened. Every memory came flooding back.

The nightmares. The voices. The blade. The release. The blood. Lots of blood. More blood than ever. The crying. The pain. The screaming.

"Griffin," I cried out, begging for him to help me. I knew he would. I knew he'd understand.

"I'm here, Bean." His hand latched back onto mine and squeezed tightly.

"They're too strong," I whimpered. I accepted defeat. The voices had won. I needed help. "I can't stop." I stared at the bandage in horror.

"Jillian, look at me," he commanded.

I turned my face and met his eyes. "It's over, Jillian. I won't let you hurt yourself anymore."

"How do I stop hurting?" I asked.

"What hurts, Jillibean?" He ran his hand over my head. "I'll make it stop."

"Promise?" I whispered.

"If you tell me what hurts, I'll make it stop. Forever."

I believed him. I didn't have the strength not to. I nodded, my eyes growing heavy.

Griffin's thumb drew circles over the back of my hand. "Jillian, I've never been so scared. I thought I was going to lose my best friend." I knew I should say something, ease his sadness and grief, but the heavy weight of sleep pressed close. I tried to stay awake, tried to focus on his moving lips—the words. "I thought I'd never get a chance to say all the things I've wanted to say," he continued.

"I'm so tired, Griff—" Sleep quieted my lips.

"No, Jillian," he said. "I lov—"

Sleep won.

"Sweetie, wake up."

A soft whisper played at my ear, and I stirred. "Hmmm...."

"Jillian, sweetie. Wake up." Mrs. Daniels brushed my hair back and smiled down at me.

"Wha...what time..." I sat up, stretching.

"It's early. About five in the morning."

I looked at Griffin, hoping and wishing for some change. "Anything?" I asked Mrs. Daniels.

"No." Her discouraged sigh hung in the air. "Bill and I talked to the doctor. His surgery went very well and the swelling is subsiding. They're going to start reducing his medication, and hopefully he'll wake up soon." She tried to smile and thought better of it, afraid to let herself hope too much.

"Really?" Fear and excitement bubbled up inside of me at the same time. I feared that hope too, but I knew Griffin didn't. He never gave up hope on me...I wouldn't give up on him.

"Really," she said, patting my shoulder. "Honey, why don't you run home for a little while?" Mrs. Daniels suggested.

"Uh-uh. I'm not leaving him." I shook my head vehemently. I refused to leave his side.

"Sweetie, Dr. Adler's fairly certain that he won't wake up until all the medication is out of his system. You can make a quick trip over to our house, or Griffin's apartment. Clean yourself up, change your clothes; it'll make you feel better." She watered the flowers that sat on the table beside his bed.

I didn't want to hear her. I shook my head, adamant against leaving him.

"Please? You have to take care of yourself. You have to stay strong for him. Go. Get cleaned up," she demanded.

I listened to her plead with me. I looked down at the rumpled clothes I'd worn for two days, and a shower didn't sound half bad. "What if he wakes up and I'm not here?" I asked.

"If I know my son, he won't wake up until you return. He'll wait for you." She winked at me and smiled.

I slid my legs from the bed and stood up. "Okay. I'll hurry." I looked down at him sleeping peacefully. The swelling in his face had gone down and he looked more like himself. I leaned down and whispered in his ear, "I'll be right back, Griff." I placed a soft kiss on his lips. "I LOVE you."

* * *

Mr. and Mrs. Daniels let me borrow their rental car, so I wouldn't have to take a cab back to Griffin's apartment. Being in Griffin's home felt more right than any part of the nightmare I'd lived for the last two days.

I showered in record time and dressed even faster. I pulled clean clothes from my suitcase and twisted my hair into a wet bun. I felt ready to fight; ready to help Griffin fight. I recalled my first couple of sessions with Dr. Hoffman, right after my accident.

Even though I knew I needed help, I wasn't ready to face my past. I was so angry with Griffin every time he drove me to her office. But he took my anger in stride. He ignored the vile words I spat at him, overlooked my childish temper tantrums. He looked me in the eye and said, "You're one hell of a fighter, Jillibean. And I'm going to be here to make sure you keep fighting."

I shook off the memory, with Griffin's voice still echoing in my head. He was a fighter, too. He was going to pull through this.

Before I left, I checked in with Chandra and Sarah. I was sure they were going out of their minds. I pressed Sarah's name on my phone and let it ring.

By the time I got to the bottom of the steps, Sarah answered. "Jillian? Jesus, what's going on? We've been going crazy since you left."

"Is Chandra there?" I asked, noticing the plural.

"Yeah, she's here. We wanted to stay together, in case you called," Sarah informed me.

I pulled a bottle of water from Griffin's refrigerator and grabbed the keys from the counter. "I'm glad you weren't alone," I said.

"How is he?" Sarah asked.

I uncapped the bottle and took a drink, swallowing. "He hasn't come out of the coma yet. We're just waiting."

"Oh." Optimism *whoosh*ed out of her like a deflating balloon.

"Sarah," I said. "Will you put Chandra on?"

"Sure."

I heard the phone being shuffled around, then Chandra's voice. "Jillian?"

"Hey, Chandra. I'm not going to be back before the end of the semester." I said with a sigh.

"I've already taken care of it, Jillian. I was on the phone for most of the day yesterday, but I got a hold of all your professors. They've all agreed to give you an extension to finish your projects and finals."

"What?" I screeched and nearly dropped my water bottle.

"It's all good. Take care of Griffin. Get him better, then you can worry about school," Chandra said.

"What about the Spring Showcase?" I stammered.

"Professor Vine agreed to let me show your line. She said you'd receive a deduction in your grade, but it's better than an incomplete."

"But I'm not finished with that last dress."

"Don't worry about it. I'll finish it." I could hear the insistence in her voice.

"Chandra, I don't know what to say."

"Jillian, we got things covered here." Sarah said, coming back on the line.

"Thank you," was all I could think to say.

*　*　*

I lay beside Griffin, watching the rain bead up on the window. The trees in the parking lot swayed back and forth, tossed by the howling wind. Streaks of lightning flashed across the sky and thunder crashed, but Griffin's room was quiet. After three weeks, the noisy machine that breathed for him had been disconnected. Griffin's body was healing, and he'd mumble things every now and then, but he hadn't regained consciousness. I hated waiting in the quiet—it felt louder than the raging storm outside. Every time a clap of thunder sounded, I'd look at Griffin's face, wanting his eyes to open. When they didn't, I prayed the next clash would be louder...loud enough to wake him up. I was thankful for the storm; it drowned out the silence.

My phone vibrated on the bedside table. I looked away from the window and reached for it, seeing a picture of a well-lit catwalk, and Sarah's name printed at the top of the message.

The Spring Showcase had started.

In the picture, Chandra stood off to the side of the stage as her model walked the catwalk wearing a vanilla-colored, tailored suit. Chandra smiled, but looked nervous.

I quickly sent a text back and told Sarah to keep them coming.

"The show's started, Griff." I held my phone up to his sleeping eyes. "Chandra looks scared to death even though her designs are flawless."

I was curled up next to him, showing him the pictures and updates from both Sarah and Chandra.

You're about to go on, Jill. Chandra texted.

YIKES! I wrote back.

Hey, did I ever tell you how pleasant Tina is? She's a real "Diamond in the Rough." Chandra joked.

I quickly typed back my response. *She's something... but from my experience, it doesn't sparkle... it stinks.*

Chandra responded, *Oh, you're right. I stand corrected. Gotta go. You're up!*

"It's my turn, Griff," I said excitedly. Even though I wasn't physically there, I still felt a little rush of adrenaline.

Sarah sent picture after picture. I felt like I was right in the mix.

Lightning lit up the room as I typed my last text to Chandra. My portion of the show was complete. *Thank you, Chandra.* I silenced my phone and laid it on the table, at peace with that part of my life. Now I just needed peace here. I reached over to the small table, beside Griffin's bed and grabbed the frames he'd given me for my birthday.

Snuggling back down beside him, I stared at my parents' images, running my finger over the smooth glass covering. I wasn't afraid to look at them anymore. Mom had been right…we *were* a part of each other. By keeping their memory stuffed in a drawer for so many years, I'd done the same thing to myself. I'd sealed away my heart, forfeiting any chance at happiness. Dr. Hoffman had once asked me if happiness was worth taking risks for. Looking up at Griffin, still uncertain of what the future held, I knew I'd risk my heart a zillion times over for just a moment of happiness with him.

I smiled, shuffling the frames, placing the one of Griffin and me on top. I traced the etching. I wanted my *promise.*

Over and over again, I ran my finger across those seven letters until my eyes grew heavy. I clutched both frames to my chest, resting them between Griffin and me. The storm outside had passed, and now all I could hear was the light rain pattering on the window. It lulled me to sleep.

* * *

In the middle of the night, I was awakened by a strange movement beside me. At first I thought I was dreaming, but when I heard his voice I gasped. I sat up straight and stared at him. His head tossed side to side. "Griffin?"

"Ugh," he groaned. "Bean?" His voice was weak and raspy.

For just a second I thought my heart had stopped beating. But watching his eyes focus onto me sent it into double time. I clasped my hands over my mouth, unable to speak.

He blinked, searching my face. "Bean?" he said again.

A smile blossomed across my face and I shook my head. "I'm here!" My voice cracked. "I'm right here." I grabbed his hand in mine and squeezed as hard as I could.

"Promise?" He asked in a gravelly voice.

I leaned my forehead on his and whispered, "Forever."

Epilogue

From downstairs came the muted chords of the guitar. Smiling, I hung the last picture on our bedroom wall. With a hammer in one hand and a couple of nails in the other, I backed off the small ladder. It was nice to be home, settled.

The last two months had been difficult and emotionally draining, but once Griffin came home from the hospital, things started to improve. I moved into his apartment and Thor moved out to get a place with Harper. I made a quick trip back east to complete the finals I'd missed, and Griffin took it easy at home, rehabilitating. Now that I'd returned, life was getting back to normal. We had at least a month before I'd have to head back to school.

Stepping off the ladder, I put the hammer and nails on to the night table and pivoted backward. Shuffling through Griffin's strewn clothes, I kicked them into a pile near the door as I caught a glimpse of the picture frames he'd given me for my birthday.

A warm smile consumed my face. Mom, Dad, and a smaller

version of me in one frame, Griffin and a much older me in another—we all smiled from behind the glass. The familiar pang of sadness pinched my heart. There'd never be a day I wouldn't miss my parents, but at least now I could smile through the sadness. Griffin was right; they were my forever…forever in my heart.

Admiring the pictures side by side, I crossed my arms and took a step back, bumping into a solid body. I glanced behind me. Griffin stood there with his arms folded across his chest. "Sorry," I said, not realizing he'd come upstairs.

Loosening his arms, he slid them over my shoulders, towering over me. With my back pressed to his abdomen, he rested his chin atop my head. "You busy?" he asked, the deep murmur resonating against my back.

I closed my eyes, committing this moment to memory…the lingering sensation of his voice still beneath my skin, his warmth, the scent of his masculine body, the oxygen in his lungs, his beating heart…*him*.

I'd never take our time together for granted.

He ran his hands over my bare arms and I sighed at the pleasure of his touch. "Not really." I rested my head against his strong chest.

Griffin pressed his palms to my shoulders and gently spun me around, folding his hands at the small of my back. I lifted my head and he fixed me with a thoughtful gaze. "Already redecorating, huh?"

"Well," I drawled, looking around the cluttered room. "This place could use the help of a good designer."

"Anyone come to mind?" He unlatched his hands, guiding them over the curve of my backside.

I cocked my head and stared at the ceiling, then shrugged, smiling. "Hmm, maybe. I think she prefers clothes to bedrooms, though."

His mouth pulled up into a playful smile, lighting his eyes. "Know what I prefer?"

I shook my head, biting my lip. "Uh-uh."

He leaned down and pressed his mouth to my ear. "I prefer bedrooms and no clothes."

His warm breath and words sent shivers down my spine, while the stubble on his cheeks and chin scratched my face, leaving a fiery trail in their wake. Besides chaste kisses here and there, the last time we'd even come close to having sex had been on my birthday. But not because I didn't want to—my body craved his touch. Recovery from a head trauma and brain surgery, however, trumped my wanton needs. He was under strict orders to abstain from all strenuous activities for at least four weeks, depending on what his body could handle. I didn't push.

Doctor's orders didn't deter him, though. In the last month, I'd exercised superhuman strength to ward off his advances, seeing to it he didn't jeopardize his health.

Has it been long enough? When his breath kissed my skin, my brain ceased to function, and my resolve disappeared. "Griff…" I trailed off, shaking my head. "I'm not so sure…"

"Jillian," he said, low and insistent. His eyes burned the color of charcoal. "I got the 'all clear' from my doctor today. As long as I'm not in any pain, no headaches, I can resume my normal level of activity."

"Really?"

He nodded.

I couldn't help but smile. "Griff, that's great news." I stretched up on my tiptoes and kissed him. He caught my face in his hands, not allowing me to retreat. His lips brushed over mine, breaking down my defenses. Then he pulled away and I slowly lowered my heels back to the carpet.

He rested his forehead against mine. "I want you, Jillibean. I promise you, I'm fine." His thumbs trailed lightly over my cheekbones. "These last eight weeks…hell, these last six months have been excruciating. I *need* to be inside you," he rasped.

I sucked in a breath. His words and his voice were my undoing. My insides melted. Smoothing my hands up his back, I drew him close and whispered in his ear, "And that's right where I want you." I stared at him, my resolve burned away by the heat we generated.

"Fuck," he moaned, crashing his mouth onto mine. Raw and hungry, he bit my lower lip, sucking it into his mouth. Circling his hands around my neck and into my hair, he pressed me closer and slid his tongue past my lips. I loved the taste of him. Our tongues swept against each other with fevered urgency while my hands kneaded the straining muscles in his back.

Again I savored this moment. "Make love to me," I sighed.

Griffin glided his hands down my back and centered them at my waist, bending slightly to pick me up. I wrapped my legs around his waist and my arms around his neck. He flexed his arms, securing my body to his, our tongues moving together.

Griffin walked us toward the bed and lowered me onto the mattress. He slowed the kiss and stood, hovering. My eyes roamed over his clothed body. Maybe I wasn't a fan of clothes anymore.

I watched Griffin's gaze follow a sensual trail over my face, down my chest, and come to rest at the hem of my dress. Starting at my knees, he slowly moved his hands up my thighs. "I'm tired of being apart, Jillian."

I nodded, finding it hard to concentrate on his words while his hands moved closer to where I wanted them. "Me too," I breathed.

A lusty smile curled his lips. "Did you make this?" He fingered the hem of my sundress before his hands disappeared beneath the lightweight fabric.

I hummed. "Mmm-hmm." His hands pressed upward while he lowered his body over mine. My muscles tightened beneath his touch.

"It's my new favorite," he whispered.

I pushed onto my elbows, our noses touching. Shifting my weight, I pulled the dress over my head and tossed it to the floor. "I was never fond of it." I pecked his lips and smiled, flopping back down.

Griffin's eyes widened. "Jillian," he stammered. "You are so damn sexy." He smirked and shook his head. With his hands, he traced over every part of my skin, even the tattered and scarred parts. He loved all of me.

Shuffling back a step, he stood and reached behind him, pulling his Chili Peppers t-shirt over his head and making quick work of the rest of his clothes, too.

My eyebrows shot up, my heart raced, and I forgot how to breathe. As many times as I had imagined Griffin's naked form, nothing compared to the real thing. I loved designing clothes, but as long as I lived, I would never want to cover up his beautiful body. It was a work of art, on display for only me.

With his hands he parted my legs, then slowly climbed on top of me. Sliding the palms of his hands over my shoulders, he dragged the straps of my bra downward, exposing my breasts. Then, ever so gently, he worked his hands to the back of my neck and lifted me up, unhooking my bra. Brushing his hands up my shoulder blades and around to the front of my body, he pulled away the pink fabric and tossed it over his shoulder.

Griffin curved his body over mine, pressing tiny kisses to my scars before drawing a line along my jaw with his nose. He inhaled. "Flowers and the ocean."

My breathing hitched and caught in my throat. My hands went to his short hair. The shaved ends tickled against my skin. So many new sensations flooded my body at once. I'd never thought I'd experience this kind of passion. Who would ever want me?

Griffin. He wanted me.

His hand moved in lazy, seductive circles over my waist, at the waistband of my panties…the only strip of clothing keeping us apart. Resting his chin against my breasts, he looked into my eyes. I could see my reflection in his dark irises. "I love you, Jillibean." His voice echoed through my body.

I drew in a large breath and watched his head rise along with my chest. "I love you," I whispered.

He tilted his head to the side and closed his eyes while I ran my fingernails over the griffin stretched across his back. "I could listen to your heartbeat all day long." His breath burned against my skin.

Keeping his ear to my heart, he worked his right hand along the length of my arm, extending it above my head, lacing his fingers with mine. His left hand moved southward, dipping his fingers just inside the top of my panties. "Hmmm," he crooned. "You're changing the beat, Jillian." He chuckled. "Much more syncopated."

My muscles clenched at hearing my name on his lips. I worked my hands to his lower back, pressing him closer while his hand slid further inside the flimsy material.

Turning his head, he leaned up and put his mouth on mine, driving his hand further into my panties. His tongue licked across my lips, and I opened to him. He plunged his tongue into my mouth, claiming me.

Oh god.

His fingers slid over me and it felt like my heart would beat out of my chest. Stars burst behind my eyelids.

Against my mouth, he murmured, "I've written songs about you—" he kissed me again— "but your heartbeat right now has to be the damn sexiest, most gorgeous song I've ever heard."

He picked up the beat with his expert fingers…playing me.

Measure after measure, my song built, and his skilled fingers coaxed noises from me that added the melody to his perfect rhythm. I squeezed my eyes shut. "Oh…my…Griffin…" I panted and arched my back. My body shuddered and my heart thumped in my chest. He slowed his deft fingers and used both hands to slowly peel my panties away.

I opened my eyes.

There was nothing between us, yet we were still so far apart.

Then he pulled away and got off the bed. *Oh no. Something's wrong.* My brain flipped through a dozen scenarios, each one worse than the previous. I sat up, chilled. "What's wrong? Are you okay? Are you hurt?"

He shook his head and smiled. "Relax, Bean." Holding up an index finger, he pulled open the drawer to his night table, rummaged through it quickly, and returned to my side, tearing open a condom wrapper with his teeth.

Oh.

My cheeks flushed as I watched Griffin roll the condom into place. His smoldering eyes never left mine, but I had to look away, distracted by the way his tattoos rippled with each contraction of his muscles.

Sliding back on top of me, he pushed me back onto the pillow. He brushed the hair away from my face and peered down. "Are you sure?" he asked.

I memorized everything...the weight of his body on mine...our hot, damp skin pressed together...sharing this experience with my best friend...

My lover.

Griffin searched my face, still waiting for my permission. I nodded. And it was all the invitation he needed. Leaning forward, he gently pressed his lips to mine, easing himself against me.

I wrapped my arms around his neck, securing my lips to his. My tongue pressed into his mouth at the same moment he pushed inside me.

The distance between us...

Obliterated.

Every nerve ending fired at once, sending a current of electricity through my body. The song my heart had played for him earlier had just been the prelude to the symphony it played now.

Griffin took it slow for my sake, filling and stretching me, then pulling away, repeating the same rhythm over and over again.

Our hands explored the landscapes of each other's bodies, our tongues danced. No space. I was all him...he was all me.

His hands ran up the length of my arms, holding them above my head. Our fingers laced together and he pressed them into the pillow. My fingers squeezed his, holding on to him with everything I had. I'd never let him go.

"Griffin," I moaned. I couldn't breathe, yet I'd never felt more alive.

Pressing further into me, he brought his mouth to mine, hard. He thrust his tongue into my mouth, and I bucked my hips beneath him.

He groaned against my mouth. "Jillian…"

Releasing my hands, he placed his strong arms at each side of my head, caging me beneath him. My hands were free to touch him. I dragged my fingers over his sweat-slicked skin, feeling him move inside me. I cried out, "Griff!" I didn't recognize my voice—primal and confident. He consumed me, body and soul.

Griffin worked his hands to my face, and I felt him shudder, "I'm so close…" he muttered, kissing my jaw.

I gripped his shoulders, feeling my muscles clench. Griffin leaned in close to my ear and whispered, "Come for me, Bean."

He thrust into me once…twice…three times…

My eyes closed and I arched my back, moving my body in time to his. My toes curled. Rainbows exploded behind my eyelids. And I was…flying.

I'd always hated flying…until now.

Then with two more long thrusts, Griffin moaned in my ear and his body trembled in my hands. He fell against me, his chest rising and falling…breathing…alive. It was the most beautiful thing I'd ever seen.

Together, we caught our breath. Griffin pressed close and kissed me, then propped his head up with his hand. He smiled and brushed my hair away from my face. "Sorry, Jillibean, I lied."

I wrinkled my nose in confusion. That was an odd thing to say after what we'd just done. "Huh?"

His fingers brushed lazily over the crown of my head. "Remember when I told you I planned to hold you hostage for days?"

"Yeah." I nodded, licking my kiss-swollen lips.

He shook his head. "Try forever."

I laughed. "Promise?"

"Damn straight." He bent close, sealed his lips to mine, closing the distance between us.

Did you love Griffin as much as we did?

Stay tuned for Griffin's story in

CAN'T GO BACK

Available Summer 2015

Did you love Griffin as much as we did

stay tuned for Griffin's story in

CAN'T GO BACK

Available Summer 2015